The

COMPLETE
STARTUP GUIDE
for the
BLACK ENTREPRENEUR

By

BILL BOUDREAUX, MBA, CPA

CAREER
PRESS

FRANKLIN LAKES, NJ

THE COMPLETE STARTUP GUIDE FOR THE BLACK ENTREPRENEUR
EDITED BY JODI BRANDON
TYPESET BY EILEEN DOW MUNSON
Cover photo by Laraine Giroir
Cover design by Johnson Design
Printed in the U.S.A. by Book-mart Press

To order this title, please call toll-free 1-800-CAREER-1 (NJ and Canada: 201-848-0310) to order using VISA or MasterCard, or for further information on books from Career Press.

CAREER
PRESS

The Career Press, Inc., 3 Tice Road, PO Box 687,
Franklin Lakes, NJ 07417
www.careerpress.com

BESt CEO and blackhomebusiness are trademarks of Minority Business Options, LLC. Its use is pursuant to a license agreement with Minority Business Options, LLC.

Library of Congress Cataloging-in-Publication Data
Boudreaux, Bill, 1955-
    The complete startup guide for the Black entrepreneur / by Bill Boudreaux.
        p. cm.
    Includes index.
    ISBN 1-56414-724-X (paper)
    1. Minority business enterprises—United States. 2. Minority business enterprises. I. Title.

HG2358.5.U6B68 2004
658.1′1′08996073—dc22

2003069598

For Linda Boudreaux,

loving wife and a true Proverbs 31 woman.

Always and forever.

Acknowledgments

First, I thank my Heavenly Father for His eternal love and the gift of His Son, Jesus Christ.

I'd like to thank my two children, Jonathan and Jessica, and my mother for their love and support.

I'd also like to thank Charmin Edwards, Mike T., Jim Smith, and my father. Their entrepreneurial spirit is a constant source of inspiration. I am particularly grateful to Mike Lewis, Jodi Brandon, and Stacey Farkas for their invaluable help and editorial contributions. Many thanks to R. Haines and H. Kiff for giving me my start on such an amazing business journey. To Angela, Carla, and the entire staff of ITS for their endless support. To Brenda, Angela B., David, Rick, and Steven for helping me keep it real through the years. To Louis "Tony" Arsene, who is like a brother to me. To Corinne Drewery and Andy Connell for music that kept me entertained through many late nights of writing. And to Kenyon, a free spirit, a gifted writer, and a friend who now lives somewhere in the Arizona Desert (I think). Thank you for never doubting.

Disclaimer

This publication is designed to provide accurate and authoritative information in regard to the subject matter covered. It is sold with the understanding that the publisher is not engaged in rendering professional services. If professional advice or other expert assistance is required, the services of a competent professional should be sought.

The application and impact of tax laws and financial and legal matters can vary widely, based on the specific and unique facts involved. The author disclaims any responsibility for positions taken or any misunderstandings in their individual cases on the part of the readers.

With respect to documents and/or information available through the referenced Websites, Minority Business Options, LLC, nor any of its employees, makes any warranty, express or implied, including warranties of merchantability and fitness for a particular purpose; assumes any legal liability or responsibility for the accuracy, the completeness, or the usefulness of any information, product, or process disclosed; or represents that its use would not infringe privately owned rights.

Websites are provided for the convenience of the user. Although every effort is made to ensure that such information is accurate and up to date, Minority Business Options, LLC does not certify the authenticity of information that originates from third parties.

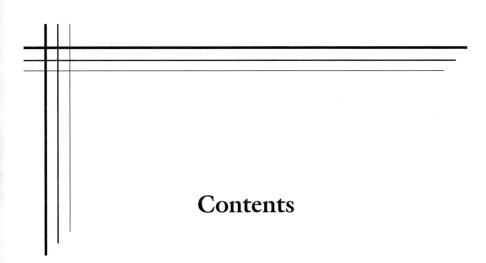

Contents

Introduction

The longest part of the journey is said to be the passing of the gate.
—Marcus Terentius Varro

What you can do, or think you can, begin it.
—Johann Wolfgang von Goethe

Carpe diem, quam minimum credula postero.
(Seize the day, put no trust in tomorrow.)
—Horace, *Odes*

A Great Journey Has Begun!

You are an entrepreneur and the time has come to organize your own business. You've imagined sitting in your home office and making the decisions that will determine your net income. You've imagined going to the post office to pick up mail that will not only include the usual household bills and credit card offers, but checks and invoices for the business you've created. Now imagine where you'd be if you had taken the steps to start your own home business five years ago. If your reaction was typical, you probably shook your head affirmatively and mumbled under your breath, "Tell me about it" or, "Don't remind me."

Many people react the same way, but don't fret. For most of us, sooner would have been better than later, but *now* is better than never. You have just passed a crossroad. You've made the decision. Finally, you're on your road to calling the shots. You have a single focus: to own and operate a business. But, chances are, you'll need some help along the way. That's where I come in—to give you a concise presentation of information to help you succeed. Not just raw business facts or 500 pages of unfocused information, but logically sequenced instruction in business strategies using language that you won't have to read four or five times to understand. Instruction that's direct and to the point. Forget the accounting jargon and legal mumbo-jumbo. Let's just talk—the way friends do.

Information Is Everywhere, but It's too Cluttered

Information is spilling out all over the place these days, especially by way of the Internet. But there's a problem—a *big* problem. The problem is especially bothersome for soon-to-be small business owners such as you, who don't have time to waste. To get the information you need, you'll have to surf the Internet for countless hours and read dozens and dozens of articles before finding something you can use, if you find it at all! An enormous amount of time is wasted surfing, searching, and sifting. In the end, you still come up short. You wind up with a bunch of puzzle pieces, but not the big picture.

There is entirely no point in searching endlessly through vast amounts of information or reinventing the wheel when trying to figure out how to organize and manage your home-based or small minority business. I've done the heavy lifting for you. These pages are chock full of practical information, templates, worksheets, and Internet resources **all in one place** and designed with a **single focus: to help give you a fighting chance to succeed in today's highly competitive business environment.** It's a war out there, and your success, as a black-owned, home-based business is needed. Take a look at these statistics.

According to year 2000 statistics published by the U.S. Census Bureau, of the total U.S. minority population, 40.6 percent were Hispanic, 39.0 percent black, 12.3 percent Asian, and 2.9 percent Native American. According to statistics published by the Small Business Administration Office of Advocacy for the same year, of minority-owned businesses, 39.5 percent were Hispanic-owned, 30.0 percent Asian-owned, 27.1 percent black-owned, and 6.5 percent Native American–owned. I know—statistics clutter the mind. So, let's put them in a table and take an even closer look.

Minority Business Ownership		
Minority Group	**Percent of minority population**	**Percent of minority business owned**
Hispanic	40.6	39.5
Black	39.0	27.1
Asian	12.3	30.0
Native American	2.9	6.5
Sources: U.S. Census Bureau, SBA Office of Advocacy Note: The columns do not add up 100% because some respondents claimed more than one race.		

Table I-A

There are many statistics to validate the fact that blacks, as a percentage of the minority population, lag significantly behind each minority group listed in Table I-A in terms of business ownership. I know what you're saying, and I said it, too: "I hope they didn't spend a lot of money trying to figure that out." And you're absolutely, dead-on right. The gap is obvious just through casual observation. Walk through most cities and towns in the United States and just look around. It's hard not to see the lack of small, black-owned businesses. Sure there is a sprinkling here and there, but they are few and far between—even in 2004.

But, let's continue to examine the table. Let's zero in on the population-to-business ratio. Take the Hispanic population, for example. Hispanics represent 40.6 of the minority population and 39.5 percent of the minority businesses—about equal and about what you would expect. Accordingly, one would expect blacks to own about 39 percent of the minority businesses, because they represent 39 percent of the minority population. As you can see, that expectation does not pan out. Blacks only own 27.1 percent. Asians and Native Americans, on the other hand, own businesses at a rate much greater than one would expect, all things being equal. But the sad fact is all things are not equal. In fact, things are inherently unequal.

"The Question"

So, right off the bat, let's deal with the most obvious issue, or, as my mother used to say, "Let's put first things first." (I think everybody's mother has said that at one time or another.) I'll put "the question" on the table. Here it is: *In 2004, is there a difference between operating a black-owned, home-based business and a home-based business that is not black-owned?* You better believe there is—in many ways. In terms of accounting and licensing and taxes, generally there are no differences, but in terms of perception, operations, capitalization, and the hurdles you must overcome as a black, small business owner, the differences, even in 2004, can be very significant, almost overwhelming—if you are not prepared. Don't get me wrong: Things have changed a lot, and for the better. But the pace is slow and the momentum seems to have dissipated.

Being aware of the environment in which black businesses must operate is not about being paranoid or negative—just realistic. Knowing the hurdles that must be overcome should not give you a reason to be discouraged. On the contrary, it should provide you with a greater incentive to learn as much as you possibly can about organizing and managing the piece of the American pie that you **fully intend** to cut for yourself.

What This Book Is *Not* About

At this point, I must tell you it is *not* my intent to focus on the political and institutional disadvantages of organizing and operating your home-based business. We will leave those discussions and political gyrations within the halls of Congress and within the walls of our universities. We'll let politicians and college professors deal with curing the ills of institutional racism and effectively applying affirmative action programs (what's left of them). As they grapple with these issues and try to resolve them, we may or may not be around to benefit from their decisions. But who's got time to wait? Not me. And not you. Many people I talk to tell me they should have been reading a book such as this five years ago. Who's got time to wait for an act of Congress? And I mean that literally! Now is the time to go into action. Waiting another month could kill a dream. Every waiting day is a day your dream is deferred. The waiting game breeds complacency. Action calls!

So, What *Is* the Focus?

You have an idea that you want to bring to the market now. If you wait too long, tomorrow someone else will have your idea. I cannot tell you how many times I've seen business ideas stolen from nascent entrepreneurs, or others with the same idea simply beat them to the draw. Your focus needs to be on what must be done to maximize your chances of success and increase your profitability—as Luther Vandross would say, "Here and Now." Your focus needs to be on today.

As a responsible citizen, keep an eye on the issues and use the power of the vote to continue pulling down institution obstacles that inhibit African-American entrepreneurship. But as a Black Entrepreneur Start-up (**"BESt"**) Chief Executive Officer (**"CEO"**), your focus is on bringing your ideas, talents, and knowledge to the marketplace, despite the obstacles—as soon as possible.

Today, success in business begins when an entrepreneur with a big idea and a gut full of fire walks the high wire of risk. It has always been that way and that's not about to change. Entrepreneurialism is capitalism at work. It involves risk and effort—always has, always will. As Mike T., a friend of mine, is noted for saying, "If it was easy, everybody would be doing it." He's right. It's not easy—for the unprepared—but nor is it hard—for the prepared. What is the common denominator? Preparation! Organizing a BESt Company is a series of small efforts that must be accomplished in a fairly systematic order. The efforts involved in organizing a business are not hard. It's the persistence and follow-through that's hard. **This book will help keep you focused as you go through the process.** A series of small steps, one at a time, will take you to your goal. Just ask any motivational guru; the first step isn't the hardest, but it is the most significant. *Entrepreneurial inertia is the tendency of a business idea to remain just an idea until some force moves upon it to make it become a reality.* Each step has its own challenges. But the challenges of subsequent steps can never be conquered until the first step is taken.

Ahead of the Curve

Entrepreneurial spirit aside (just for a second), there is a flip side to the home-business coin. The home-business boom is quietly coming. Frankly, employees are growing weary of layoffs, wages with little upside potential, and little or no opportunity for advancement. These factors, coupled with the tragic events of September 11th and dramatic increases in technology, are causing aspiring BESt CEOs to quietly promise themselves: *It's now or never.* As this quiet revolution takes place, for once, you can be ahead of the curve instead of behind it. Wouldn't that be a nice plus—a pleasant change?

The Bottom Line

The bottom line is this: When it comes to selling your products and services, the only color that should truly matter is green. Skin color should not matter, but the cold reality is that many times it does. Nevertheless, racial difficulties notwithstanding, your efforts to succeed in business will be doubly difficult if you just start doing things without a well-thought-out plan. This book is designed to hold your hand and lead you step by step through the process of gathering the information and understanding needed to organize and manage a successful home-based business.

Even though technology and raw drive are crucial to overall success, they are not enough to keep your business ahead of the competitive curve. There is no substitute for having overall business knowledge of your total operating environment—a clear understanding of the big picture. I am not saying that you should be an expert in every aspect of your business—that is impossible—but everything should be familiar to you.

Doing Your Part

When you are successfully running your home-based business, you will be doing your part to level out a very unlevel playing field. It is my hope that each person who is endued with an entrepreneurial spirit accepts the challenge of starting his or her own home-based business. As more African-American entrepreneurs accept the challenge and are successful, that hard, unlevel playing field will be leveled out, house by house, street by street, and community by community.

Doing My Part

This book is written by an African-American entrepreneur for the growing African-American home-based and small minority business market. I've been there. I know the issues and struggles, from capitalizing on a shoestring to dealing with the stigma of stereotyping. My zeal is focused on one goal: that by the end of this book, you will have a leg up on how to organize and manage your business from your home on a full-time or a part-time basis, and do so successfully, despite the upfront hindrances.

From time to time, I get the following question: *With your credentials, why don't you work for a large company where there is stability and longevity and where you know your next paycheck is just a week away?* In the first place, there is no such thing as corporate longevity and security anymore. Remember Enron? Global Crossing? But even if there were, the answer quite simply is that I enjoy being in the mix, rolling up my sleeves, and wearing many hats. As the owner of a home-based business, it falls on me to understand and to be able to do many things. I am called on to understand every position, from cashier to clean-up crew, from customer service representative to collection agent, from deliveryman to shipping and receiving foreman, from Web designer to copywriter. Although some people might find such responsibility burdensome, even unbearable, I do not. I enjoy calling the shots. I like being the boss. I enjoy it so much that I want to motivate many others who have the desire to be the boss, but might need just a bit of encouragement to take the proverbial plunge.

Regardless of what type business you have decided to enter, there are many tasks to complete before you can read your first set of financial statements or spend your first dollar of profit. The path to get from where you are now to where you hope to be is peppered with countless land mines and a few deep pits. My job is to walk with you down a winding path. Along the way I will point out land mines and deep pits, and hopefully you won't lose a foot or fall in over your head.

Before we get started, there is one crucial point to keep in mind: **No two businesses are ever exactly the same.** This book is a guide. Your success will be the result of your smart work. Some say hard work, but I'd rather the emphasis to be on working smart. So here is our first BESt Principle:

BESt Principle #1 ||||➡ WORK SMART.
LEAVE THE HARD, UNFOCUSED WORK TO THOSE WHO DON'T DO THEIR HOMEWORK.

This Book is About Hustle, not Wishful Thinking

This is a book about organization and management and methodically working toward a goal, not about getting rich quick. As conventional wisdom says, "If it seems too good to be true, it probably is." So our focus is on *doing what it takes,* and not *waiting around for something good to happen.* If you are more prone to "waiting around," then buy a lottery ticket and hope against reason. Most probably, you'll wind up with a drawer full of losing tickets and many regrets from a lot of missed opportunities. There is an old saying credited to legendary Hall of Fame football coach Chuck Noll: *Good things happen to those who wait, but only what's left by those who hustle.* Ain't that the truth.

A Turning Point

Starting your own home-based business is a turning point in your life. I know you have thought about taking this step many times, and finally something has brought you to this place. You may have invented a new product, been laid off, decided it's now or never to pursue your passion, or you may simply want to supplement your current income. Whatever the goal, it's your goal and I'm glad you set it. My advice to you is to get informed, get organized, and, as Martin Lawrence would say, "Gits to steppin'!" (or going back a little further, back in the day, as Arsenio Hall used to say, "Let's get busy!").

Chapter 1

Get Focused—Quick!

If you want to be truly successful invest in yourself to get the knowledge you need to find your unique factor. When you find it and focus on it and persevere your success will blossom.

—Sidney Madwed

Gather in your resources, rally all your faculties, marshal all your energies, focus all your capacities upon mastery of at least one field of endeavor.

—John Haggai

To find out what one is fitted to do, and to secure an opportunity to do it, is the key to happiness.

—John Dewey

Take doctors, for example. The medical profession is very specialized, and necessarily so. There are cardiologists, dermatologists, and ophthalmologists, to name just a few of the many specialists broadly classified as doctors. Medical care has become so specialized, and there is so much available knowledge, that it is impossible for one doctor to stay abreast of all the approved surgical procedures and available drug treatments that can benefit each patient. In fact, even general practitioners are specialized. General practitioners, or family doctors, diagnose and treat a certain range of ailments, and that's it. If a particular patient's ailment is outside a general practitioner's schedule of procedures, he or she will refer that patient to an appropriate specialist—and rightly so.

This example allows us to quickly understand how futile it would be for a doctor to hang out a shingle saying, *"I can do it all...eye care, heart rehab, skin disease...bring it on."* Not only would that be foolhardy, but it would also be an invitation to disaster—and many lawsuits. Medical care requires focus. Organizing your BESt Company requires the same concentration of focus. You need to decide exactly what products you plan to offer or what services you plan to provide. Without proper focus, new businesses try to be all things to all people and that is a **critical error.**

BESt Principle #2 IIII➤

SPECIALIZE.
FOCUS ON YOUR STRENGTHS.
DON'T TRY TO BE ALL THINGS TO ALL PEOPLE.

In my attempt to begin focusing your efforts, let's first agree on the definition of a home business. Then we will look at a list of ideas for new home businesses.

1.1 What is a Home Business?

If you have a burning idea to market a product or service and a workspace somewhere in your home, you have both elements essential to becoming a home-based, BESt Company.

Actually, there is nothing mysterious about a home business. There is no intricate formula. Quite simply, *a **home-based business** is any operation that sells goods or provides services for profit from a private residence.* A private residence does not have to be a house that you own. It could be a house that you rent or even an apartment.

Back in the Day

Back in the day people worked at home after they got laid off or fired and just couldn't find any "legitimate" work. To camouflage the fact that work was being done from a home base, soloists would play recordings of ringing telephones and the low rumble of conversations coming from "adjoining offices." These sounds gave callers the illusion of a busy office, filled with the sounds of activity and success. To work at home was generally met with a healthy dose of skepticism by potential customers. That was then. **Things have changed**—a lot!

Today, launching and running a business out of your home is perfectly acceptable. In fact, many view it as the smart and creative thing to do! The perception of the soloist working from a home base is one of admiration and courage. It takes a courageous person to turn dreams into reality, not to mention the pioneer spirit that has to be present to strike out on your own, to chart your own course, and go where you've not gone before.

This perception is changing because customers realize that technology has increased the capacity and professionalism of soloists. A single person can now accomplish jobs that once took several people several days to do—and can do so just as effectively. This increased capacity translates into lower cost without having to sacrifice quality. Today's home business is *definitely* not your father's home business!

Technology provides small, one-person operations with many of the capabilities of Fortune 500 companies. *Did you hear what I said?* I said **Fortune 500 Companies!** I have seen work produced in a small, home office that rivals the combined effort of the entire administrative staff of an international consulting firm. The pervasiveness of technology such as wireless communication, personal digital assistants (PDAs), video conferencing, and desktop publishing has reduced the cost of technology so that it is affordable to all businesses, even those in their infancy, operating out of one office.

I'm sure you've heard this one before, but I'll mention it again, as it's a good illustration: *Apple Computers, founded in 1978, was once a home business!* According to its annual reports, the company achieved sales of more than $8 billion by 2000 and employed approximately 95,000 by the second half of 2002. How's that for inspiration? But before we get carried away with inspiration, remember the old adage: *Success is 1 percent inspiration and 99 percent perspiration.* So, for every one word of inspiration, we need to accomplish 99 tasks. Well, maybe not 99, but you get the idea.

When you have a moment, type **"started as a home-based business"** in a search engine on your Internet browser and notice the amount of hits that come up. Then, read a few. You'll be surprised how many of today's small, medium, and large businesses were once home-based operations. It wasn't long before Apple Computer was no longer run out of a garage, and, perhaps, in a couple years you'll have to move your BESt Company into a multi-office complex, too. But that's another problem, a good problem—one I'm sure you'll be able to deal with when the time comes.

Once a Home Business, Always a Home Business?

From our discussion in the previous section, that is clearly not the case. But in some cases, a home might be forever suitable. For example, some barbers, electricians, contractors, and architects might find working at home ideal and never intend to change their setup. These businessmen and women can acquire the tools of their trade and organize them within their homes in a way that does not distract from the natural flow of family life. They wouldn't have it any other way.

1.2 Home Business vs. Physical Storefront

A storefront was once the ultimate goal for a BESt Company, or any business for that matter. *A storefront is the physical presence (brick and mortar) that a business occupies other than the owner's home.* For example, your local drug store or department store has a storefront. As technology has grown, storefronts are no longer necessary. Some businesses, such as Internet wholesalers, have the potential to become international businesses without ever investing a nickel in a brick-and-mortar storefront.

According to a recent report from International Data Corporation, worldwide Internet spending was expected to exceed $1 trillion by the end of 2001, and by 2003 was on its way to an amazing $3 trillion! That's *trillion* with a "t"—in worldwide sales to governments, businesses, and individuals. Let that sink in for a moment. From offices, homes, local libraries, or wherever they can make an Internet connection, consumers are purchasing an amazing amount of goods and services via the Internet. Also, according to *Computer Industry Almanac*, the number of worldwide Internet users is projected to be more than 700 million by 2005. For these consumers, a *physical* storefront is totally unnecessary.

Notice I italicized the word *physical*. Even though you may not need a physical storefront if selling via the Internet, it is highly recommended that you have an electronic storefront that is savvy and well done. (We'll talk more about electronic storefronts in the section on advertising.)

1.3 The Pros and Cons of Operating a Business at Home

It would be nice to say that being your own boss is easy and that there is no downside. But, and I'll quote my buddy again, *"If it was easy, everybody would be doing it"*—and doing so successfully. As with most major pursuits, there are advantages and disadvantages. Many experts say that operating a home-based business requires a greater degree of sacrifice than your typical 8-to-5 job. You may be totally aware of the sacrifices and rewards of going solo, but for the sake of emphasis, let's review.

Advantages

➤ *The satisfaction of being your own boss.* This can be very strong as you mature in a position on someone else's job. As you consider what you do on your job, you may determine that you could be doing the same thing for yourself. But be honest here. Don't let a boastful attitude or a fuss with your boss distort reality. Truly count the cost before going into business. Don't find yourself in the heat of battle only to realize that being your own boss just isn't that important after all.

➤ *No commuting.* Let me give you a personal testimony of the time I save by getting off the road. For years, I commuted from Thibodaux to New Orleans on a daily basis. The time spent commuting round-trip was 2.5 hours each day, or 625 hours per year. When you run the numbers you'll find that comes to an incredible 26 full 24-hour days of commuting—each year! That is a solid month of doing nothing but driving to and from someone else's company. Now that's just crazy.

This type of commuting is not at all uncommon—millions of people do it. According to the U.S. Federal Highway Administration, the U.S. national average is 444 hours of commuting per year, or almost three weeks. Now remember: That's the average. Some commuters spend less than three weeks on the road, but some spend much more. You can redeem that time in some ways, for example, listening to books on tape or CD or learning the words to the latest songs on the radio. Or, for those with a sweet tooth, you probably know where every Krispy Kreme donut shop is along your commute. For the most part, however, commuting time is just a big, total waste.

➤ *Lower operating costs (as compared to the cost of operating a storefront).* Office rent is a significant expense that is avoided by operating from home. Plus, you don't have to pay two water bills, two utility bills, two security bills, and so forth. You will, however, have to pay two phone bills. (More on that later.)

➤ *Can begin as a part-time business that can later become full-time.* This is an effective way to minimize initial up-front costs. It can also keep a source of revenue coming in until your business can sustain itself. Be cautious, however, not to let this steady income diminish your drive to go all the way. If you keep something to fall back on, avoid the tendency to do exactly that—fall back. Fall back into the same routine, fall back from your enthusiasm, fall away from fulfilling your dream.

BESt Principle #3 ⫸

COMMIT TOTALLY.
ONCE YOUR MIND IS MADE UP,
DON'T LOOK BACK AND DON'T HALF STEP.

➤ *Increased tax benefits.* Home business deductions, write-off of equipment purchases, and so on.

➤ *A flexible work schedule.* Although this is clearly an advantage of being your own boss, it should not be abused. You may be tired of routine on somebody else's job, but you still need to have a routine for your own business. One of the frequent complaints I hear about black-owned businesses (especially small, home-based businesses) is that they don't keep regular business hours. That is a fatal flaw. Nothing destroys goodwill quicker than your customers not being able to depend on you to serve them at their (not your) convenience.

➤ *Cost savings on child care.* There can usually be someone to receive smaller children after school. Even though this is an advantage, don't let this anchor you to home base. Have an alternate plan if you need to be away to attend to customer needs or to attend an out-of-town conference.

➤ *An outlet for creative talents.* If you have a creative flair, you will have many opportunities to express yourself for example, design letterhead, Websites, advertising campaigns, flyers, slogans, and office décor).

➤ *Opportunity to employ other members of the family*, but only if they are will-ing to take their employment seriously. You should not let any family member abuse privileges by getting away with things that no other em-ployer would tolerate.

Disadvantages

➤ *Loss of fringe benefits (perhaps for an extended period of time)*. Fringe ben-efits such as health insurance and matching 401(k) contributions may cause many to think twice before going solo, especially the loss of health insur-ance. Fortunately, there are a growing number of insurance companies that cater to the specific needs of soloists.

➤ *Long work hours.* This is a given. If there is anything that needs to be done, you will either have to do it yourself or supervise. You may not work 24/7, but you're on the job 24/7.

➤ *Living space is limited.* Business space may limit and interfere with the natu-ral flow of family life. Obviously, this is less of an issue for a single person.

➤ *Perceived availability.* Family might make more demands on your time be-cause you're "available." (We will discuss this more in the next section.)

➤ *Neighbor complaints.* Neighbors may object to business activity (increased automobile traffic, increased pedestrian traffic, signs, UPS and Fed Ex delivery trucks coming and going at odd hours, and so forth).

➤ *The need for strict discipline*. This might be difficult for some until a differ-ent, more stringent work ethic is established. You can't let things slide and get to them when you feel like it.

1.4 Where Does Family Fit In?

Family support is an extremely important factor in the ultimate success of your BESt Business—perhaps the most volatile variable. Some days your fam-ily will be in your corner 100 percent; other days you will feel as if you're getting no support. You must be able to strike a balance between business activities and family life.

If you were holding down a job on somebody else's payroll, there would be certain built-in limitations. You would not be able to personally respond to every issue your family has. Accordingly, they must be willing to give you the ability to erect similar dividing walls between personal and business activities. You may be able to make regularly scheduled ball games, but should not be made to feel guilty if you have to work through a ball game to resolve business issues or if you can't watch your 2-year-old while your spouse catches a "quick flick" with friends. Having your toddler unplug the fax machine in the middle of a transmission might be cute once or twice, but such distractions can very quickly become counterproductive when a phone call has to be made requesting that the fax be sent again—not to mention the fact that it can make you look entirely unprofessional. Worst of all, customers will consider you an amateur.

Ultimately, your ability to plan effectively depends on your family's willingness to allow you to schedule regular working hours. Notice I did not say normal working hours. A straight eight-hour "normal" workday probably will not suffice in a BESt Company. Remember: You're the CEO!

Hold a Formal Family Meeting

Do not make assumptions about your family's role. Don't just assume they will give you the space and time needed. Call a formal meeting. They need you to express verbally what's expected of them, what's appropriate, and what's not. Here are some suggestions to help maintain a clear distinction between business life and family life.

➤ **Manage time effectively in order to keep regular business hours.** (We will explore effective time management in detail in Chapter 12.)

➤ **Allow for family time.** Allow time for eating out, going to the movies, taking vacations, ball games, and so forth. It's important to start on the right foot. Make sure your family, especially your spouse, knows that business will not usurp family life. Otherwise, resistance might form early on, and your support system will evaporate quicker than hailstones on a hot roof...will have the duration of a Louisiana winter...last about as long as...well, you get the point.

➤ **Continue to share chores around the house.** And, where it makes sense, allow qualified members of your family to share some responsibilities in the business. Of course, anyone who is on the payroll will have a specific job to do. Don't allow your family members to turn your business into their hobby.

➤ **Meet routinely.** Meet every three months or so on a semi-formal basis to take a pulse of current family feelings. Be willing to listen to their complaints as well as their praises. This practice helps minimize miscommunication or, worse yet, shutting of meaningful and constructive communication.

Build a Business, not an Idol

A major reason for starting your own business is to have more control over your schedule, to put away that 9-to-5 grind across town or, more likely, in a different town—one that's an hour's commute away. That does not necessarily mean that you will have more time; it simply means that, for the most part, you will be able to control the time that you do have. To control your time, you must run your business and not let the business run you. Do not erect a golden calf that you must bow to before you can take a lunch break or decide to spend time with your family. You want a business, not an idol. Effective time management will help maximize productivity and allow the greatest degree of flexibility regarding time issues.

Keep a healthy perspective and maintain proper priorities. On your list of priorities, family must always be higher than business. I have been in business many years and have seen many things, but I've yet to hear about anyone on their death bed saying, *"If only I'd spent more time at the office."* No, the regret is always about neglecting family for business, or family for anything else. If you don't neglect them and if you keep your promises, your family will become your loudest, most enthusiastic cheerleaders. Your business efforts will be more focused, and family time more joyful.

1.5 New Business Ideas

Deciding on a business pursuit ranges from turning your hobby into a business opportunity to purchasing an ongoing business or even buying a franchise. I deeply believe most people know exactly the business they would like to pursue. As you finalize your decision, consider the opinions of your friends and family. But, as with all situations pertaining to your BESt Company, the final decision is yours to make. There are aids and questionnaires designed to take inventory of your skills and desires. For a few ideas, check out this Website:

BESt Website ▐▐▐▶

www.newworkplace.com
Why is it helpful? It can guide your thinking about new business opportunities, and it offers insight from entrepreneurs who are currently operating various businesses.

The information on this site (and many others) can help guide your thinking about the type of business that best suits you. But, as I said, this is your baby and you get to name it.

Table 1-A shows a partial list of home-based business ideas. Chances are, you already have a clear idea of what you're interested in. It's probably a field or a skill you know extremely well, and that's good. Although it's not impossible, it is extremely difficult to maintain a high level of enthusiasm and confidence in a business that you do not know very well. Already your plate is full with other issues. For example, the last thing you need is to open a tax service never having done a tax return. That's akin to trying to carry water uphill in a bucket with a gaping hole in the bottom. It can be done, but not very efficiently. You will have to make many trips and try to control the leakage, and, despite your best effort, your shoes are going to get awfully wet and muddy in the process. An incredible amount of energy will be wasted, and you will always be behind the curve compared to those who are expert in that area. *Expert* is loosely defined as those operating without a defective bucket—those with sufficient knowledge in a particular area. The smart move is to create a business where you are the expert, where you can set the standard. Recall BESt Principle #1: Work smart. Expend energy on growing the business rather than exhausting attempts to overcome a significant deficit in technical knowledge.

The following list doesn't begin to include all the possibilities, but it is representative of the kinds of businesses that could be managed by one person (or a few persons) from a home base:

Accountant	Computer Repair	Gift Baskets	Parking Lot
Advertising Agency	Computer Tutor	Graphic Designer	Maintenance
Adventure	Craft Business	Hairdresser	Personal Coach
Tourism	Day Trader	Herbs/Vitamins	Pet Groomer
Antique Dealer	Delivery Service	Business	Photographer
Appliance Repair	Desktop Publisher	Home Healthcare	Picture Framer
Appraiser	Disc Jockey	Service	Portrait
Artist	Dog Obedience	House-sitting Service	Photographer
Auto Dealer	Trainer	Housecleaning	Private Investigator
Barber	Embroidery Business	Importer	Public Relations
Bed & Breakfast	Event Planner	Interior Decorator	Reflexologist
Bookkeeper	Executive Recruiter	Internet Trainer	Repairs
Candle Maker	Exporter	Landscaper	Resume Writer
Carpet Cleaner	Financial Planner	Manicurist	Screen Printer
Caterer	Fitness Trainer	Medical Biller	Seamstress
Child-care Provider	Freelance	Medical	Tailor
Chimney Sweeper	Photographer	Transcriptionist	Technical Writer
Collection Service	Freelance Writer	Newsletter Publisher	Travel Agent
Computer	Fund Raiser	Online Retailer	Web Designer
Consultant			Yard Maintenance

1.6 Whatever You Do, Don't Rush

In the beginning stages of organizing your business, your greatest asset—enthusiasm—can turn on you. You'll be investing large amounts of time and energy (and yes—money), but don't get in a hurry. I know that once you make up your mind to do something, it's *forget the details; Full speed ahead!* You want to forge ahead without delay—the old *Ready, SHOOT, Aim* philosophy.

Well, go on—forge ahead! But not at the expense of half-doing the planning and organizing processes. What seems like a year of delays will be nothing more than a few weeks of due diligence. Don't get in a hurry and do things half-cocked. As my former colleague J. Whitting once said, "The faster you go without a plan, the further you lag behind the train." I love a good quote, as evidenced by the quotes at the beginning of each chapter. (Some folks I quote you'll know, others you won't.) I also listen closely to what friends and business acquaintances say, and some of what they say I also commit to memory—either because it's profound or just plain funny. This is both, but you have to know what he meant! The idea here is that those who have laid tracks know exactly where they're going. So they can forge ahead at full speed. Without a plan, you're all over the place; lots of smoke, but no fire; sound and fury, but no substance. You'll spend exorbitant amounts of time on tasks that should have low priority (buying office furniture, for example) and not enough time on tasks of greater importance. You wind up with a beautifully appointed home office and no customers to appreciate it. Why? Because days were spent picking out a desk and lamp rather than working on your marketing plan. It just seemed too difficult to deal with at the time. Remember: The easiest thing in the world to do is spend money on office equipment. Writing checks for office furniture will make you feel as though you're making progress—and you are: in depleting valuable start-up capital by overspending it. Proper planning will help prioritize tasks, keep spending in check, and keep you on track.

I'm not saying to be the tortoise in a one-man race, but I am cautioning you against rushing the process along. This book *is* the **Quick-Start** version. Without this guide you would have to figure out all these individual items one at a time. No matter how anxious a home-builder is, raising walls and adding a roof before a foundation is poured is just plain foolish.

Understand the Rules, Know the Players, and Stay on Course

Organizing and managing your BESt Company will be a multifaceted undertaking. You place yourself at a major disadvantage if you jump in feet-first without understanding all the players and the rules to their games. For example, the IRS has different requirements than state sales tax authorities do. State sales tax authorities have different requirements than do local governments. Suppliers want one thing, and bankers want something else. The Small Business Administration will require all types of information. It falls upon you and your representatives to know what each player requires. Believe me, ignorance is no defense, nor do you want to hide behind its temporary bliss. Eventually, the bliss of ignorance comes crashing down in the form of IRS penalties, lost contracts, and unnecessarily strained relationships with bankers and suppliers.

According to the Small Business Administration, only 67 percent of small businesses survive the first two years. About 50 percent survive after four years. Early on, the two most common reasons for failure are poor management and insufficient cash flow. In the early stages, poor management is characterized by poor planning, unbridled optimism, and the *tendency to veer off course*. As a result of being overly optimistic, it's all too common for entrepreneurs to underestimate the time required to produce desired business results. Do not rush the planning process. Keep a cool head, focus quickly, remain focused, and prioritize, prioritize, prioritize.

BESt Principle #4 ▐▐▐➡ PLAN TO STICK TO YOUR PLAN. DEVIATE ONLY WHEN IT MAKES $ENSE.

Chapter 2

Setting Up Shop

The most important work you and I will ever do will be within the wall of our own homes.

—Harold B. Lee

A man travels the world over in search of what he needs and returns home to find it.

—George Moore

2.1 Carving Out a Space

No matter what type of business you're planning to enter, you'll need a dedicated workspace, usually an office or a studio. **Question: *Do you have such a room?*** Hopefully the answer is yes. Don't try spreading your work on the coffee table or across your bed or the kitchen counters. It will be difficult enough trying to fight the distractions of your personal life without having to deal with some topic on *Oprah* that catches your attention or gathering up your stuff every time the doorbell rings. It is crucial to have a designated space where you can work undistracted, where documents and files can be laid out without being disturbed, a place where the environment, especially sound, can be controlled to some degree. It is difficult to concentrate and block out dialogue from a TV program or music with distracting lyrics.

Your workspace may begin in the den, garage, basement, a detached office, or the RV parked alongside your house. The most significant factor in allocating workspace is finding the physical space that matches the demands of your business. Because this is going to be a place that you will spend one-third to one-half of your life, find the best fit and personalize it. This is going to be your domain, or as Jay S, taught his 3-year-old to say of his home office, "That's Daddy's green room—his profit center, where Daddy makes our money!"

Unlike the cramped cubicle you left back at the J-O-B, your walls do not have to be IBM blue and hospital gray, with cold steel shelving and #2 pencils sticking from a coffee mug with *You have to be insane to work here* or *You want it when?!?* imprinted across the front. These are your new digs. You get to decide on furniture, wall color, plants, lamps, and shelving. My personal preference is a light, airy décor with a tropical island motif. I find natural wood floors with white walls very attractive. I also enjoy paintings of beach landscapes with magnificent sunsets and swaying palms and lots and lots of light streaming through the windows. What's your preference?

Apart from the aesthetics and the creative pleasure of carving out and personalizing office space, there is another important reason to maintain a separate business area. It involves the tax advantages you can receive for the business use of your home. You will need specific advice from your tax-preparer, but I'll note some of the issues that need to be discussed. This area tends to be a bit technical, so stick with me. I'll make it quick.

2.2 What the IRS Has to Say About Where and How You Set Up Your Facilities

IRS Tests

To be able to claim expenses for the business use of your home (also called a home-office deduction), you must meet certain requirements. The requirements of the home-office deduction are strict. The IRS calls these requirements "tests" because you must pass these "tests" or "conditions" to determine whether or not the use of your home could qualify for a business deduction. Notice the word *and* that separates Test 1 from Test 2.

TEST 1: USE. Your use of the business part of your home must be:

    A. Exclusive (however, there are exceptions that we will discuss later), **and**

    B. Regular, **and**

    C. For your trade or business.

AND

TEST 2: ACTIVITY. The business part of your home must be one of the following:

    D. Your principal place of business (we will define this later) where you meet or deal with customers in the normal course of your business, OR

    E. A separate structure (not attached to your home), in which case you merely have to use it in connection with your business.

That's it in a nutshell—these are the tests. I will explain each part in detail, but let me make a point right off the bat. If you qualify for the home-office deduction, take the deduction! Such a statement might seem obvious, but it is not always heeded. I have seen seasoned businessmen fearful of claiming a deduction for the business use of their home. They give illogical reasons such as, *I just don't want to give the IRS a reason to look at my tax records too closely* or *I just can't afford to go through an audit, so I'll just forfeit that deduction—it's no biggie* or *I hear that is a hot-button deduction—let's not go there.*

Read the wise words of Judge Learned Hand in his dissenting opinion in Commissioner v. Newman, 159F.2D 848, 850-851 (CA2 1947).

"Over and over again courts have said that there is nothing sinister in so arranging one's affairs as to keep taxes as low as possible. Everybody does so, rich or poor; and all do right, for nobody owes any public duty to pay more than the law demands: taxes are enforced exactions; not voluntary contributions."

As this opinion makes abundantly clear, it is always in your personal best interest to make sure that you arrange your affairs to take advantage of every deduction to which you are entitled. The deduction for *home business use* is no exception.

Let's continue our discussion about what is required to take the deduction. Remember: There are two tests: use and activity.

First, we will discuss **use**. Use must be ***exclusive*** *use,* ***regular*** *use, and* ***trade or business*** *use.* Then, in the section that immediately follows use, we will discuss **activity**, which include *principal place of business, customer activity,* or *separate structure.*

Exclusive Use...Simplified

In keeping with my promise, I will not throw out a lot of accounting jargon or tax-speak. I will keep this as simple as possible. As the heading indicates, this discussion will be about exclusive use...simplified. (In fact, the next few sections deal with tax issues and they will all be simplified.)

To qualify under the *exclusive use test,* you must use a specific area of your home **only** for business. The area used for business can be a room or other separately identifiable space. Notice the word *space.* The space does not need to be marked off by a permanent partition.

You **do not** meet the requirement of the *exclusive* use test if you use the business space for both business and for personal use. Also, you do not meet the exclusive use test if you use that portion of your home for investment activities.

Example: *You're a freelance writer and use a den in your home to write magazine articles for a client. Your family also uses the den for recreation* *(watching television, playing games, etc.). Because the den is not used exclusively for your business, you cannot claim a business deduction for its use.*

Exception: You can take a deduction for home-business use without meeting the exclusive use test if either of the following applies:

> ▷ You can claim business use of your home if your home is the only fixed location of a **retail** or **wholesale** business. In that case, you use part of your home for the storage of inventory or product samples.

> ▷ You use part of your home as a day-care facility. Be aware, however, that there is an additional time restriction concerning the actual time of day the center is open and operational.

Whew!! Take a breath! Even though I am keeping this simple, are you beginning to see the importance of having a tax professional on your team? Tax laws are very complex, with many twists and turns. I will continue this discussion because it is the crux of what constitutes a home business, but don't feel overwhelmed by this short section. Typically, all it takes is a little time to digest this new information before it begins to make sense. Okay? Let's press on.

Regular Use...Simplified

To qualify under the *regular* use test, you must use a specific area of your home for business on a **continuing** basis. You do not meet the test if your business use of the area is only occasional, even if you do not use that area for any other purposes.

Trade or Business Use...Simplified

You must use part of your home in connection with a trade or business. If you use your home for a profit-seeking activity that is not a trade or business, you cannot take a deduction for its business use.

> **Example:** *You use part of your home exclusively and regularly to read the* Wall Street Journal *and several financial magazines, to monitor your portfolio by computer, and to complete other activities related to your own investments. However, you do not make investments as a broker or dealer. Because your activities are not part of your trade or business (that is, you are not a stockbroker or investment consultant), you* **cannot** *take a deduction for the business use of your home.*

Principal Place of Business...Simplified

Your home must be the principal place of business for your business. To determine if your home is your principal place of business, you must consider certain conditions:

> ▷ Your home is used exclusively and regularly for administrative or management activities of your business.

▷ You have no other fixed location where you conduct substantial administrative or management activities for your business.

Place to Meet Clients or Customers...Simplified

You physically meet with clients or customers on the premises, and the use of your home is substantial and integral to the conduct of your business. Using your home for occasional meetings and telephone calls will not qualify you to deduct expenses for the business use of your house.

Separate Structure...Simplified

You can deduct expenses for a separate freestanding structure, such as a studio, garage, or barn, if you use it exclusively and regularly for your business. The structure does not have to be your principal place of residence.

Okay, those are the conditions. Let's review. Remember: There are two tests, and each test has several parts. Take a look again.

TEST 1: USE. Your use of the business part of your home must be:

A. Exclusive, **and**

B. Regular, **and**

C. For your trade or business.

AND

TEST 2: ACTIVITY. The business part of your home must be one of the following:

D. Your principal place of business where you meet or deal with customers in the normal course of your business, **OR**

E. A separate structure (not attached to your home), in which case you merely have to use it in connection with your business.

Expanded Home-Office Deduction

Beginning on January 1, 1999, the deduction for the business use of a home was expanded to include self-employed people who have no other place where they conduct substantial managerial and administrative duties for their business.

To deduct for a home office under the expanded rules, all rules apply except that the space does not need to be a separate room, nor does it have to be a place where you meet regularly with customers. Nevertheless, it still must be a place used exclusively for the business (that is, no personal activities can take place).

BESt Companies that benefit from these expanded rules are those that work at a job site but have no place, other than their home offices, to do their invoicing and other administrative duties.

Example: *A carpenter whose principal work place is the job site can now take a home-office deduction if he or she maintains a home office to take care of administrative duties (prepare invoices, review contracts, pay bills, etc..), regardless whether or not he meets with customers or clients on a regular basis.*

Special Note

Remember: When discussing the *home-office deduction,* we are talking about whether or not you can write off a portion of the cost of your home and the expenses associated with running your home, such as utilities, homeowners insurance, and so forth. We are not talking about other business expenses, such as telephone expense, legal expense, or auto expenses (to name a few). Telephone, legal, auto, and other expenses are allowable even if you do not qualify to take a deduction for the business use of your home. However, if you have a home business, chances are you will pass the tests to take a home-office deduction.

Finally, and perhaps the most overlooked benefit to claiming a home-office deduction, is your ability to deduct more car expenses. If you do **not** take a home-business deduction, the miles driven to your first job site or appointment and the miles back home in the afternoon are considered non-deductible commuting miles. Those miles can be very significant, and, in most cases, consist of the greater part of miles driven on any given day.

 Keep that treadmill and weight set out of your home-office. Bringing exercise equipment into your home office introduces personal activity into the workspace and generally voids your ability to take a home-office deduction. Also, have a legitimate business explanation before bringing a big-screen TV or billiard table into your home office.

A Point Worth Repeating: Taking a business tax deduction for the business use of your home is a convoluted tax matter. You should seek the assistance of an experienced tax advisor for proper advice on your specific situation before making any final decisions. This discussion is meant to familiarize you with the requirements that must be met to qualify for a deduction. Having read the discussion, when you do meet with your CPA, you'll be able to listen intelligently to what he or she is saying, then ask very specific and relevant questions.

2.3 Getting the Feel of the Place

Apart from meeting the requirements imposed by the IRS to be able to take a tax deduction for the business use of a home, there is another good reason to carve out a designated area for your workspace as early in the organizing process as possible: Doing so allows you to begin a gradual transition from the structured mentality of a 9-to-5 employee to becoming a versatile BESt CEO.

In your 9-to-5 days, there was a reception area, a waiting area, restrooms, multiple offices, and so on. Your BESt Company will generally be restricted to a single room or area. You must structure your workspace to offer enough functionality so that customers are not inconvenienced. You also want the space to have a natural, unfettered flow.

For example, before going out and buying an office full of new furniture and office equipment (I know it's hard to resist), bring in that old desk with the missing drawers and a couple of folding chairs. Get a feel for your new space. Feel the way you flow in and out—not in some mystical way, but in a real, practical way. You want to make sure you have enough room to move about and operate. Ask yourself the follow questions:

1. Will customers be walk-ins or by appointment only?

2. How much furniture is needed to accommodate customers?

3. If clients have to wait to be served, how will they be accommodated? Where will they sit?

4. Is a coffee machine or a small refrigerator necessary to minimize travel from the kitchen to the office?

5. How will restroom requests be handled?

6. Will I be able to hold a private conversation while others are waiting?

I know it is immediately satisfying to spend a bunch of money on office furniture and equipment—the bigger and more plush, the better. It makes us feel legitimate and successful. Well, resist the urge. Think through every purchase. Don't buy a big, oversized desk simply because it looks good. Work out what will work best, given your space limitations and budget. You shouldn't have to unplug and move your fax machine every time someone wants to use the restroom. Think flow, both of people and of work procedure.

2.4 Business Entrance

The objective in configuring the best layout for your home office is to minimize the number of times customers or clients will run into family members or those calling on family members. For example, clients can get spooked if they ring a doorbell that is answered by your disappointed daughter who has just ran from a back room expecting to see her boyfriend. Clients should never feel unwelcome or as if they are intruding. Their visits should be anticipated, private, and welcomed.

Try to have a clearly marked, separate entrance to your business, if possible. If that is not possible, certainly not having a separate entrance is no deal breaker. Perhaps you can request that your family and their visitors use a seldom-used side or back entrance to minimize the chance of running into customers.

2.5 Office Essentials: A Word of Caution

Once you have identified a space, do not rush out and get in debt by purchasing a bunch of high-tech gadgets and a sleek modular workstation with a contemporary, ergonomic, high-back executive chair made with full-grain leather. You don't have to spend a fortune for good, functional equipment that will serve the purpose, especially office furniture and fixtures. Previously owned furniture is usually an excellent option—especially file cabinets, tables, and shelving. That being said, here are a few words to the wise.

A Comfortable Chair...Ahhh!

If you have responsibilities that will force you to have considerable "seat time," do yourself a favor and buy a chair that fits your body frame and preferences. Again, be forewarned: Higher cost does not necessarily mean greater comfort. One of the most comfortable chairs I own cost $60 brand new, right out the box! One of the most uncomfortable chairs I ever used was from my days as a 9-to-5er. It was a $400 leather chair with tacked upholstery and a high back. A beautiful chair, yes, but the most uncomfortable ever! It had a rigid bar across the front that would put pressure on the back of my thighs. It was torturous. I'd squirm the entire time I was seated. Generally, you get what you pay for, but sometimes the better deal is also the cheapest. The best way to buy a suitable chair is not from a catalogue, but to actually "test sit."

What About Used Stuff?

As I mentioned, I do not hesitate to suggest used furniture, but I generally do not suggest purchasing used computer equipment. Technology is moving too quickly and cost continues to fall too rapidly to scrimp on computer equipment. Without doubt, a computer will become a close ally in your daily effort to manage your BESt Company. Buy new computer equipment. Those will be some of the best dollars you'll ever spend.

2.6 Essential Equipment

Determine exactly what you need to run your business, make a list, and stick to it. In addition to office furniture and fixtures (desks, chairs, file cabinets, and so forth), here is a list of items you should have to present the proper image of professionalism.

➤ **A dedicated phone line.** A dedicated business line is not a luxury for a home office or an expense you only allow yourself once you are profitable enough to afford one. It is essential. I can't begin to tell you the horror stories I've heard involving teenagers with subwoofers buzzing from their boom boxes, or small children taught to answer business calls politely but who spook clients because they sound like just what they are: polite kids! A second phone line with voice mail gives you control over the professional image you want to project. If you think you can't afford a second phone line, eliminate some other expense to cover the cost. This is a "must have."

Note: Having a deluxe telephone is also a plus. I use a Panasonic (model KX-TG2000B). It has all the functions of a typical phone, but it also has an all-digital voice-mail system with auto attendant. Auto attendant eliminates the need for a receptionist in your office and also prevents messages from getting lost. You can set the voice-mail system to automatically answer all incoming mail with a personalized greeting and route callers to their desired extension, your cell phone, or a voice mailbox.

Following is contact information for three companies that offer a wide variety of telecommunication equipment that can handle the needs of most small businesses.

Company	Phone Number	Website
Motorola Personal Communications	800–331–6456	*www.motorola.com*
Panasonic	800–414–4408	*www.panasonic.com*
Uniden America	800–297–1023	*www.uniden.com*

➤ **Business cards.** In many cases, a business card is all a potential customer ever sees of your business. When you leave it with people you meet, it becomes a convenient reference should they decide to do business with you. I believe that first impressions are lasting ones. If your business card does not present a professional image, nor will your company. If you create your own cards with desktop publishing, try to avoid the cheap paper with the jagged, serrated edges. And please, please do not use a dot-matrix printer. The print quality is simply too poor.

➤ **A computer and printer.** An up-to-date computer and printer are simply essential to your business success. There are so many variables to consider when deciding on a system, that I have chosen to place the discussion of computer specifications outside the scope of this book. I will, however, mention that when deciding on a particular system, look for durability, ease of use, and, most importantly, customer support. And, of course, decide whether a desktop or a laptop will better serve your needs. My personal choice of computer equipment is a Dell laptop. Dell's products are reliable and, in my experience, customer service is very good.

 **BESt Website** Ⅲ➤

www.dell.com

In 2003, Dell reported that it has approximately 40,000 employees and revenues of $36.9 billion for four quarters. The company has ranked fourth on *Fortune* magazine's "Most Admired" lists. It was also named among the top-10 most trusted and respected companies by a *Wall Street Journal* poll. By any measure, Dell has an excellent reputation.

➤ **A fax machine.** Just be aware that most computer printers now have fax capabilities. Connecting a fax machine to a separate line provides maximum flexibility and 24/7 coverage for incoming documents.

➤ **An Internet Service Provider (ISP).** There is no doubt about it: Not being wired is a competitive disadvantage. Dial-ups, cable access, and digital subscriber lines (DSLs) are all options for your Internet connection. DSL and cable connections are quickly becoming the connections of choice for businesses and individuals. Of course, only pay for what you need. If your company does not need the fast-access capability, you can save $20 to $30 or more each month on this one expense. Be forewarned, however. If you ever experience the speed of cable or DSL access, chances are you will never be able to endure the comparable crawl of dial-up access.

➤ **A cell phone.** With the flexibility offered in the zillions of talk plans, cell phones are quite affordable for almost every budget. Because you may not have the luxury of a secretary initially, there is no better way to receive calls when you're on the go.

After securing these essentials, create a second list of other devices, such as a high-speed printer, copier, or deluxe phone system, that will help increase productivity. However, you should not delay the start of your business before you can afford a deluxe phone system or high-speed printer. In time, you will be able to acquire all that you need to increase productivity.

Chapter 3

Legal Requirements

There once was a young man from Lyme
Who couldn't get his limericks to rhyme
When asked "Why not?"
It was said that he thought
They were probably too long and badly structured and not at
all very funny.

—Anonymous

It can be very difficult to find the rhyme and reasoning behind the requirements that local, state, and federal governmental agencies impose on all businesses, both large and small. Thanks to politics and political stakeholders of all stripes, legal requirements and tax matters can be quite confusing, and decisions during the organizing process, once made, are often very difficult or impossible to undo. This chapter will help BESt CEOs better understand legal structure, zoning requirements, and general tax issues that must be dealt with at the time a company is being birthed. The goal is to acquaint the CEO with these issues so that they might be well thought out before any final decisions are made.

3.1 Deciding on a Legal Structure

One of the first critical decisions is to select a legal structure for your business. You, with the assistance of your accountant or attorney, must choose a legal structure that will best suit your needs and the needs of your business. The five principal types of business structures are:

1. Sole proprietorship.

2. Partnership.

3. Regular corporation (also called a "C" corporation).

4. "S" corporation.

5. Limited liability company.

Sole Proprietorship

A *sole proprietorship* is a business owned and operated by one person. You and your business are one; there is no distinction. Wherever you are, that's where your business is. If you move from New Orleans to Los Angeles, the business moves from New Orleans to Los Angeles as well. Move again to Denver, so does your business.

To establish a sole proprietorship, you need only obtain the operational licenses necessary to begin operations. Because it's so easy to adopt, many small businesses operate under this structure. However, just because many home-based businesses are sole proprietorships, don't automatically assume that a sole proprietorship is the best legal structure for your BESt Business. Every business is unique. Consider the pros and cons of a sole proprietorship.

Advantages

➤ Fewer formalities and fewer expenses involved in forming and operating a sole proprietorship. No partnership agreement is needed, nor do you have to register with the Secretary of State, as is the case with corporations and limited liability companies.

➤ As the sole owner, you have complete control over all decisions. You have no one to answer to but yourself. For many, this is a very compelling advantage.

➤ Structure can be easily terminated.

➤ No separate tax return. Income-tax filing is a part (Schedule C) of your annual personal tax return.

Disadvantages

➤ You are personally liable for any debts or damages your business incurs. This means that your personal property, such as your house, car, or other property, could be subject to the liabilities of your business. Ouch! Without question, this is the greatest disadvantage for most people.

➤ Difficult to secure financing. Your bank is in essence lending directly to you, so your company's ability and your ability to borrow money is essentially the same. If the bank considers you a poor credit risk, your company will likewise be viewed as a poor credit risk.

➤ There is a perception of "smallness." Some companies are resistant to doing business with companies they perceive as small. The fact that you won't be able to use the **"Inc."** designation or the word *Corporation* in your name could invite closer scrutiny.

➤ As the sole owner, all managerial responsibility lies on your shoulders. That makes for some very long days.

Partnership

General, Limited, and *Limited Liability Partnerships* are found frequently in today's business environment. According to the Uniform Partnership Act, *a **partnership** is an "association of two or more persons to carry on as co-owners of a business for profit."*

Partnerships generally are guided by a written partnership agreement. The Uniform Partnership Act does not specifically require a written agreement, but to not have one is to invite unnecessary and inevitable misunderstanding. A written partnership agreement is *strongly* recommended. The agreement spells out what the partners are to contribute to the partnership, the division of profits and losses, and the general duties of the partners.

Advantages

➤ As a result of partners pooling their assets and talents, a partnership generally has more resources than a sole proprietorship.

➤ A partnership does not pay federal income tax. An information tax return (Form 1065), which shows what income, losses, tax credits, and so forth passed through to the partners, must be filed. But, again, this is only an informational return.

➤ Liability can be spread among all partners.

➤ Less expensive to organize than a corporation.

➤ Synergy of combined effort of the partners. A synergistic effect essentially means that 1 plus 1 equals 3—or, the sum of the whole is greater than the individual parts. Almost always, two people working together can typically accomplish more than two individuals working separately.

Disadvantages

➤ Agreement among partners can be fragile. Strife among partners is not uncommon. Very important to have a partnership agreement, which minimizes misunderstandings and strife.

➤ Limited life. Each time a new partner is admitted or withdraws, a new partnership agreement is needed.

➤ Unlimited liability. Each partner has an unlimited personal liability for the debts of the partnership. If a partnership cannot pay its debts, the partners must use personal assets to pay partnership debts.

➤ Can be expensive to buy out a partner.

Corporation

Corporations are complex legal entities. They are defined as *"an artificial being, invisible, intangible, and existing only in contemplation of the law."* Essentially, what that means is that a corporation is a distinct, legal entity separate from the individuals who own it. It is, if you will, an artificial person.

It is *essential* for you to obtain competent legal advice if you are thinking about forming a corporation. Mistakes in formation can easily be made that can damage the veil of protection offered by a properly formed corporation. In other words, you'll think you are protected from personal liability, but the limited liability protection offered by a corporation may be harmed by some novice mistake. Be careful!

The Secretary of State for your state has a Website (see Table 3-B starting on page 44) that spells out all the requirements for incorporation. Among the requirements, you will have to file *articles of incorporation* and corporate *bylaws*. Articles of incorporation state the powers and limitations of your company. Bylaws serve as the constitution for governing the corporation.

Advantages
➤ The owners' (stockholders') liability is usually limited to their investment. This means that in the event of a lawsuit, the owners' personal assets are protected.
➤ Corporation continues to exist even if a stockholder dies.
➤ Business ownership is represented by shares of stock, which are readily transferable.
➤ Generally easier to raise capital.

Disadvantages
➤ More complex and difficult to set up than other business structures. Generally requires legal assistance.
➤ Double taxation. First, corporations pay their own income taxes on corporate income; then stockholders pay personal income tax on the dividends that they receive from corporations. This issue is currently being addressed by Congress. President George W. Bush has proposed to eliminate double taxation. The final result is pending. [*Note: Specific tax issues are exceedingly complex and totally beyond the scope of this guide. Whenever tax issues are discussed, it is only to broadly orient the reader. Your CPA or attorney can provide specific advice.*]

Limited Liability Company

*A **Limited Liability Company** ("LLC") is a hybrid type of legal entity—it has qualities of both a corporation and a partnership.* As does a corporation, an LLC must also register with the Secretary of State. LLCs provide protection from personal liability similar to a corporation, but with the tax benefits of a partnership. Unlike a corporation, where the owners are called stockholders, owners of a LLC are called members.

Advantages
→ Limited personal liability for the owners.

→ No federal taxes.

→ No limit of the number of members.

Disadvantages
→ Complex rules. It is *essential* that an attorney familiar with LLC law be consulted when considering this legal structure.

→ No "continuity of life" as with a regular corporation.

3.2 Is It Necessary to Hire an Attorney to Incorporate?

The Internet is ablaze with services that will walk you through the process of forming a corporation or LLC for approximately one-fourth the cost of hiring an attorney. For example, to hire an attorney to incorporate your BESt Company in your state might run as much as $850, maybe more. On the other hand, using these self-incorporation services on the Internet costs approximately $250. A fantastic savings of $600! This seems to be a quite attractive option—and it is—but be forewarned! It is very easy to make serious and costly mistakes when you self-incorporate. Remember: Your business structure is the foundation of your business. If the foundation is ill-formed, the business can be exposed to unnecessary taxes and liability. Unless you are very comfortable with business law, I would recommend that you seek competent advice when forming a partnership, corporation, or LLC.

3.3 Which Business Structure Is Best?

You will have to decide very early in the organizing process which business structure is best for your unique set of business and personal circumstances. I know I'm pounding this issue, but this decision should not be made without first consulting your CPA and/or attorney. This is a very complex and technical issue with far-reaching consequences. The decision you ultimately make can affect how you will withdraw funds from your business, how you pay yourself, and the amount of your annual tax liability. Let me repeat that: The decision you ultimately make can affect the amount of your *annual* tax liability!

In order to make the best decision, you should have a planning session with your hired professionals. Give them a full appreciation of your plans, your goals, and the procedures you will employ in day-to-day operations.

Of course, the future being veiled, it is difficult to know ultimately what will happen. But as I have been declaring and you are beginning to recognize, not being able to foretell the future is no excuse for shabby planning. Your first choice regarding business structure should reflect the best information available regarding your vision and intent.

 When deciding on a business structure, don't underestimate your potential. Many small, home-based businesses become extremely successful in a relatively short period of time. Starting as a sole proprietor may seem like a "no-brainer," but as the company grows, you may become very concerned about limiting your personal liability. And, as I mentioned, limited liability is not available to sole proprietorships. In some cases, switching from one business structure to another is so costly and complicated that it becomes virtually impossible to accomplish without adversely affecting the company's cash flow. (See section 12.8 for a discussion on cash flow.)

For many BESt CEOs, the most appealing consideration when deciding which business form to adopt is the limited liability offered by corporations and LLCs. But bear in mind that, as a home-based small enterprise, most lenders will still require you to execute a personal guarantee for loans. When you sign a personal guarantee, the limited liability of a corporation or LLC is sidestepped and claims can be made against your personal property just as if the corporation or limited liability company did not exist.

Even without the benefit of limited liability, more than 70 percent of all businesses in the U.S. are sole proprietorships.

Source: bizstats.com

3.4 The Best Legal Structure for Your BESt Company—Part II

It is not remotely possible to give specific advice regarding the legal structure that will best serve the needs of you and your business. As a BESt CEO, you will be required to wear many hats, but you must know your limitations. No one expects you to wear the hat of a CPA or an attorney. **The bottom line is this**: To avoid legal problems later on, you must obtain professional counsel prior to making a final decision regarding business structure—period. Enough said.

3.5 What Is a Tax Year?

Federal and state taxing authorities are interested in the results of your business performance. They are interested in how much your business makes in order to assess their share of taxes. Because federal and perhaps state and local tax returns are filed on an annual basis, you must decide on an annual accounting period called a tax year. *A **tax year** is a period of 12 consecutive months for which a company or business calculates earnings, profits, and losses.* The tax year is also used as a benchmark to compare a company's growth and progress from year to year.

There are three kinds of tax years:

⊳ **Calendar tax year.** A period of 12 consecutive months beginning January 1st and ending December 31st.

⊳ **Fiscal tax year.** A period of 12 consecutive months ending on the last day of any month other than December. For example, you could have a fiscal tax year that runs from July 1st through June 30th.

⊳ **52–53 week tax year.** Allows a business to always end its tax year on the same day of the week. For example, you may want your tax year to always end on the last Monday in March.

Your tax year should reflect your natural business cycle. In other words, try to time your tax year in such a way that it will end when inventory is at its lowest point. If your BESt Company does not have inventory, time your tax year to end when general business activity is at its lowest point. If you operate a business as a *sole proprietor,* however, the tax year for your business must be the same as your individual tax year. (In most cases that would be a calendar tax year.)

Be aware that for some business formations, special rules may apply. For more information about tax years, see *www.irs.gov* and do a search for Publication 538.

3.6 Account and ID Numbers You'll Need (and When to Apply)

Employer Identification Number. *An **Employer Identification Number** ("EIN") is a nine-digit number assigned to all companies, including corporations, partnerships, and limited liability companies. The IRS uses this number in the same fashion as it does social security numbers for individuals.* EINs are used on many forms, including your federal income tax return, loan applications, contracts, and so forth. Use Form SS-4 to apply for an EIN. (See *www.irs.gov* to download a copy of Form SS-4 and/or to get instructions on how to complete the form.)

You should only apply for an EIN once you've decided on the business structure and the tax year. In fact, these three issues are generally dealt with at the same time. When you talk to your CPA about business structure and establishing a tax year, filing for an EIN is a natural outcome of those discussions.

The IRS has made the process of obtaining an EIN incredibly easy. The IRS requires that companies applying for EINs do so according to the state in which the business is located. Many BESt CEOs let their CPAs obtain their EINs. Some CEOs, however, feel competent enough to acquire their own. Depending on your location, use Table 3-A to determine the service center that would handle your request.

Contact Number to Obtain an EIN	
Location of BESt Company	CALL or FAX your EIN application to the following number:
Connecticut, Delaware, District of Columbia, Florida, Georgia, Maine, Maryland, Massachusetts, New Hampshire, New Jersey, New York, North Carolina, Ohio, Pennsylvania, Rhode Island, South Carolina, Vermont, Virginia, West Virginia	Brookhaven IRS Center Attn.: EIN Operation Phone: 866–816–2065 Fax: 631–447–8960
Illinois, Indiana, Kentucky, Michigan	Cincinnati IRS Center Attn.: EIN Operation Phone: 866–816–2065 Fax: 859–669–5760
Alabama, Alaska, Arizona, Arkansas, California, Colorado, Hawaii, Idaho, Iowa, Kansas, Louisiana, Minnesota, Mississippi, Missouri, Montana, Nebraska, Nevada, Oklahoma, North Dakota, New Mexico, Oregon, Puerto Rico, South Dakota, Tennessee, Texas, Utah, Washington, Wisconsin, Wyoming	Philadelphia IRS Center Attn.: EIN Operation Phone: 866–816–2065 Fax: 215–516–3990
If you have no legal residence, principal place of business, or principal office or agency in any state:	Philadelphia IRS Center Attn.: EIN Operation Phone: 866–816–2065 Fax: 215–516–3990

Table 3-A

Call the telephone numbers in Table 3-A only to apply for an EIN. Call the IRS's toll-free number (800–829–1040) or the number listed in the government pages of your telephone book for any other tax-related inquiries or questions.

Other Identification Numbers. There is no uniformity from state to state or county to county (or, as is the case in Louisiana, parish to parish) with regard to specific registration requirements for your BESt Business. Businesses have to apply to many different departments and agencies, depending on the transaction type (for example, occupational licenses, sales taxes, unemployment insurance, state income taxes, and so forth). Although there are many registrations to consider, it is important to realize that some will apply and some will not. For example, some states do not assess or collect state income taxes. Obviously, if you live in a state with no state income taxes, you will not have to apply for a state withholding tax number. The following list gives the more common types of business registrations that most businesses typically need to apply for.

➤ **State withholding tax.** As an employer, you may be required to withhold state income taxes from your employees' paychecks. Registering for a state withholding tax number allows companies to report to the proper authorities the state taxes withheld from employees' wages.

➤ **State employment tax.** Registration allows the employer to report the mandated contributions to state unemployment insurance coiffeurs.

➤ **State sales tax.** To facilitate the reporting of sales taxes collected by merchants that, in turn, must be remitted to the state.

➤ **County/parish occupational license.** Registration and payment of a fee gives a business the right to "do business" within a certain jurisdiction.

➤ **County/parish sales taxes.** To facilitate the reporting of sales taxes collected by merchants that, in turn, are remitted to the county or parish where the sale was made.

➤ **Local taxes.** Specific to each locale. Contact your local governmental officials for specific details.

The bottom line is that you must call or visit the various state and local agencies to determine their specific requirements. You can save yourself a great deal of time and effort by first contacting your State Secretary's office. Most State Secretaries have a "one-stop shop" where you can register with all the appropriate governmental agencies and taxing authorities.

The following table is a convenient resource to locate your Secretary of State on the Web. Generally, these Websites are filled with resources that you will find extremely helpful, especially in the beginning stages of business formation. Be prepared to search around a bit for the information you need. If you have difficulty, use the included phone number to get assistance. And don't be bashful. Usually, the personnel that handle such inquiries are very helpful.

One-Stop Licensing Resources		
State	**Website Address**	**Phone (General Info)**
Alabama	*www.sos.state.al.us/*	334–242–7205
Alaska	*www.gov.state.ak.us*	907–465–3520
Arizona	*www.sosaz.com/*	602–542–7386
Arkansas	*www.sosweb.state.ar.us/*	501–682–1010
California	*www.ss.ca.gov*	916–653–6814
Colorado	*www.sos.state.co.us*	303–869–4860
Connecticut	*www.sots.ct.us*	860–509–6212
Delaware	*www.state.de.us/sos/*	302–739–3811
District of Columbia	*www.dc.gov/*	202–727–1000
Florida	*www.dos.fl.us*	850–245–6500
Georgia	*www.sos.state.ga.us*	404–656–2817
Hawaii	*www.hawaii.gov/*	866–462–3468
Idaho	*www.idsos.state.id.us*	208–334–2300
Illinois	*www.sos.state.il.us*	312–793–3380
Indiana	*www.in.gov/sos/*	317–232–6576
Iowa	*www.sos.state.ia.us/*	515–281–5204
Kansas	*www.kssos.org*	785–298–4564
Kentucky	*www.sos.state.ky.us/*	502–564–3490
Louisiana	*www.sec.state.la.us*	225–922–0433
Maine	*www.state.me.us/sos/*	207–626–8400
Maryland	*www.sos.state.md.us/*	410–974–5521
Massachusetts	*www.state.ma.us/sec/*	617–727–7030
Michigan	*www.michigan.gov/sos*	517–322–1460
Minnesota	*www.state.mn.us/ebranch/sos/*	651–296–2803
Mississippi	*www.sos.state.ms.us/*	800–256–3494
Missouri	*www.sos.state.mo.gov*	573–751–4153

One-Stop Licensing Resources		
State	**Website Address**	**Phone (General Info)**
Montana	www.sos.state.mt.us	406–444–3665
Nebraska	www.sos.state.ne.us	402–471–4079
Nevada	www.sos.state.nv.us/	775–684–5708
New Hampshire	www.sos.nh.gov	603–271–3242
New Jersey	www.state.nj.us	609–984–1900
New Mexico	www.sos.state.nm.us/	800–477–3632
New York	www.state.ny.us/	518–474–4750
North Carolina	www.secstate.state.nc.us/	919–807–2166
North Dakota	www.state.nd.us/sec/	701–328–2900
Ohio	www.state.oh.us/sos/	877–767–3453
Oklahoma	www.sos.state.ok.us/	405–521–3771
Oregon	www.sos.state.or.us/	503–986–2204
Pennsylvania	www.dos.state.pa.us	717–787–1057
Rhode Island	www.state.ri.us/	401–222–2357
South Carolina	www.scsos.com/	803–734–2170
South Dakota	www.state.sd.us	605–733–3537
Tennessee	www.state.tn.us/sos	615–741–2286
Texas	www.sos.state.tx.us/	512–463–5555
Utah	www.utah.gov	877–988–3468
Vermont	www.sec.state.vt.us/	802–828–2363
Virginia	www.soc.state.va.us/	804–786–2441
Washington	www.secstate.wa.gov/	360–902–4151
West Virginia	www.wvsos.com/	304–558–8000
Wisconsin	www.wisconsin.gov	608–266–8888
Wyoming	soswy.state.wy.us/	307–777–7378

Table 3-B

3.7 Zoning Requirements

All cities and towns (municipalities) have established zoning ordinances to protect community standards and property values. They are also used to control the type and level of activity that takes place within any given area. Even though zoning is a universal concept, local zoning laws on home-based businesses vary considerably from community to community. There is no "one-size-fits-all" zoning code.

Some zoning ordinances limit all in-home businesses; others will look the other way if your business is discreet and not disruptive to your neighbors. For example, if you maintain a bookkeeping practice or have a company that designs Web pages, you could do amazing business without calling attention to yourself. Your neighbors would never guess a business was right next door. On the other hand, discretion is totally out the window if you sell used cars, run a trucking service, or provide a daycare service for preschoolers. Fortunately, most communities do allow home-based businesses.

In addition to the types of work that can be done from home, your specific community might have something to say about other issues, such as the use of on-street and off-street parking, whether or not signs are allowed, the size and construction of signs, the number of employees you may hire, and the hours you may legally operate. Obviously, this list is incomplete. For peace of mind and the ability to operate in the most open manner, it pays to give your *local planning commission* a call to find out what you can and cannot do. This is especially important before making any investment or irreversibly modifying your home to accommodate customers.

Common Licenses and Permits		
Licenses and Permits	**Description**	**Where to Go**
Health Department Permit	Needed when food is sold directly or indirectly to customers	Local health department
Liquor Licenses	Needed when wine, beer, and hard liquor are sold	Local beverage control agency
Sign Permit	Needed when the municipality has specific restrictions on signs	Local municipal government
Occupational License or Business License	Grants businesses the right to operate within a particular jurisdiction	Local municipal government

Table 3-C

Chapter 4

Business Insurance

They're funny things, accidents. You never have them till you're having them.

—Eeyore, in *Pooh's Little Instruction Book*

I don't want to tell you how much insurance I carry with the Prudential, but all I can say is: when I go, they go too.

—Jack Benny

4.1 Luck Is No Substitute for Insurance

One step forward, one hundred steps backward. That's what it's like when some unfortunate event occurs and there is no insurance in place to cover losses. Sometimes the losses can be insurmountable. As much effort as it takes to launch or grow your BESt Business, the last thing you need is a financial setback due to a lack of insurance.

It is easy to rationalize not purchasing adequate insurance. I've heard them all. See if any sound familiar: *I'll be extremely careful....I just don't have the funds....I'm pretty lucky, I'll just roll the dice....I just started; I don't have that much to lose....If I have to start over, so be it.* Some comments are haughty, others simply naïve. But you can bet they all sound pretty hollow and short-sighted when disaster strikes. And by disaster, I don't mean some catastrophic event of biblical proportions. A disaster could be a small fire, a burglary, or someone tripping over a garden hose that slipped off its rack. Anything could happen, and, at some point, generally does. Please don't get me wrong, I am not a harbinger of doom, but I've seen months and even years of effort spent growing a business simply go down the drain due to some uninsured and untimely incident. And the sad fact is this: All such incidents are untimely.

Generally, accidents couldn't happen at a worse time—regardless of when they happen. When you think of the risk, investment, and sweat that go into growing a business, it just makes sense to protect your investment.

4.2 Which Types of Insurance Should You Consider?

There's a glut of insurance products on the market, and the process of purchasing insurance can be quite overwhelming. To simplify the matter, we will focus on the basic insurance needs of a small company and how to get the most bang for your insurance buck. The basic insurance needs of a business include, but are not limited to, the following:

> ‣ Auto.
> ‣ Property.
> ‣ General liability.
> ‣ Umbrella coverage.
> ‣ Workers' compensation.

Other insurance products should be considered based on the nature of your specific industry. For example, accountants should consider carrying professional liability insurance, such as errors and omissions.

4.3 Auto Insurance

If your BESt Company uses an auto for business activities, you need to have automobile coverage that will protect you from accidents that occur while you or your employees are engaged in business activities (for example, picking up inventory or supplies, ferrying customers, or visiting clients). Your personal automobile policy may cover limited business uses, but you need to verify that with your insurance agent. Be sure to ask very specific questions! Inform the agent about the exact nature of your business and the situations in which an automobile will be used. Probably, however, a separate business auto insurance policy will be needed. Again, your insurance agent can help you make the proper decisions.

Auto Insurance Cost-Saving Ideas

Even though auto insurance tends to be relatively expensive, there is quite a bit of flexibility in its cost structure. Usually, the most effective cost savings strategy is to simply adjust your policy deductible. Deductibles can range from $100 to $1,000 or more. As the size of the deductible increases, the amount of the premium decreases. The idea is that you assume some of the risk of loss in order to have a lower premium. Obviously, the caution here is to make sure you can pay the deductible in the event of an accident.

Another cost savings, especially pertaining to older cars, is to eliminate specific types of coverage. If the book value of an auto is approaching zero (which means that its value is substantially depreciated) and there is no outstanding mortgage balance, you might consider removing the collision and comprehensive coverage altogether. Comprehensive coverage helps pay for damage resulting from fire, theft, vandalism, and some natural disasters. Collision insurance covers damage to your vehicle from collisions with other cars or objects. It covers only your car and not the object it hits.

A third cost savings tip is to ask your agent if the auto premium is discounted when the amount of miles driven is local or below some minimum. For example, if all your business miles are local, there might be a cost savings (as opposed to the company that accumulates heavy mileage or does interstate driving).

4.4 Property Insurance

Property insurance protects business assets from damage or loss from fire, explosion, natural disasters, vandalism, and so forth. The current trend by agents is to quote property insurance written on an all-risk basis, with exceptions spelled out. So unless an exception is specifically spelled out, the property insurance will cover the loss. Exceptions can include losses resulting from flooding, and hailstorms, for example. Conversely, some property policies will only protect your business property from specific perils or risks spelled out in the policy. All-risk coverage is highly recommended as long as you specifically review the policy's exclusions and evaluate the impact such risk would have on your company.

Property Insurance: Replacement Cost vs. Actual Cash Value

"Replacement cost" and "actual cash value" refer to the different methods insurance companies use to calculate the amount it will pay for a loss that you incur. Payment based on the replacement cost of damaged or stolen property is usually the most favorable figure from your point of view, because it compensates for the actual cost of replacing property. For example, if your laptop is stolen, a replacement cost policy will reimburse you the full cost of replacing it with a new (and similar) laptop. The insurer will not take into consideration the fact that the laptop was used in business every working day for the past year, causing a considerable amount of wear and tear.

In contrast, actual cash value, also known as market value, is equal to the replacement cost minus any depreciation. That is, the insurance company determines the amount of wear and tear on the property. In the case of the stolen laptop, the insured would receive an amount equal to the replacement value less a deduction for wear and tear.

The only difference between replacement cost and actual cash value is a deduction for wear and tear. If possible, you should insure your property with *replacement cost* insurance as opposed to *actual cash value* insurance.

4.5 General Liability Insurance

General liability coverage protects your BESt Company's assets against claims of bodily injury or property damage caused by you or your employees that occur on or away from your premises. Such injuries might result from a faulty product, operational problems, independent contractors, a disputed service, or many other reasons that might be attributable to the operations of your business. The policy also contains specific exclusions generally covered by some other policy, such as auto insurance, health insurance, or workers' compensation. However, "no fault" coverage for medical payments is usually included in general liability policies, subject to a modest limit such as $5,000 per person.

Do not assume that your homeowner's policy will cover your BESt Company. It probably doesn't! This is especially true if you have customers or delivery persons expressly coming to your place of business to transact business. Carefully review your homeowner's policy with your agent. Be prepared to purchase additional liability insurance for your BESt Business.

The cost of general liability insurance depends on the type of business, the size of the business, and the safety standards of the industry. The premium is based on the company's exposure to different types of risks. For example, a general liability policy for a building contractor is more expensive than for a janitorial service. An agent can easily estimate the annual premium for this type of coverage based on the size of your business as determined by payroll costs, square footage, or some other quantitative factor.

General Liability Insurance Cost-Saving Ideas

First, work with your agent to determine adequate liability coverage. Generally, experts suggest $2 to $3 million in liability coverage should be sufficient. But again, your business may need less (or more) depending on your specific risk factors. Also, make sure you shop around for the best buy. Even though you may have a long relationship with a particular insurance broker, he or she may not be giving you the best deal. Finally, ask about discounts. Oftentimes, insurance companies offer premium discounts to businesses that carry several different types of coverages with the same insurance company or agency.

4.6 Umbrella Policies

An umbrella policy, as the name implies, provides an extra layer of coverage when the limits of other policies are reached, or for liabilities not covered in any other policy. For example, suppose you are responsible for the injuries of someone and their treatment costs $400,000. If your general liability policy only covers $300,000, then the additional $100,000 would be picked up by your umbrella policy.

Allow me to quickly dispel a common misconception: Umbrella policies are not just for the wealthy. Umbrella policies are very affordable and are easily coordinated with other policies to give added protection and peace of mind.

4.7 Workers' Compensation

Workers' compensation is a system of benefits provided by state law to cover most full-time and part-time workers from job-related injuries. Workers' comp is mandated by state law in all 50 states and varies state by state. Workers' comp usually consists of three tiers, two compulsory and one voluntary:

➤ **Medical bills and lost wages.** All necessary medical services reasonably required to treat an ill or injured employee. This tier of the insurance also covers reimbursement for lost wages when an employee is under a doctor's orders not to report to work due to a job-related injury or illness.

➤ **Employer's liability.** Covers the company in the event a spouse or child of an injured or killed employee decides to sue.

➤ **Voluntary coverage.** Protects employers from the acts of their employees. For example, employers would be protected against lawsuits that result from age or sexual discrimination, and so forth.

Each state has different requirements that determine when a company must purchase workers' compensation. Factors such as the number of employees and the type of industry often come into play. For example, in some states, any business with five or more employees or any company in the construction industry is required to carry workers' comp. Also, in many jurisdictions, corporate officers are considered to be employees and, therefore, are included in the count for determining whether an employer is required to purchase the coverage. Your insurance agent will be able to give you specific advice.

The cost of workers' compensation insurance varies according to the type of business in which you are involved and the estimated payrolls. Classifications are assigned to business categories, and rates vary according to each classification. For example, a delivery service business might have a classification for the driver, a classification for those involved in sales, and a classification for those involved in administration. Each classification has a different rate, depending on the relative risk of injury involved in each job function. Thus, these classifications become the basis for the estimated premiums. At the end of the policy year, the insurance company will audit payroll records and adjust the estimated premium to reflect the actual payroll expenses.

4.8 The Bottom Line

A good insurance plan begins with a realistic assessment of risks. The CEO can implement many actions to reduce risks and thus minimize the likelihood of loss. For example, fire extinguishers, alarm systems, and periodic maintenance of equipment can all work together to reduce risks. A reduction of risks generally leads to a lower incidence of claims, which, in turn, is one of the best ways to keep costs as low as possible. At the end of the day, however, no matter how safe you try to be, accidents will happen. The key is to protect your investment and, in the event of loss, to have coverage in place to keep you from having to start all over.

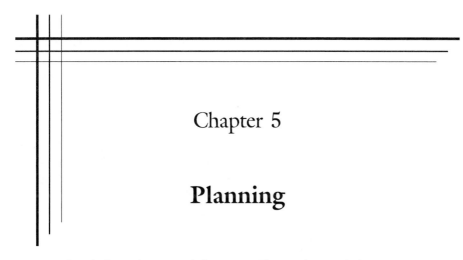

Chapter 5

Planning

Good plans shape good decisions. That's why good planning helps to make elusive dreams come true.

—Lester R. Bittel, *The Nine Master Keys of Management*

Plans are only good intentions unless they immediately degenerate into hard work.

—Peter F. Drucker

Without a solid foundation, the grandest house is destined to fall into a heap of rubble. Banish the thought: ***I'm too small to need a business plan.*** No, you're not! That sort of thinking will put you at a competitive disadvantage no matter how solid your business idea is or how popular your products are. A good plan is a prelude to good action. It focuses thoughts and desires into goals—goals that can be measured and modified. Without a plan, you will approach situations without a clear pattern of execution—in effect, a soldier without a battle plan. Consequently, you'll wind up expending more energy and receiving less in return; spending more money and receiving less value; and accepting mediocrity, rather than demanding excellence.

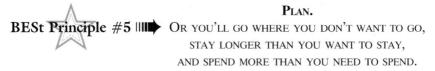

PLAN.
BESt Principle #5 ▐▐▐▶ OR YOU'LL GO WHERE YOU DON'T WANT TO GO,
STAY LONGER THAN YOU WANT TO STAY,
AND SPEND MORE THAN YOU NEED TO SPEND.

The Difference Between a Strategic Plan and a Business Plan

You may hear the term *strategic plan* mentioned from time to time. A business plan is not a strategic plan. A strategic plan is a planning tool for the management of larger companies to identify and address external opportunities and threats to a firm, to identify internal strengths and weaknesses, to formulate strategy to deal with competitive issues, and to allocate the resources of the firm. Strategic plans are broad in scope and do not focus on specific action. You **will not** need a separate strategic plan.

A business plan is action-specific. It can be compared to a simulation—a practice run. A well-thought-out business plan will allow the BESt CEO to think out the results of decisions before they are actually implemented. Business plans also anticipate the resources that will be needed to accomplish BESt Goals. Where strategic plans tend to be abstract, business plans are more concrete. BESt Companies can easily combine the features of both plans into a comprehensive business plan. You **will** need a business plan.

5.1 FAQs: Business Plans

What Is a Business Plan?

➤ Follows a fairly common format.

➤ Written by the BESt CEO, with input from hired professionals as required (CPA, insurance agent, attorney, and so forth).

➤ Describes legal structure of the BESt Company.

➤ Describes competition.

➤ Describes how the company will operate in the marketplace.

➤ Describes how the company will be financed and managed.

➤ Projects revenue and expenses to determine if the BESt Company is potentially profitable.

Why Should I Prepare a Business Plan?

➤ Serves as a guide for decision-making.

➤ Serves as a checklist for organizing and managerial purposes.

➤ Serves as a tool to help obtain financing; banks expect to see one. It is highly unlikely that any company, home-based or otherwise, will obtain significant financing without a business plan.

➤ Allows you to think through your operation before "going live." As you draft your plan you will quickly see strengths and weaknesses as they are revealed. For example, if you haven't identified your competition, perhaps you may be planning to offer the same service that can be obtained across town for 15 percent less than your price. Planning helps you to "see" these situations.

➤ Helps you to estimate your true cash needs.

➤ Provides a "yardstick" that can be used as an assessment tool. The objectives and strategies outlined in the document can be reviewed periodically to see how close reality is lining up to the plan.

➤ Provides a basis for the next plan. There is no sense in reinventing the wheel each time you need to update your business plan.

When Should I Prepare It?

➤ The more information you possess the more accurate your plan, but...

➤ Don't wait until you've opened the doors for business. Organizing activities can be facilitated by your written business plan.

➤ After you have completed all the legal requirements outlined in Chapter 3, that is, after you determine what business structure works best (sole proprietorship, partnership, corporation, or limited liability company); filed to receive an EIN; and decided on a tax year. Again, those three first steps go hand-in-hand.

5.2 Before You Go Into Battle, Count the Cost

Before going to battle, find out as much as you can about the hostile environment of small business. Planning helps organize that process. You might feel overwhelmed about putting your ideas and thoughts on paper. Invariably, the following question is asked: *Why so much thinking and planning and writing? Can't we just get started already?* The answer is: *Yes, you could.* But running a business is like fighting a war. I know—you would rather be on the front line drumming up business than crouched over a desk drawing up battle plans. And you will be—soon. But right now, you need to understand the lay of the land (the business environment). You need to find out where the land mines are buried (legal requirements and responsibilities), where the enemy is crouched (the competition), and where the opportunities are hidden (potential profits).

Imagine paratrooping into hostile territory without knowing the lay of the land. You'd be a sitting duck. You better believe your competition knows the lay of the land. So be patient and do your homework. The process may seem as if it goes on and on and on and on, but it does not. As a child, as I anticipated Christmas gifts, I used to think that Christmas Eve was the longest night of the year. Of course, it was no longer than any other night; it only seemed that way.

The length of time it takes to gather information and write a business plan depends on the type of business, the systems you must create, and the amount of resources you have. At any rate, there's a lot to do. Hopping around on one foot, with one hand tied behind your back, trying to do a little of this and a little of that just will not cut it—you have to know where you're going. Right now, your job is to determine the best route.

5.3 Developing a Business Plan

Section 5.4 will introduce you to the various elements that are included in a typical business plan. As I've mentioned several times before, every business is unique, and there is no one correct way to write a business plan. Nevertheless, each plan has essentially the same elements.

Your business plan is a practical document, yet it must convey all the enthusiasm and passion you have about your BESt Company. To be taken seriously, it must:

1. Project a professional image.

2. Have facts that are verifiable.

3. Include financial projections that are reasonable.

People who are experienced and practical in financial matters will read your plan. They will be able to distinguish between hype and reasonableness. You must keep it real. I'll give you a sample of a business plan (starting on page 64) to use as a guide for your own unique business plan. I also have a business plan questionnaire in Appendix A, plus several business planning Websites in Appendix B that you'll find very helpful.

5.4 General Elements of a Business Plan

If you do not have all the finances necessary to start your business, the first person who will receive your plan will probably a banker. As a lender, he or she probably receives many business plans throughout the year. After a while, they all start to look the same. That's not necessarily a bad thing—assuming yours is well prepared. A well-presented plan, free of typographical and computational errors, will receive the attention it deserves. That is the banker's responsibility, and to do less would be unethical and negligent.

Business plans have become so commonplace that there is almost, but not quite, a standard format. As you prepare your own business plan, you may wish to arrange the sequence of topics differently. However, the following represents the contents of a typical business plan.

Title Page. The title sheet should be attractively formatted and uncluttered. The reader should be able to identify the demographic information about the company at a glance. The title page contains the business name, address, phone number, fax number, and e-mail address. This will be the first page of your report. Make it inviting, neat, and orderly.

Table of Contents. List each section of the document by page number. The readers of your plan are quite busy. The better your plan is organized, the more likely they are to give it adequate consideration. Better organization also cuts down on the number of questions.

Executive Summary. The executive summary is a concise overview of your plan, preferably one page. It is generally the last section written. This is the section where your overall business strategy is described. The executive summary gives a bird's-eye view of the company. It should be written concisely and cleanly.

Industry Analysis. The industry analysis includes current economic conditions and industry trends. Trends reveal the direction of the market—that is, whether or not the demand for your particular products and/or services is growing, declining, or relatively stable.

Company Overview. This describes the form of business organization, whether you will operate as a sole proprietor, partnership, a corporation, or a limited liability company. The company overview provides the address of the business, which, for a home-based business should be the same as your home address, unless you have a separate entrance with a different address. This section also contains the following information:

▷ The date founded.

▷ Ownership data.

▷ A brief history of events leading to the founding of the company.

▷ A brief summary of products and services.

Products and Services. This section contains a detailed description of all products and services, including features and benefits.

Advertising and Promotion. From a practical standpoint, this section of the business plan is the most important. It explains exactly how you plan to entice potential customers to do business with your BESt Company. Before you can market effectively, you must know who comprises your market— that is, you must know your intended customers and their buying habits. Getting a full description of the composition of your market and their buying habits could be a time-consuming and costly affair. Nevertheless, the more you know about those you are selling to, the better you can tailor advertising dollars. The following advertising and promotion questions should be answered:

1. Who are the BESt Company's customers (age, sex, occupation, and so on)?

2. What is the present size of the market? What will be your share? How do you plan to increase your share?

3. How do customers get their information? What publications do they read? What radio stations do they listen to?

4. Which advertising media would be most effective? In other words, how can you reach the greatest number of potential customers for the least cost?

5. How will you convey your image? For example, how will customers view your printed material? Your business environment? Appearance? Voice-mail messages? Promotional gifts? Will you be perceived as trendy? Conservative?

6. How will you measure the effectiveness of your advertising campaign?

In some cases it is not possible or practical to identify all the potential customers that comprise your market. For example, using e-mail and Internet access, a computer consultant could theoretically work for any company anywhere in the world. Trying to define a market so large, complex, and fuzzy would be difficult indeed. For BESt Companies, I have coined a concept I call demographic relevant range. *The demographic relevant range ("DRR") is a manageable geographic area consisting of potential customers that a small business could effectively serve.* The key phrase is "effectively serve." Many BESt Companies can serve distant clients, but can they do so in a cost-effective manner? There is great benefit in periodically being "face to face" with a customer. The cost of business travel, for example, can quickly mount if several plane trips and hotel stays are required to effectively service an account. Such mounting cost tends to make effectively servicing distant clients cost prohibitive.

The DRR depends on the exact nature and capacity of the BESt Company in question. Some BESt Businesses, such as Internet companies, can include the entire world as a potential market; others, such as child-care services, are limited to a single county or community. My market, for example, consists of all small, African-American businesses in the United States. This book does not address organizing and managerial issues in China. A Chinese businesswoman living in Beijing would not profit from this book as much as an African-American living in Atlanta. I should not spend time trying to develop a Chinese market—or, for that matter, French or Korean markets. Trying to develop markets that are irrelevant to my business is a pointless waste of time and resources.

Sales Strategy. Advertising strategy brings customers to the door; sales strategy involves getting the order or signing the contract. Marketing gets the message out; sales strategy sells the products. Sales strategy uses elements such as price, freight options, and sales discounts to close the deal.

Competition. It has been said that those who are most successful in business know almost as much about their competitors' businesses as they do their own. Conversely, those who assume they have *no* competition are prone to failure. Ask the following questions when developing this section:

1. Who are your five nearest competitors?

2. Do you have a niche market to focus on? A niche market is a group of potential customers with a strong desire for your products or services. The group is large enough to provide the volume of business your BESt Company will need to survive but small enough that it might be overlooked by your competition.

3. What competitive advantage do you have over your competitors? Be specific.

4. Are their sales increasing, decreasing, or steady? Why?

5. What is their pricing strategy?

6. What are their strengths and weaknesses?

7. Are there substitutes for your product or service?

Management and Operations. This section will focus on the qualifications of the BESt CEO and professional consultants associated with the company. Include a firm profile of your lawyer, CPA, and insurance agent. You want to assure potential lenders that you will not try to handle transactions that are out of your realm of expertise.

▷ *Resume of Owner.* Providing your resume is especially important if you plan to secure capital from a source that doesn't know you from Adam. Your resume will include your work history and experience with the products or services that your BESt business will offer. The more experience you possess, the better.

▷ *Professional Consultants.* No one is born with an innate ability to create financial statements or write contracts. These skills require extensive training. Even then, CPAs and attorneys require ongoing training to keep up to speed on new laws and regulations. You definitely need these guys in your corner.

Financial Statements. Because your business is an upstart, your financial statements will be projections based on your best guess regarding sales and expenses. Bridle your enthusiasm and keep it real when preparing financials. Sales, for example, are not numbers just "picked from the blue," they are determined by market size, pricing strategy, and managerial abilities. Projections have to make sense.

The following reports should be included in the financial section of a business plan:

▷ Financial assumptions.

▷ Amount of start-up money.

▷ Personal financial statement of owner (prepared within 90 days).

▷ Projected income statement (3 years).

▷ Projected balance sheet (3 years).

▷ Projected statement of cash flow (3 years, monthly the first year).

5.5 Case Study of a Typical Business Plan

Businesses are born in the minds of entrepreneurs either out of need or out of vision. An idea can come while eating in a restaurant, commuting to work, or standing in the shower—or in countless other ways. Or it may be a long-standing notion that just simmers in the back of your mind for months on end. I was using a friend's fishing camp, watching the midnight news, when I had the idea to develop seminars for BESt Companies. C. Edwards, a New Orleans-based client, said she was washing her car when the idea to create a line of hair accessories popped into her head. Great ideas take no predictable path. Developing a business plan is similarly unique, but there are many similarities that exist among all business plans that we need to investigate.

To follow the flow of the planning process and to see how all the necessary information is organized, let's develop a business plan for a fictitious company. Let's think of something interesting, something that's fairly simple and straightforward. As I mentioned, I love the island motif and all things tropical, so let's develop a business plan for a small, two-person cosmetic business we'll call *Jamaica-Max Tropical Cosmetics, LLC*. We'll use this company throughout the rest of this text for all our examples.

One last point before we introduce the company that will be the subject of our case study. The facts considered in *our* business plan are generally important to *all* companies. Obviously, we can't cover every unique situation. As I said, there is no exact process to planning, nor are there "canned" responses, although many would make you think so. Every plan has to have some customization, no matter how intuitive and comprehensive the template. My example will guide you as you write yours. But, in every sense, the final version of your business plan will essentially be in your own words and include your unique facts. All final decisions will be yours. You're the boss, so don't be afraid to call the shots. After all, that is why you are going into business for yourself.

Meet the Thorns

Max and Jamaica Thorn are a happily married, African-American couple originally from Belize. In 1980, while both were in their early 20s, the Thorns married and within weeks left their Central American country and immigrated to the United States. Their first move was to the Greater Houston area. They lived with relatives for about two years before establishing their own household. As soon as they were eligible, they became naturalized citizens.

In the spring of 1986, to celebrate their sixth wedding anniversary, Max and Jamaica decided to take a trip to New Orleans to attend the New Orleans Jazz and Heritage Festival. They stayed in a small bed and breakfast comfortably nestled under the sprawling oak trees on Esplanade Avenue. They both fell in love with the French Quarter and the city's lazy Creole charm. Later that year, they decided to relocate to New Orleans, and they purchased a three-bedroom house less than a mile south of Lake Ponchatrain.

Jamaica Thorn, now 44, has been a flight attendant with Tri-National Airlines for 16 years. Maxwell Thorn, 45, has spent the last 14 years as an oilfield supplies salesman for Nolan Corporation. Maxwell, who insists that his friends call him Max, also teaches Spanish courses in the evening for the Orleans Parish Adult Education program. The Thorns have two teenagers: Malik, 17, and Marcia, 15.

In the wake of September 11th, Tri-National Airline gave Jamaica a furlough without pay. That was the third time she had been laid off, the first being in 1995 and the second in 1998. Each time, the company hired her back as business picked up, but the uncertainty of continued employment was disrupting her lifestyle. Also, with each rehire, she lost some of her perks. First, the company cut her vacation time from three weeks to two, and in 1998 they stop subsidizing her health insurance. After nearly 15 years on the job, Jamaica was losing ground. At 44, she was working harder than ever, making less money per working hour, and becoming increasingly frustrated. Five years ago, she began to moonlight as a door-to-door cosmetics representative.

Jamaica is tall and stunningly beautiful. Standing eye to eye with Max, her baby-clear complexion is the color of raw honey. She still has the poise and sophistication of an international supermodel, and hardly a week passes that someone doesn't encourage her to try her hand in the fashion business. Two months after being laid off for the third time, Jamaica and Max are having breakfast together on the patio of their home. Jamaica sips cranberry juice from a tall glass, looking at Max as he proofreads her resume.

She is preparing to interview with several companies, but her heart isn't in it. For years, she had been thinking about starting her own cosmetics line. If it was going to be done at all, it had to be now. Max is also a bit concerned about the oilfield business, which is notorious for wide swings in sales volume. It seems as though the historically up-and-down market had entered a sustained downturn. Several of Max's long-term co-workers had recently received pink slips. His still-youthful face is beginning to show lines of worry.

Let's listen in on their conversation on this warm and sunny late autumn morning (with their permission, of course).

"You know, Max, I just can't get excited about my interview with Crescent City Travel, or any of these travel agencies."

Max looks up, slips his slender eyeglasses from his cleanly shaven face and places them on the table next to his coffee mug. He nods his head knowingly. "I can see that," he says. "I can't say I blame you. Sixteen years is a big chunk of time to have to start over. I think—"

"More than enough," she interrupts and begins paging through a small wire bound journal she had been reviewing. "I think the time is right to start what we've been talking about for years—our own line of cosmetics. Our own business."

"Well yes, I know we've talked," Max agrees reluctantly, "but you do have the interview scheduled," he reminds her. "Besides, why now?"

"Because I'm working harder than ever, making less money... basically just spinning my wheels." She sits her glass on a neatly folded napkin. "We've been talking and dreaming about starting our own business for years. Why not now?" she insists. "Do you know what we could do if we had our own business? All the energy we put out for others can go right into our own company."

Max lowers his head and rubs his bottom lip contemplatively. "Something that we could build for ourselves," he says with increasing interest.

"Exactly!"

"You and me," he says with his eyes still lowered, still in heavy thought.

"Yes!" she agrees excitedly. "You could continue working while I organize and get everything in place. I've already lost my hospitalization and vacation time, and there's no guarantee the airline is going to call me back. Plus, this travel agency is mostly a commissioned job. It's all so iffy. I say, let's do our own thing."

"Are you sure, Jaye?" he asks, using his most affectionate term of endearment. "I mean, this is quite a big step."

"That's all I've been thinking about for the last few years," she assures him. She closes her journal, picks up her glass, and takes another sip. Max is now fixed on the resolute determination of her jaw and how he could see the motion of her mind in her eyes. He's seen it all before. He is quite familiar with her determination once her mind is set. "We should have done this years ago. And, I know, if I start another job, there's no telling when we'll have the opportunity we do now," she reasons.

"What about investment?" Max asks.

"We can work it out," she assures him. "No doubt, there are a lot of factors. But we'll create a plan and go from there."

Max shook his head reluctantly at first, but then with increasing excitement. "Umph…I feel you…what you're saying. It is time," he thinks aloud. "What will we call it—our new company?"

"Mmmm…MJ Cosmetics? Easy Beauty Products?" Jamaica throws out a couple of ideas she had toyed with the past few months.

"I know," Max says enthusiastically, "how about Jamaica-Max Cosmetics?"

"Yes!!" they both agree in unison.

Two weeks later, the Thorns finished the following business plan.

The characters and circumstances included in the case study are purely fictional. Any resemblance to actual persons or events is unintentional. In the interest of conserving space, the sample business plan is run continuously on the following pages. When creating your own business plan, start each section on its own page.

Jamaica-Max Tropical Cosmetics, LLC
Every Color Under the Sun

BUSINESS PLAN

555 Main Street, Suite 200
New Orleans, Louisiana
E-mail: mt@jamaicamax.com
Phone: 985–555–1234

Table of Contents

Executive Summary

The objective of this plan is to obtain a $ 50,000 five-year bank loan and a $10,000 line of credit for Jamaica-Max Tropical Cosmetics, LLC ("Jamaica-Max"). The funds will be used to finance the purchase of inventory, displays, and equipment and to cover any cash shortfall until cash flow breakeven is achieved.

Jamaica-Max was founded in November 2003 and is located at 555 Main Street in New Orleans, Louisiana. The company was formed as a limited liability company in the state of Louisiana. Jamaica-Max will use a network of retail outlets, beauty shops, day spas, and the Internet to distribute a cosmetics line in the Southeast region of the United States, including Louisiana, Alabama, Mississippi, and the Florida panhandle. The Company's product line will include high-quality lip covers, moisturizing creams with SPF protection, face powder, nail polish, custom-blended foundations, and other products that are formulated to provide long lasting, natural, sun-kissed beauty for active women who enjoy "tropical days that fade into Reggae nights."

Jamaica-Max will create its own brand by labeling high-quality products manu-factured by *Create Your Own Line, Inc.*, a cosmetics company that manufactures unlabeled products for independent distributors. By employing this strategy, the management of Jamaica-Max will be able to control the promotion and packaging of its ActiveIslander image, including the store displays and the Internet Website. Consistent presentation of the ActiveIslander image will reinforce the casual atti-tude of the Jamaica-Max philosophy, reinforce the company's expertise, and cre-ate brand loyalty with the customers. All packaging will include a tropical island motif including botanical prints against muted earth tones that suggest the tropi-cal ease of island activity.

To achieve the company's goals, Jamaica and Max Thorn will invest in con-sumer marketing and advertising programs, modify a detached garage into a dis-tribution center, and create a secure Website for online Internet sales.

Industry Analysis

According to the Yahoo/AC Nielsen Internet Confidence Index, U.S. consumers were expected to spend $14.8 billion online in the first quarter of 2003, or approxi-mately $60 billion on an annualized basis. Also, according to recent statistics pub-lished by the U.S. Census Bureau, the cosmetics industry in the Gulf South region grossed $267 million in sales during the most recent reporting period. These statistics indicate that both the cosmetics industry and Internet sales continue to experience sustained growth. This sustained growth will provide Jamaica-Max with the opportu-nity to introduce its line, develop its distribution network, and capture market share.

According to the Southeastern Federation of Beauty Shops ("SFBS"), sales to minority women in the Louisiana/Mississippi/Alabama area for over-the-counter cosmetics were $118 million, with the average sales ticket at $31.82. The manage-ment of Jamaica-Max estimates that 85% of its sales will come from women of color—both African- and Hispanic-Americans. The five-year forecast by SFBS is considered strong.

Imagery, mood, lifestyle, and impulse buying have always been the primary factors for buying cosmetics. In order to sell cosmetics on the Internet, the imagery must be distinct and powerful. Internet imagery is difficult to achieve, yet, according to statistics released in the February 2000 edition of *Women's Wear Daily*, online sales of personal care products were approximately $1.2 billion at the end of 2003. Accordingly, the management of Jamaica-Max has a reasonable basis to anticipate that it will achieve sales projections, estimated at 23% of company revenue, from Internet sales, given an effective advertising campaign. To encourage site loyalty of Internet visitors and shoppers, the Jamaica-Max site will include editorial content, an advice column, and links to other sites that address women's issues. To keep the site fresh, Website editorial content will be updated weekly.

Company Overview

Mission

Jamaica-Max's mission is to sell Tropical Cosmetics and the Jamaica-Max philosophy to women of all ages, but especially to women in their mid-30s to late 50s, who have older children and who are transitioning from soccer mom to ActiveIslander woman.

Jamaica-Max Tropical Cosmetics plans to achieve its sales goal by providing natural, high-quality products that provide long-lasting beauty at a reasonable price. Jamaica-Max will also provide friendly, value-added service and quick delivery of Internet sales. As the company grows, it will continue to meet the increasingly complex challenges of competition and changes in the marketplace without compromising product quality or customer service. *Customer service* and the tropical island lifestyle will be key elements in Jamaica-Max's marketing strategy.

As the children of ActiveIslander women become more independent, these women find time on their hands to enjoy guiltless activity. The fast pace of chauffeuring, chaperoning, and soccer games gives way to a more tropical pace, where days fade into nights and living is active, easy, breezy, and carefree. Jamaica-Max Cosmetics wants to be this woman's first choice in cosmetics and beauty products.

Business Description/Legal Structure

Jamaica-Max was founded in November 2003 by Max and Jamaica Thorn, a husband-and-wife team originally from Belize, now naturalized citizens of the United States since 1986. Jamaica-Max is a limited liability company. The company is located at 555 Main Street in New Orleans, La. The company's primary business activity is to distribute its own line of quality cosmetics.

Strategic Alliances

Jamaica-Max will not manufacture its products. The company will enter into a strategic alliance (as a customer) with *Create Your Own Line, Inc.,* which is an FDA-approved manufacturing facility that specializes in formulating and blending customized products that beauty professionals can brand as their own. *Create Your Own Line, Inc.* works with each customer on an individual basis to blend the exact colors that will satisfy customers' requirements. Products range from botanical-based formulas to cosmeceuticals, plus *Create Your Own Line, Inc.* maintains a library of thousands of shades. As a result of this relationship, Jamaica-Max will develop a customized line of eye-, lip-, nail-, and skincare products.

Website

In May 2004, Jamaica-Max will launch its Website: *www.jamaicamax.com.* The site will feature a complete description of all products and services. It will also provide *shopping cart*™ in a secure online environment where shoppers can feel safe about placing orders over the Internet.

Retail Displays

To develop brand loyalty, Jamaica-Max will create a standard display system, featuring images of palm trees and various elements of island lifestyle. The management of Jamaica-Max plans to use this consistent theme on its Website.

Products

Jamaica-Max offers the following products:

ActiveIslander Lip Cover. The ActiveIslander Lip Covers are smear proof, long-lasting, and provide outstanding moisturizing quality. Loaded with moisturizers and Vitamin E. Leaves a smooth, non-tacky finish. Jamaica-Max maintains 30–40 tropical colors for sale at all times.

ActiveIslander Face Cream. Contains two powerful antioxidants: vitamins C and E. Specially formulated to reduce facial pores. Replenishes dehydrated skin and gives a luscious "dewy" appearance.

ActiveIslander Shine-Free Face Powder. Oil control formula keeps your face island breezy for hours. Hypoallergenic formula will not clog pores.

ActiveIslander Nail Polish. 25 exotic island colors, from Hibiscus Red to Gardenia White to Coconut Brown. Resistant to chipping. Easy touch-up. Brush design eliminates streaking.

ActiveIslander Sun Screen SPF 15. Long-lasting. Provides optimal sun protection and produces smooth, moist, younger-looking skin.

ActiveIslander Custom Blend Foundation. Custom blending eliminates color confusion. Contains oil-free SPF protection. Glides on for effortless application and precise blending. Contains antioxidant vitamins C and E.

ActiveIslander Cosmetic Brushes. Hand-crafted, all-natural. Handles are made from close grain hardwoods, attached to nickel ferrules. Superior in quality, workmanship, and durability.

Advertising and Promotion Plan

Customer Profile

Jamaica-Max's customers are women who routinely visit day spas, specialty shops, and their beauticians for hair, face, and nail care. They are women of discriminating taste, yet on a budget. They have an island attitude, where life is invigorating and exciting, but at a leisurely pace.

Jamaica-Max will target its products to women between the ages of 35 and 55, whose children are either older teenagers, in college, or married. These women are interested in changing their level of physical activity from non-stop hectic to leisurely active. They are interested in travel and the tropical lifestyle. They are neighborhood joggers—not marathoners; health club swimmers—not iron women; and local cyclists—not triathletes. After working out, they want cosmetics with natural ingredients that enhance rather than cover up their natural beauty.

Market Plan

Jamaica-Max's customer base will be made up of neighborhood beauty shops, specialty shops, and day spas that will buy the product and sell it to their customers. Beauty shops and day spas will account for 54 percent of the company's revenue, 23 percent will consist of sales to small, specialty shops located in malls and strip shopping centers, and 23 percent of Jamaica-Max's revenue will come form Internet sales.

Jamaica-Max Leisure Cosmetics Sales Mix	
Customer Type	**Projected Sales (%)**
Beauty Shops	36%
Day Spas	18%
Specialty Shops	23%
Internet Sales	23%

Jamaica-Max's primary marketing strategy is to help customers establish a purchased and consignment inventory mix. Jamaica-Max will sell all skin, eye, and hair products but will consign nail products and cosmetic brushes. This arrangement will allow retailers to carry the complete product line at approximately 75 percent of the inventory cost.

The company will also develop printed advertising materials (flyers, brochures, line sheets, and catalogs) that will explain the products, their application, and their benefits. The printed material will be developed via desktop publishing. Desktop publishing will allow pricing and delivery information to be kept current. The advertising materials will be distributed to customers on a monthly basis. Each mailing will also include monthly specials and sale items.

To promote the ideas and products of the company, Jamaica-Max has determined that the Southern Women's Lifestyle Show is a "must do" trade show. The Southern Women's Trade Show is sponsored by the Southern Women Organization, which is headquartered in Atlanta, Georgia. The show has 250 exhibitors, more than 100,000 square feet of exhibition floor space, and 30,000 attendees over a four-day period. The trade show will be held in Jacksonville, Florida, during the week of October 17, 2004 though October 20, 2004.

To further promote the ideals and products of the company, Jamaica-Max has agreed to participate in the New Orleans Allied Health Show. This is a local event that is primarily attended by residents from the Greater New Orleans area, including Terrebonne, Lafourche, St. Charles, St. Bernard, Jefferson, and St. Tammany parishes. NOAB is usually held in the Ponchatrain Center during the early fall.

The primary advertising medium to be used by Jamaica-Max is printed ads in local and regional magazines. The company will also develop radio ads that will run on radio stations WYLD and WQUE in New Orleans and WBLK in Atlanta.

Sales Strategy

Jamaica-Max will position itself as a cosmetic line for women transitioning to another phase of life: women who enjoy the richness of an active life as well as the tranquility of a leisurely stroll, preferably along a soft white beach and beneath a cool, twilight sky. Jamaica-Max will offer these women quality products in exquisite packaging. The name Jamaica-Max and its exquisite packaging will conjure up images of island living.

The benefits of adopting this sales strategy are as follows:

+ Immediate brand recognition.
+ Highlights natural ingredients.
+ Appealing to Baby Boomer generation
+ Emphasis placed on ease of application.
+ Promotes popular island lifestyle living.

Sales Programs

Direct Sales. Jamaica-Max expects approximately 77 percent of its potential revenue will be generated by selling directly to the beauty salons, day spas, and specialty cosmetics shops as they respond to the company's advertisements and via word-of-mouth.

Internet Sales. Jamaica-Max expects to launch its Website on May 1, 2004. The company is the registered owner of *www.jamaicamax.com* and *www.jamaicamax.biz.* The site will feature a complete description of all products and services. It will also feature a ***shopping cart*** application in a secure online environment where shoppers can feel safe about placing orders over the Internet.

Jamaica-Max will offer free shipping on all Internet orders of more than $50.

Competition

The primary competition for Jamaica-Max products in the local market are Kleen Fashions, Inc. and Arnell Miller Cosmetics. Both lines are based in New Orleans and are generally sold in specialty stores and beauty shops in the Southeast region of the United States. Both lines also offer blended foundations and quality application accessories, such as chrome and glass handle brushes and high polish magnifying mirrors. In addition to those brands, Jamaica-Max must also compete against many national brands, such as Mayfair Cosmetics and Code One Fashion Cosmetics, which are sold in a variety of stores, from Wal-Mart to Saks Fifth Avenue.

Competition from companies that sell door-to-door, such as Avon and Mary Kay, is also significant. The marketing effort of Jamaica-Max will have to go head-to-head with such firms and present itself as a more desirable alternative. An informal survey of Jamaica Thorn's current customers indicates that they tend to have several different lines in their possession during any given period of time. The most significant factor in making a selection among the alternative cosmetic lines is product quality, followed closely by ease of application and image. Because most of existing lines are comparable in quality, the management of Jamaica-Max believes that effectively marketing the ActiveIslander image will allow Jamaica-Max to capture market share.

Management and Operations Plan

Management

Max and Jamaica Thorn co-manage Jamaica-Max Tropical Cosmetics, LLC. Max and Jamaica Thorn are also its owners and founders.

Over the past five years, Jamaica Thorn has worked as an affiliate for International Woman Cosmetics, Inc., a distributor of women's beauty products. She has developed a client base of approximately 120 customers, many of whom have been customers for all five years. Mrs. Thorn understands the cosmetics industry, and her strength is customer service, which is vitally important in this industry. Mrs. Thorn will serve as the President of Jamaica-Max. Her duties will include sales, customer service, and packaging.

Max Thorn has been an oilfield sales manager for 14 years and has taught Spanish in an adult education program on a part-time basis for more than 10 years. Mr. Thorn is very knowledgeable about accounting and desktop computing. His duties will include advertising, accounting, billing, and collections. He will also share packaging duties with Mrs. Thorn.

Jamaica Thorn

Jamaica Thorn spent five years as an independent distributor of International Women's Cosmetics, Inc., a privately owned company with annual sales of $10 million, 42 full-time employees, and 200 distributors. Jamaica has highly effective management skills. She has been particularly successful in being able to increase market penetration with innovative marketing strategies. Jamaica has expertise in all phases of purchasing and selling. She also acquired the distribution rights for two national brands, Tropical Oils and Lotions and Charming Lip Products. Jamaica is well traveled and speaks fluent Spanish.

PROFESSIONAL BACKGROUND

International Women Cosmetics, Inc.; New Orleans, LA   **1998–present**

Sales Representative (part-time)—Built a client base to 120 regular customers. Sales have averaged more than $3,500 per month for the past 12 months.

- Established personal sales quotas and monitored the monthly progress using Microsoft Excel.

- Developed sales literature to hand out to potential customers responding to company advertisements.

- Had full purchasing responsibility.

- Rented a local hotel meeting room for "Makeover Day" in 2002. Picked up 12 regular customers. Event was published in the local newspaper. Was deemed an "astonishing success" by the local media.

TriNational Airline; New Orleans, LA   **1987–2003**

Note: Prepare a section that details each position held by the BESt CEO or manager that showcases relevant experience in the business the BESt CEO is intending to organize. Do not be concerned about "gaps" in the resume; the focus of this resume is to highlight business experience rather than to find a job.

REFERENCES

1. John Q. Public, CEO of International Women Cosmetics, Inc.
   123 First Street
   New Orleans, LA 12345
   Phone 985–555–1231
   Fax 985–555–1232
   E-mail: jqp@inwomen.com

   Note: Additional references would be included as required.

Maxwell Thorn

Max spent 14 years as the export sales manager for Nolan Corporation, a privately owned oilfield supplies company with annual sales of $6 million and 23 employees. Max is highly organized and has met his annual sales quotas for each of the last 10 years. Max has worked on a team to acquire the distribution rights for more than 50 national brands.

PROFESSIONAL BACKGROUND

- Increased annual sales from $100,000 per year in 1998 to more than $200,000 for year ended December 31, 2002.

- Increased gross profit margin from an average of 22 percent to 29 percent during the same period. At present, according to the National Safety Suppliers Group, Nolan's gross margin is 26 percent greater than the industry average.

- Grew customer base from 16 to more than 50.

- Initiated a relationship with EXIM Bank to insure sales to foreign companies.

Nolan Corporation; New Orleans, LA   1990–present

Export Sales manager for oilfield supplies division, which serves more than 80 customers in 10 countries, including Venezuela, Mexico, Panama, and India. Responsible for soliciting accounts, preparing bids, and providing individualized customer service.

REFERENCES

1. John J. Business owner, CEO of Nolan Corporation
   123 Third Street
   New Orleans, LA 12345
   Phone 985–555–1231
   Fax 985–555–1232
   E-mail: jjb@njosinc.com

2. Jennifer A. Entrepreneur, President of MMR Safety Supplies, Inc.
   123 Fourth Street
   New Orleans, LA 12345
   Phone 985–555–1233
   Fax 985–555–1234
   E-mail: jae@mmr.com

Operations

Jamaica Thorn will operate the business on a full-time basis. Max Thorn will devote at least 20 hours each week to the business. He will discontinue his duties as a part-time adult education teacher, effective May 1, 2004. As business increases, the Thorns will hire the necessary full- and part-time employees.

Max and Jamaica are cross-trained in all functional areas. This will ensure that the business will continue to run smoothly despite illness or scheduling issues. At present, Max and Jamaica are each responsible for the following functions:

Jamaica Thorn   Mrs. Thorn will serve as the President of Jamaica-Max. Her duties will include sales, customer service, and packaging.

Max Thorn   Mr. Thorn's duties will include advertising, accounting, billing, and collections. He will also share packaging duties with Mrs. Thorn.

Professional Support

Corporate Attorney	CPA Firm
John K. Attorney	John K. Accountant, CPA
123 Fifth Street	123 Six Street
New Orleans, LA 12345	New Orleans, LA 12345
Phone 985–555–9999	Phone 985–555–7777
Fax 985–555–8888	Fax 985–555–6666
E-mail: jka@lawyermail.com	E-mail: jkacpa@cpamail.com

Financial Plan

The financial plan is based on an estimate of the most likely set of market and economic conditions for the three-year period ending December 31, 2006. It reflects the best estimate of management's intended course of action under those conditions. Some assumptions used in the preparation of the financial plan, although considered the most reasonable by management at the time of the preparation, might not be borne out or substantiated by evolving events.

Financial Assumptions

In assembling the financial plan, management made a number of important assumptions:

A. The company included in its forecast sales a client base that Jamaica Thorn has supplied and serviced for the past five years. Sales are projected to increase approximately 50% each year for the next three years.

B. **Labor.** It is anticipated that Max and Jamaica Thorn will provide all labor until sales reach approximately $400,000 per year, at which time the first employee will be added. In 2004, Jamaica will draw $3,000 each month and Max will draw $1,000 each month. In 2005, Jamaica will draw $3,500 and Max will draw $1,500 each month. In 2006, Jamaica will draw $4,000 and Max will draw $2,000 each month.

C. **Property and Equipment Depreciation.** Property and equipment are carried at cost and are considered to be either seven-year or five-year property per Modified Accelerated Cost Recovery (MACRS). Maintenance and repairs are expensed as incurred. Expenditures, which significantly increase value or extend useful life, are capitalized.

D. General Assumptions.
   - Interest Rate—8%
   - Sales on credit—75%

Sources and Uses of Investment Capital

Jamaica-Max Tropical Cosmetics Sources and Uses of Investment Capital		
Sources of Capital		
Owners' Investment	$19,500	
Term Loan	50,000	
Total Sources of Capital		$69,500
Uses of Capital		
Monthly Operating Costs	$23,500	
Fixtures and Equipment	40,000	
Starting Inventory	6,000	
Total Uses of Capital		$69,500

Sales Forecast

Jamaica-Max Tropical Cosmetics, LLC Sales Forecast For three running years ending December 31, 2004, 2005, and 2006				
Customer Type	2004	2005	2006	Total
Beauty Shops	$49,500	$74,250	$111,375	$235,125
Day Spas	25,000	37,500	56,250	118,750
Specialty Shops	31,250	46,875	70,312	148,437
Internet	31,250	46,875	70,313	148,438
Total	$137,000	$205,500	$308,250	$650,750

Projected Income Statement

Jamaica-Max Tropical Cosmetics, LLC						
Projected Income Statement						
For three running years ending December 31, 2004, 2005, and 2006						
	12/31/2004		12/31/2005		12/31/2006	
	Amount	Ratio	Amount	Ratio	Amount	Ratio
Sales	137,000	100.00%	205,500	100.00%	308,250	100.00%
Total Cost of Sales	54,000	39.42%	82,200	40.00%	123,300	40.00%
Gross Margin	83,000	60.58%	123,300	60.00%	184,950	60.00%
Expenses						
Advertising	2,400	1.75%	3,000	1.46%	4,500	1.46%
Auto	1,000	.73%	1,500	.73%	2,250	.73%
Bank Charges	120	.09%	300	.15%	450	.15%
Depreciation	8,000	5.84%	12,800	6.23%	7,600	2.47%
Insurance-Auto	3,000	2.19%	3,400	1.65%	5,050	1.64%
Insurance–Liability	800	.58%	1,000	.49%	1,400	.45%
Insurance–Health	2,500	1.82%	2,750	1.34%	4,150	1.35%
Interest	3,638	2.66%	2,956	1.44%	2,192	.71%
Legal and Accounting	1,200	.88%	2,400	1.17%	3,600	1.17%
Office Supplies	1,200	.88%	2,000	.97%	3,000	.97%
Promotional Samples	1,000	.73%	2,000	.97%	3,000	.97%
Repairs and Maint.	1,200	.88%	1,800	.88%	2,700	.88%
Supplies	1,300	.95%	1,200	.58%	1,800	.58%
Telephone	1,800	1.31%	2,400	1.17%	3,600	1.17%
Utilities	600	.44%	900	.44%	1,350	.44%
Total Expenses	29,758	21.73%	40,406	19.67%	46,642	15.14%
Net Income	53,242	38.85%	82,894	40.33%	138,308	44.86%

Projected Balance Sheet

Jamaica-Max Tropical Cosmetics, LLC Projected Balance Sheet As of December 31, 2004, 2005, and 2006			
	12/31/2004	**12/31/2005**	**12/31/2006**
Assets			
Current Assets			
Cash	22,997	43,885	99,403
Accounts Receivable	17,138	25,706	38,559
Inventory	4,949	7,425	11,137
Total Current Assets	45,084	77,016	149,099
Fixed Assets			
Furniture and Fixtures	8,000	8,000	8,000
Equipment	32,000	32,000	32,000
Less: Accumulated			
Depreciation	(8,000)	(20,800)	(28,400)
Total Fixed Assets	32,000	19,200	11,600
Total Assets	77,084	96,216	160,699
Liabilities and Members' Equity			
Current Liabilities			
Accounts Payable	10,809	16,214	24,320
Current Maturities	9,167	9,931	10,800
Total Current Liabilities	19,976	26,145	35,120
Long-term Liabilities			
Notes Payable—FirstBank	41,533	32,366	22,435
Less: Current Maturities	(9,167)	(9,931)	(10,800)
Total Long-term Liabilities	32,366	22,435	11,635
Members' Equity			
Members' Equity*	24,742	47,636	113,944
Total Members' Equity	24,742	47,636	113,944
Ttl Liabilities and Members' Equity	77,084	96,216	160,699
Net of members' draw			

Pro Forma Cash Flow (3 years)

Jamaica-Max Tropical Cosmetics, LLC Pro Forma Cash Flow For three running years ending December 31, 2004, 2005, and 2006			
	12/31/2004	**12/31/2005**	**12/31/2006**
Cash Received			
Cash from Operations			
Cash Sales	$34,250	$51,375	$77,063
Cash from Receivables	$85,613	$145,566	$218,334
Subtotal Cash from Operations	$119,863	$196,941	$295,397
Expenditures			
Expenditures from Operations			
Payment of Accounts Payable	$63,899	$106,886	$157,948
Total Spent on Operations	$63,899	$106,886	$157,948
Additional Cash Spent			
Long-term Liabilities Principal	$8,467	$9,167	$9,931
Draws by Members	$48,000	$60,000	$72,000
Subtotal Cash Spent	$120,366	$176,053	$239,879
Net Cash Flow	($503)	$20,888	$55,518
Cash Balance	$22,997	$43,885	$99,403

Monthly Pro Forma Cash Flow (Year 1)

Jamaica-Max Tropical Cosmetics, LLC
Monthly Pro Forma Cash Flow (Year 1)
For twelve months ending December 31, 2004

	Jan	Feb	Mar	Apr	May	Jun	Jul	Aug	Sep	Oct	Nov	Dec
Cash Received												
Cash from Operations												
Cash Sales	2831	2856	2856	2856	2856	2856	2856	2856	2856	2856	2856	2856
Receivables			8494	8569	8569	8569	8569	8569	8569	8569	8569	8569
Ttl Cash from Operations	2831	2856	11350	11425	11425	11425	11425	11425	11425	11425	11425	11425
Expenditures												
Exp from Operations												
Payment of A/Payable		1837	9782	1828	10823	1818	10814	1809	10804	1799	10795	979
Ttl Spent on Operations		1837	9782	1828	10823	1818	10814	1809	10804	1799	10795	979
Additional Cash Spent												
L/T Liabilities Principal	680	685	689	694	698	703	708	712	717	722	727	732
Draws by Members	4000	4000	4000	4000	4000	4000	4000	4000	4000	4000	4000	4000
Ttl Additional CashSspent	4680	6522	14471	6522	15521	6521	15522	6521	15521	6521	15522	5711
Net Cash Flow	-1849	-3666	-3121	4903	-4096	4094	-4097	4904	-4096	4904	-4097	5714
Cash Balance	21651	17985	14864	19767	15671	19765	15668	20572	16476	21380	17283	22997

Personal Financial Statement of Owner

At this early stage of your business existence, the owner **is** the business. Even if you have decided to organize as a corporation or adopt a limited liability company legal structure to limit your personal liability, most banks will not extend significant credit without a personal guarantee. To assess your ability to repay a debt, bankers will want to have a current picture of your financial condition. A CPA could easily fulfill this request by preparing your personal financial statement. Note also that the SBA and most banks would happily provide you with a blank copy of their own standardized personal financial statement form.

5.6 A Few Concluding Thoughts

Creating financial statements tends to be the most challenging task in preparing a business plan. Even practitioners with high levels of experience prefer using simple, inexpensive business plan software that saves time and helps minimize the possibility of forgetting to include some item in their calculations. Palo Alto Software is among the best and least expensive (approximately $100). It is easy to use, and it will help you create a balance sheet, income statements, and cash-flow statements almost simultaneously. Through a series of questions, the program accepts the responses and internally prepares the financial statements. All of the formatting and classification issues are dealt with seamlessly and behind the scene.

 **BESt Website** ⅢⅢ➤

Business Plan Pro Software

www.palo-alto.com

This software offers 400-plus sample business plans. Simply enter your information and the program will guide you to a finished product that is preferred by banks, the SBA, and venture capitalists.

The time spent preparing your business plan is essential. It allows you to work out on paper what's in your head. And like the chef who constantly tastes his food as he prepares it, at times you may be tempted to throw out the entire batch and start over if it doesn't suit your taste or if you're missing a certain ingredient. For instance, when you see that you'll need $50,000 and you only have $2,000 in the bank you may feel discouraged. I want you to be aware of that feeling, because it will come. I also want you to know that it's temporary. The best thing you can do when discouragement comes is to toss it out, but maintain your desire, drive, and plan to be in business. Whatever you do, don't dwell on what you lack. Just keep planning!

Finally, the contents of your plan are thoughtful and methodical, but very rarely will things go exactly as intended. When actual results differ from your plans, seeing that difference early will allow you to deal with it more effectively. Your thinking should be: Recognize and correct. Then, plow on!!!

BESt Website ➠

www.sba.gov
The Small Business Administration's Website contains a library of resources linked to hundreds of sites offering research material on every area of planning a business.

Chapter 6

Funding

Everybody likes a kidder, but nobody lends him money.

—Arthur Miller

Lack of money is no obstacle. Lack of an idea is an obstacle.

—Ken Hakuta

So we went to Atari and said, 'Hey, we've got this amazing thing [the Apple Computer], even built with some of your parts, and what do you think about funding us? Or we'll give it to you. We just want to do it. Pay our salary, we'll come work for you.' And they said, 'No.' So then we went to Hewlett-Packard, and they said, 'Hey, we don't need you. You haven't got through college yet.'

—Steve Jobs

Someone once said there are three kinds of people in this world: those who make things happen, those who watch things happen, and those who wonder what happened! I know you are definitely not in the third group. If you were, you wouldn't be reading this book. Far too often, though, even the most ambitious people find themselves in the second group. What separates those who make things happen from those who watch things happen? The main reason is a lack of funds or "a lack of jack," as Chris T., a former student, once quipped when I queried the members of one of my accounting classes about the significance of negative cash flow. There's no telling how many businesses have failed to get their ideas off the ground due to a lack of finances—or, even more frustrating, insufficient financing. Imagine having a great product and getting the business up and running, only to have it die on the vine due to a lack of sufficient capital. Nothing is more frustrating, or more tragic.

There are thousands of Websites spewing all sorts of disjointed information about where and how to get financing for your business. At the end of the day, the whole process of surfing and reading is just that: surfing and reading. Trying to find a financing source can be confusing, misleading, overwhelming, frustrating, and incredibly time-consuming. As I have done up to this point with other issues that are time-consuming, I will point out a Website or two that provide the needed information in the most organized and concise manner.

To start your BESt Business, you may need as little as $1,000 or as much as $1,000,000—maybe more. Probably, however, your financial needs, in terms of a business loans, are going to be relatively small. Finding the needed capital is not difficult, but no one is simply willing to give away money or invest in every jackleg plan that comes along. Those who offer grants (money that does not have to be repaid) similarly require significant justification and documentation before a check is cut. Contrary to popular belief (and the $400 and $600 tax rebates coming out of Washington these days), not even the federal government will simply write you a check without sufficient cause. Also contrary to popular belief, grants to finance business endeavors are relatively rare. For the most part, the money you need will come from some sort of loan.

You've already taken a big step toward securing financing by learning to write an effective business plan. You now have a document to lay on potential lenders' desks, something they can read to understand your vision.

6.1 Reality vs. "Pie in the Sky"

Before approaching a lender, let's get one thing straight. There is a great difference between "taking a business risk" and "going after a pipe dream." When it comes time to put up cash, your plan must convey that your business idea is solid, your business plan is realistic, and you have a handle on every aspect of the business. And for those business functions for which you're not totally competent, such as preparing your year-end tax return, pursuing a deadbeat customer, or drawing up a contract, there are people in place to handle those jobs. If those issues are settled, and they should be by now, then the next hurdle is ready to be jumped. And, of course, that hurdle is making a reasonable financial request.

In financing, there are three questions that must be answered:

1. How much money does the business need?
2. Where does the money come from?
3. What do lenders look for?

6.2 Computing Start-Up Capital Requirements

As with most issues for your BESt Company, the quick answer is that it depends. Every business is different, with different cash needs. You can, however, estimate your cash needs by using the worksheet (Figure 6-A) on page 84.

Instructions: Your BESt Company will incur two different types of costs: monthly and one-time.

> ▷ Start with the one-time costs column and enter an amount for each item as appropriate.

> ▷ Repeat the procedure for monthly cost.

> ▷ After you have identified all one-time and monthly cost items, add each column and enter the total in the *estimated total* row.

Note: The sufficiency factor for one-time costs is one (1)—you only expect to incur these costs once. The sufficiency factor for monthly costs depends on the nature of your business. The quicker you can convert sales to cash, the lower the sufficiency factor. In our example, we will use a sufficiency factor of 3, which means that you are giving yourself a three-month buffer before relying on cash flow to pay the bills of your BESt Company.

Once you have determined your cash needs, you will need to estimate how much you can contribute to the total estimated cash requirement and how much you will need to find somewhere else. For example, if estimated start-up costs amount to $125,000 and you can only contribute $25,000, then the balance of $100,000 must come from some other sources.

CAUTION ⫸ Figure 6-A is not intended to be given to bankers and other potentially interested parties. It is primarily for you to determine start-up cash requirements. If you start handing this worksheet out to bankers, they may scrutinize it beyond what is required to secure a loan. For example, they may see your anticipated draw and consider it too high. Certainly, you're not trying to hide anything, but giving out too much information can work against you in the same way as not giving enough information can. As any good attorney will tell you, only answer the question that is being asked.

Your true cash requirements may seem to be a dizzying amount to you. That's okay. Bankers and financiers deal with capitalizing businesses all day long. What's a large amount to you is probably a reasonable request to them. We will talk about sources of capital in the next section, but let me say at this point that whatever the cash requirement is—it is. Don't underestimate. It's far better to be going after what you realistically need than to underestimate your requirement and doom your company before it gets off the ground or, as I said earlier, to watch it die on the vine.

Start-Up Cost Worksheet			
Item **1**	**Comments** **2**	**One-Time Cost** **3**	**Monthly Cost** **4**
Legal and Professional Fees	Formation of business structure		
Furniture and Fixtures	Office furniture, computer, display cases		
Decorating	[Continue using brief comments to describe the cost]		
Licenses			
Deposits			
Starting Inventory			
Salary/draw of BESt CEO			
Other Wages			
Payroll Taxes			
Advertising			
Supplies			
Freight			
Telephone			
Internet Service			
Other Items			
Estimated Total		$	$
Sufficiency Factor*		1.0	3.0
Factored total (multiply estimated total in each column by sufficiency factor		$	$
Total estimated start-up cash required (add columns 3 and 4 above)			$
*Sufficiency Factor: Because you will need to purchase certain items only one time, the sufficiency factor is 1.0. For those expense items that you will incur monthly, you'll need to project enough cash to cover the expenses until expenses can be paid out of the cash flow of the business. In this example, 3 months of start-up cash is estimated to be sufficient.			

Figure 6-A

6.3 Where Does the Money Come From?

The main reasons many companies can't find funding are:

▷ They have no plan.

▷ They don't know whom to ask.

▷ If they do have a plan, they present it poorly.

▷ They're looking for a "free lunch."

We've already talked about planning; so scratch through the first line. Before we begin our discussion on "whom to ask," let me say that all BESt Companies need to be doubly prepared (so to speak) before presenting anything, especially a loan request. Right out of the box, those to whom you present your plan will probably be more skeptical than usual. Why? Because small black businesses draw skepticism. I know it shouldn't be that way, but many times it is. I also know that this is probably not news to you; you've been down that road before. Just be prepared for baseless skepticism so it won't throw you off balance. Money separates families and best friends. Don't expect any favors, especially when it comes to finding funding in the private sector.

Commercial Bank Loans. Start with the bank where you keep your personal accounts. This is the most likely source for financing your BESt Company. Call your account executive and arrange a meeting where you can present your plan and talk about terms and conditions. Unless the deal that your account executive offers you is a no-brainer, don't stop there. Shop other banks and compare their terms and requirements with those of your original banker.

Whichever bank you decide to work with, ask for an *unsecured term loan* or an *unsecured line of credit*—first! You just might qualify. *A **term loan** provides a fixed amount at the beginning of the borrowing period and you make monthly payments over the life of the loan.* On the other hand, a **line of credit** works more like a credit card. Once approved, a certain credit limit is established that sets the maximum that is available to a borrower within a specific period. Draws can be made against a credit line as needed.

For micro loans (those less than $10,000), and depending on your credit history, some banks will not require any collateral. For example, if you have a good credit history, the bank where you do your personal banking might be willing to give you a $5,000 unsecured line of credit. However, if your cash needs are greater than $5,000, expect to sign a personal guarantee. Also expect to sign a personal guarantee if your credit history is blemished.

Venture Capital. A word of caution: A venture capitalist, by definition, is an opportunist. **Be careful releasing your business plans to just anyone, regardless of his or her supposed integrity.** I don't mean to be cynical, but I've seen good ideas stolen from naïve, cash-starved entrepreneurs by those possessing a lack or scruples and the wherewithal to capitalize upon them.

I even hesitate to mention this alternative because very few small or home businesses are capitalized by venture capitalists. The average deal size that catches a venture capitalist's eye is upwards of $5 million. Plus, venture capitalists expect huge returns on their investments. Nevertheless, a good, home-based Internet company might have blue-sky potential. A venture capitalist group might be interested in such a firm, but their interest in a bicycle rental shop or welding contractor is probably not going to be there. The bottom line is this: Most BESt CEOs should not waste their precious time chasing venture capitalists. Consider other options; there are easier ways to get money into your company.

Small Business Administration. You have probably heard about that great big bureaucratic Santa Claus called the Small Business Administration ("SBA"). The SBA is a governmental agency specifically created to stimulate small business opportunities. Many people think that when all else fails, the SBA will lend money to whoever walks through the door. This is not true, although many would stake their lives to the contrary. The SBA is not Santa Claus, but it does have many loans programs to help stimulate small business development. They are, however, no less tolerant of a shaky business plan than your local bank. In fact, SBA loans generally come from local banks, not the SBA! Allow me to repeat that: **The SBA will guarantee SBA loans, but it is your local bank that funds them.** The SBA simply provides a loan guarantee that will help you obtain money from your local bank by shifting the risk from the bank to the federal government. To quote Marcia H., an old business acquaintance of mine, "All over the business world, and yes, including the federal government, to sell a deal, things just have to make sense."

Loans guaranteed by the SBA usually offer more attractive terms than conventional loans. They usually provide lower interest rates and longer repayment terms. This translates into a lower monthly payment and a smaller total cash payout. Most significantly, these more liberal repayment terms work to improve cash flow. (We will discuss cash flow in Section 12.8.)

(The SBA is such an important source to small upstart businesses that I have included a separate chapter to discuss the various loan programs it offers. We will pick up our discussion of various SBA programs in Chapter 7.)

Angel Investors. So-called "angel" investors are similar to venture capitalists, but tend to be a bit more informal. The term *angel*, only about 100 years old, comes from the practice of wealthy businessmen investing in Broadway productions. Your angel could be a wealthy local businessman who has committed himself to helping small upstarts, a group of professionals seeking alternative investments, an investment club, or your brother-in-law.

This group of investors has a review process that is generally less structured than professional venture capitalists'. Less structure, however, does not necessarily translate into quick turnaround. Often, angels take as long as 60 to 90 days to make a decision to fund or not to fund a loan request. Fortunately, however, they typically do not require the rates of return on investment that venture capitalists require. Still, you must be able to demonstrate that their return on investment will be at least what could be earned on investments of similar risk.

Angels tend to keep their money in the neighborhood. Angels in Denver tend not to invest in firms in New Orleans. Also, these kinds of arrangements tend to be legally complex. Angels have issues that may not be as cut and dried as the SBA or your local bank. For example, there may be community property issues if the angel has a spouse. This is a situation where a good, experienced attorney has no substitute.

Here is the hundred-thousand-dollar question: How do you go about meeting an angel? Well, always start with the assumption that someone you know will know the angel personally. For example, your brother might work with someone who is in an investment club that is looking for local opportunities. Ask around and, if you catch a potential angel's interest, subscribe to the *incremental information method.* To use this method, start with a phone call and, as increased interest is shown, follow up with a summarized soft copy (e-mail) of the business plan. If continued interest is shown, follow up with a face-to-face meeting where you deliver a complete hard copy of your business plan.

 Be extremely careful to whom you release a copy of your business plan. Keep a record of the people and companies plans are sent to. If interest decreases, be sure to request that the plan is returned to you.

Friends and Family. Many writers discourage this source of financing your business. I will not discourage friends and family as a source of funding, but I will say that only those who fully understand the inherent risks associated with operating a business should be approached. I think it is important for you not to approach those close to you who either don't fully understand the inherent risks or who can't afford to have their investment tied up for an indefinite length of time. The last thing you want is to have a relative calling several times a week looking for a lump-sum payback.

401(k) Funds. A 401(k) account is a tax-deferred savings account that was established and administered by your previous, or soon-to-be-previous, employer. Regardless of the reason you leave a company, even if you leave to start your own business, in most cases you can leave your 401(k) account intact and under the administration of your ex-employer. Securing funds from a 401(k) is fairly easy, but there are several legal and accounting issues that *must be resolved.*

This is a funding source that you should approach with great care. The tax implications are fairly complex, and simply cashing in your 401(k) can be an extremely costly decision. You should definitely consult with your tax-preparer before drawing on this source.

In spite of these cautions, a 401(k) can be an immediate source of finances for your new business. If you consider your 401(k) as a possible source, generally the funding will be in the form of a loan against the balance in the fund. There will be administrative costs and interest expense associated with the loan. The administrative costs are paid to the fund administrator for handling the transaction. Because the money comes from your account, though, it is your money you're borrowing. Consequently, the interest you pay is credited to your account, which is tantamount to paying yourself interest. But once again, **look before you leap!**

Other Sources. Obviously, this list is not exhaustive. I've only included the sources where the probability of successfully obtaining funding is high and relatively immediate. It is not possible to produce an exhaustive list of possible sources of funding. For example, some states have economic stimulation programs for small, minority businesses, as does the federal government. Then there are private institutions, foundations, and philanthropic initiatives from industry.

 **BESt Website** ⫸

www.businessfinance.com
America's business funding directory, this site lists 4,000-plus sources for business loans and venture capital.

6.4 What Do Professional Lenders Look For?

When it comes to borrowing money, lenders want to know one thing: Can you repay the loan? Because your business will not have a history of activity, the lender will look at your personal history to determine your credit worthiness. Of course, once you have been in business awhile, the emphasis shifts from your personal credit worthiness to the credit worthiness of your small business.

Here is a short checklist that most lenders will use to determine your credit worthiness:

❑ **Bills are paid on time.** Lenders view you as a good credit risk when you are conscientious about paying bills on time. Your credit history should reflect a pattern of on-time payments. This does not mean that your pay history has to be flawless. If you were 30 days late paying a credit card or if you were late once or twice on your auto loan, such incidents generally are not "show stoppers." The overall pattern is the important factor.

Review your own credit history and make sure there aren't any surprises. If there is a blemish, be able to explain it. Have an explanation and not an excuse. Many times your credit history can contain entries that are there in error. Someone with a name similar to yours might have his or her delinquent records show up on your account. A call followed by a letter to the reporting agency can usually take care of such problems.

❑ **The debt load is reasonable.** Do not overextend your debt. If your current debt load is too high, lenders will tend to back away from the deal. A reasonable debt load is one that can be amortized and repaid out of cash flow after all other expenses are paid, including a reasonable draw or salary for the owner of the BESt Company.

❑ **Credit inquiries are kept in check.** Numerous credit inquiries undermine your efforts to obtain credit. Too many of them can indicate that you're "credit-hungry" and that you're either in or headed for financial trouble. Creditors may also have reason to believe that you have received funding from sources making the inquiries and that many of those loans have not yet appeared on your credit report. Be careful how often you allow potential lenders to run credit checks. Do so only if the deal looks as if it's about to happen.

6.5 The Bottom Line for Finding Funds Is Still Your Business Plan

None of these investor groups know what's inside your head. The more complete and informative your business plan, the more likely you will be given serious consideration and a favorable decision. Having a face-to-face meeting with any of the lenders mentioned in this chapter is not a substitute for a well-prepared business plan. It is extremely difficult to review and sell the totality of your idea in an hour or over dinner. You might focus on your resume and completely forget about marketing strategy. The bottom line is this: To receive maximum consideration from prospective lenders, be able to leave a well-thought-out business plan in their hands.

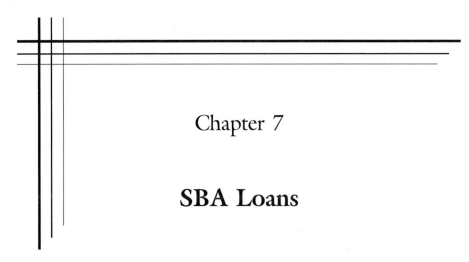

Chapter 7

SBA Loans

We can loan you enough money to get you completely out of debt.

—Sign on a bank

7.1 Overview of SBA Guaranteed Loan Programs

S-B-A. Whenever I mention those three letters, which invariably come up in almost any discussion of small business finance, and especially among BESt Companies, I get two reactions: hot indignation or glowing accolades—rarely indifference. Why such a vast difference of opinion about an entity that is supposed to deal fairly and consistently with its business customers? Can the U.S. Small Business Administration (SBA) be accused of impartiality? I suppose if you introduce politics and human nature, anything's possible in any given situation. Even though many complain, the SBA does a good job in fulfilling its mission, which is to maintain and strengthen the nation's economy by aiding, counseling, assisting, and protecting the interests of small businesses.

The SBA was established in 1953, and by 1954 the organization was already guaranteeing bank loans and making direct loans to small businesses. Despite the complaints from the negative side of the aisle, the data from the last 50 or so years seem to paint a different picture—one that is quite compelling to observe. For instance, from 1991 to 2000, the SBA has helped almost 435,000 small businesses get more than $94.6 billion in loans, more than in the entire history of the agency before 1991. In fact, according to statistics it publishes, the SBA's current business loan portfolio consists of approximately 219,000 loans at a value of more than $45 billion. That's not too shabby. The portfolio guaranteed by the SBA is perhaps the largest portfolio of small business loans in the world. It seems small businesses are benefiting greatly—but, are they really?

What blurs these dizzying statistics is the fact that the SBA defines small businesses as those companies with 500 or fewer employees. You and I both know that 500 employees might be small to the federal government, but it is colossal to us. This liberal definition of small business tends to mask some of the frustration experienced by truly "small" entrepreneurs and especially owners of BESt Companies. There is no question that small business is being helped, but the needs of truly small businesses are being obscured by statistical averages.

More fundamental than the frustration caused by the definition of what constitutes a small business is an attitude that strikes a little closer to home. The gulf between the two extreme opinions regarding the value of the SBA to a BESt Business can be summed up in two words: *varying expectations.* So, let's address these expectations and bring them into line by quickly dispelling the three most common myths that small businesses hold about the SBA:

1. The SBA makes business loans.

2. The SBA awards many grants.

3. SBA loans are "cheap."

The SBA makes business loans. False. *Except for a very limited number of direct loans, the SBA does not "make" loans by "cutting checks" and depositing them into your bank account.* What the SBA does, and does fairly well, is guarantee loans that have been submitted by financial institutions on behalf of a particular small business—or, as in your case, your BESt Business.

To decide on a loan request, the SBA evaluates a business in the same way that banks do. But before we continue our discussion about what the SBA does and does not do, let's talk for a moment about the difference between a local bank and the SBA. Here is the main difference, and it's a big difference: If a bank is tentative about extending a loan to a business because (1) there is insufficient collateral, (2) there is a higher risk level than the bank is comfortable with, or (3) the fact that the company is an upstart (without a history of performance), then the bank will turn to the SBA in an attempt to shift its risk by obtaining a loan guarantee that is backed by the federal government. The SBA has a higher tolerance for such loans.

The loan guaranty program is one of the SBA's primary lending programs. The SBA, through its loan guaranty program, assumes the substantial portion of the risk that would ordinarily be shouldered by the bank, if the loan was funded without such a guaranty in place. Bear in mind that the bank still "cuts the check," but the SBA assumes most of the risk in the event of default.

The SBA awards many grants. False. The truth is quite contrary. The SBA has very few grant opportunities, and those that are available are extremely difficult, if not impossible, for the average company to obtain. Despite what you've heard, the SBA is not in the business of funding grants to businesses.

I can't tell you how many times prospective business owners have approached me and asked about the "free money" that the government has for disadvantaged, minority businesses. The confusion generally exists because the SBA does have several programs (including the 8(a) program, which we'll discuss in Chapter 8) to facilitate disadvantaged companies in their efforts to do business with the federal government. These are "set-aside" type programs, not grants.

Most government agencies do have some grant monies available for various reasons, and so does the SBA. However, the money is not easy to get. Generally, it is available to those companies willing to commit to a period of research and development to create new products, technologies, or processes.

SBA loans are cheap. **False.** SBA loans are not cheap. There is no such thing as a non-interest-bearing loan from the SBA, or loans below the prime interest rate. *The **prime interest rate** is the rate that lending institutions offer their best customers.* Interest rates on SBA loans are higher than the prime rate. In addition to the interest on SBA-guaranteed loans, there is also a guaranty fee of approximately 3 percent based on the dollar amount of the guaranteed portion of the loan. I know that's a mouthful; let me give you an example to illustrate what is meant by guaranty fee.

Let's say that a BESt Company goes to its local bank to borrow $50,000 and that the local bank is hesitant about lending the entire $50,000 to a new company without a basis in collateral, or because it is an upstart, or due to the fact that the bank simply doesn't like the prevailing market conditions for a particular industry. This is exactly the sort of situation where the SBA shines for small businesses. SBA participation, however, has a price: the interest rate and the guaranty fee. If the SBA decides to guarantee this loan, the bank would fund the entire $50,000 but would have guarantees from the SBA for a certain percentage, say 80 percent. Therefore, 80 percent of $50,000 (or $40,000) of the loan value would be guaranteed by the SBA. Because $40,000 is the amount guaranteed, a guaranty fee of $1,200 ($40,000 × 3%) would have to be borne by the BESt Company—on top of interest costs.

Computation of SBA Guaranty Fee	
Loan Request	$50,000
Amount guaranteed by the SBA	$50,000 × 80% = $40,000
Guarantee fee	$40,000 × 3% = $1,200

Table 7-A

I'm not saying that the costs are oppressive; I'm simply driving home the point that the loans are not cheap.

A Rumor That's Actually True

From time to time, clients have asked the question, "Is it true that the SBA's repayment policy is very liberal?" Yes, that's actually true. Apart from guaranteeing loans that banks won't otherwise touch, perhaps the second biggest advantage that the SBA offers is a longer amortization period than most commercial loans. *An **amortization period** is the length of time that it takes to completely pay off a mortgage through repayment of the principal and the accumulated interest.* A seven-year working capital loan is not uncommon. Such terms can greatly facilitate cash flow. The SBA realizes that cash flow is vitally important to all businesses, but it is critical for upstarts. They generally do not have cash reserves to tap if cash flow goes negative. The following amortization periods are fairly typical of SBA loans.

SBA Loan Amortization Rates	
Working capital	Up to 7 years
Fixed assets	Up to 10 years
Construction or real estate	Up to 25 years

Table 7-B

Your local bank and the SBA will evaluate your loan request on the same general basis: Can the loan be repaid? Though the SBA places priority on your ability to maximize cash flow, demonstrated willingness to repay the loan is still important. What is demonstrated willingness, you ask? Good question. It is your willingness to personally guarantee a business loan—to put your money where you mouth is. Personal guarantees involve risking personal assets. What the SBA is saying is this: Demonstrate to us that you feel as positive about your business as the numbers in your business plan indicate. This is yet another reason to make sure your business plan is realistic.

7.2 When Does the SBA Get Involved in the Lending Process?

Allow me to bring out a nuance about dealing with the SBA. There might be some confusion as to when and how the SBA initially gets engaged in the loan process. For example, does the BESt CEO have to call an SBA representative? Or does the bank make the call? Is a visit to the local SBA office required? Exactly what is the protocol, and which documents does the SBA want to see in order to make a loan decision?

When you first walk into the bank, the process is not unlike any other loan. As a business owner, you pay your banker a visit to discuss the financial needs of your BESt Company. The SBA is generally not even mentioned until the bank has determined that it is not willing to make the loan without an SBA guarantee. Once you and your banker agree to involve the SBA, the process continues to move forward. Don't expect to go talk to an SBA representative at this point. Your banker continues to handle the request as he or she would normally, except that now another party—the SBA—is involved. Its involvement, though, takes place in the background. The SBA will want the same financial information the bank required: tax returns, financial statements, credit history, debt schedules, and so forth. Apart from the fact that the bank is seeking to transfer the bulk of its risk to the SBA, the transaction continues in a virtually seamless fashion.

7.3 SBA Loan Programs

Because approximately 90 percent of all businesses in the United States are classified by the SBA as "small business" and are eligible for SBA financial assistance, there is little doubt that your BESt Company will be eligible for SBA financial assistance. However, there are some exceptions. (Please see Section 7.4 for a list of businesses that are prohibited from receiving loan guarantees.) Also note that SBA financial assistance is not available to a company that dominates its field, is not independently owned, or is able to obtain bank or other private financing without assistance from the SBA.

The SBA has quite a number of programs available. We will focus our attention on the most popular programs and those that are most popular with BESt Companies:

 ▷ 7(a) loans.

 ▷ MicroLoans.

 ▷ LowDoc procedure.

Before I launch into this discussion, let me preface by saying that there is a vast amount of information available on each of these programs. This chapter is only a brief introduction to each of these programs. You can request additional free information by contacting your local SBA office or accessing its Website. (See Appendix D for the telephone numbers, addresses, and Website for the SBA.)

In the following sections, a detailed description of each of these popular programs will be discussed. Our discussion will focus on the following issues for each type of program, if applicable:

 ▷ Eligibility requirements.

 ▷ Maximum loan amounts.

 ▷ Maturity terms.

- ▸ Interest rates.
- ▸ Percentage of guaranty.
- ▸ Guaranty fee.
- ▸ Prepayment penalties.

7.4 7(a) Loan Guaranty Program ("Guaranteed Loans")

The 7(a) Loan Guaranty Program is the most basic and widely used type of lending program. The program operates through private-sector lenders, called participants. They are called participants because they participate by facilitating the 7(a) program at the local level. Not all banks participate, but most do. Remember: The SBA itself has very limited funds for direct lending.

Eligibility requirements. Eligibility depends on business type. Generally speaking, religious organizations, lending institutions, businesses that are involved with gambling activities or pyramid schemes, and companies that deal in speculative investments or rent real estate are not eligible to receive SBA financial assistance.

Company size is also a significant criterion to determine whether or not a particular business is eligible to receive SBA financial assistance.

Size Requirement for SBA Eligibility	
Manufacturing	Range of total number of employees must be equal to or less than 1,500; actual limitations differs by industry.
Wholesale	Up to 100 employees are permitted.
Service	Eligibility is determined by sales volume, not number of employees. Maximum annual sales can range from $3.5 to $14.5 million, depending on industry.
Retail	Maximum annual sales can range from $3.5 to $13.5 million, depending on industry.
General Construction	Maximum annual sales can range from $7 to $17 million, depending on industry.
Special Trade Construction	Average annual receipts cannot exceed $7 million.
Agriculture	Annual sales receipts cannot exceed $0.5 to $3.5 million, depending on industry.
	Source: Small Business Administration

Table 7-C

Maximum loan amounts. There are a few exceptions, but generally, the maximum amount the SBA can lend is $2 million (remember that when the word *lend* is used, you should be thinking *loan guarantee*). Accordingly, the maximum SBA exposure is $1 million. Thus, if a business receives an SBA guaranteed loan for $2 million, the maximum guaranty to the lender will be $1 million or 50 percent. There is no minimum amount the SBA will guarantee, but most banks and lending institutions shy away from processing commercial loans of less than $25,000.

Maturity terms. This refers to the length a loan. Loan maturity depends on the type of loan requested. All loans can be paid out sooner without being subject to prepayment penalties. This is an important benefit, especially for companies that experience significant growth and find themselves with surplus cash. At present, lenders generally adhere to the following guidelines:

▷ Working capital loans: five to seven years.

▷ Fixed-asset loans: seven to 10 years.

▷ Real estate and building loans: up to 25 years.

Interest rates. Interest rates are based on the prime rate as advertised in the *Wall Street Journal.*

Loans of $50,000 or more:

Loan maturity of less than 7 years:	prime plus 2.25%
Loan maturity of 7 or more years:	prime plus 2.75%

Loans between $25,000 and $50,000:

Loan maturity of less than 7 years:	prime plus 3.25%
Loan maturity of 7 or more years:	prime plus 3.75%

Loans of less than $25,000:

Loan maturity of less than 7 years:	prime plus 4.25%
Loan maturity of 7 or more years:	prime plus 4.75%

Percentage of guaranty. The SBA can guarantee up to 85 percent of loans of $150,000 and less, and up to 75 percent of loans in excess of $150,000 (generally up to a maximum guaranty amount of $1 million).

Guaranty fee. Depending on the loan amount, the SBA charges the lender between 1 percent and 3.5 percent for the security and privilege of guaranteeing the loan. With the approval of the SBA, the bank or lender, in turn, passes the guaranty fee on to the borrower.

Prepayment penalties. Some lenders penalize you for paying off the loan balance faster than the stated loan maturity. Prepayment penalties can amount to as much as several percentage points of the amount of the unpaid mortgage balance.

7.5 MicroLoans

Right at the beginning of the Clinton administration, the SBA made the MicroLoan program available to certain eligible small businesses. It provides very small loans to start-up, newly established, or growing small business concerns. Under this program, the SBA makes funds available to non-profit community-based lenders called intermediaries, which, in turn, make MicroLoans to eligible borrowers. The SBA chooses to work with these local agencies because they are more familiar with the community and usually have direct knowledge of its needs and economics. According to SBA statistics, the average size of a MicroLoan is about $10,500. Applications are submitted to the local intermediary where the credit decisions are made.

Please note that these intermediaries are non-profit, community-based organizations. They are not for profit banks. (See Appendix C for a list of MicroLoan intermediaries.)

Eligibility requirements: This program was established to primarily benefit minority- and women-owned companies. The companies most likely to benefit are small, home-based companies very much like your BESt Company.

Maximum loan amounts: MicroLoan is definitely an appropriate name for this program. Loans range anywhere from $100 to a maximum of $35,000.

Maturity terms: This depends on the earnings of the business and planned use of the funds. MicroLoans must be paid within the shortest terms possible, but no longer than six years.

Interest rates: The interest rate on MicroLoans cannot exceed the New York prime rate plus 4 percent. (The prime interest rate is the rate that banks will lend money to their most-favored customers. New York prime is simply a widely quoted prime rate, one that is monitored in most financial publications and Websites.)

Collateral: Each intermediary lender has its own lending and credit requirements. However, business owners contemplating application for a MicroLoan should be aware that intermediaries will generally require some type of collateral and the personal guarantee of the business owner.

Technical assistance: Each intermediary is required to provide business-based training and technical assistance to its microborrowers. Individuals and small businesses applying for MicroLoan financing may be required to fulfill training and/or planning requirements.

7.6 LowDoc Procedure

Unlike 7(a) and MicroLoans, the LowDoc program is **NOT** a type of loan; rather, it is a procedure (a delivery method) that helps streamline the application and lending process.

Before 1993, banks and other lenders were resistant to doing business with small businesses with loan needs generally less than $100,000. According to the lenders, this group of borrowers was less sophisticated and had less available financial information, and the loans were much less profitable. The SBA responded to their concerns by introducing the LowDoc program, which eased the documentation requirements of lenders as they processed these smaller loans. Once a small business borrower meets the lender's requirements for credit, the lender may request a guaranty from the SBA through SBA LowDoc procedures. It's a quick, two-step process:

STEP 1: The borrower completes the front of the SBA's one-page application, and the lender completes the back.

STEP 2: The lender submits a completed application to the SBA and receives an answer within 36 hours.

Eligibility requirements: A business is usually eligible for the SBA LowDoc if:

▷ The purpose of the loan is to start or grow a business.

▷ The existing business employs no more than 100 people and has average annual sales for the preceding three years not exceeding $5 million; the business and its owners have good credit; and the business owners are of good character.

Maximum loan amount: $150,000

Maturity terms: The length of time for repayment depends on the ability to repay and the use of the loan proceeds. Maturity is usually five to 10 years. For fixed asset loans (such as heavy machinery) it can be up to 25 years.

Interest rates: Interest rates can be negotiated between the borrower and lender, may be fixed or variable, are tied to the prime rate (as published in the *Wall Street Journal*), and may not exceed the SBA 7(a) program maximums.

Guaranty fee: The fee is 1 percent on guaranteed portion. The SBA will guarantee up to a maximum of 85 percent.

Collateral: To secure the loan, the borrower must pledge available business and personal assets. Loans are not declined when inadequate collateral is the only unfavorable factor. Personal guaranties of the principals are generally required.

7.7 Veterans Assistance

As the SBA rightly claims on its Website, the United States owes a great deal to its veterans. The SBA has taken a proactive role in bringing together many resource partners that are dedicated to veteran entrepreneurship. The SBA also has a number of programs that provide technical assistance to veterans and disabled veteran entrepreneurs who are interested in getting into business or expanding an existing business. (Visit *www.sba.gov* for details.)

7.8 SBA Paperwork

The SBA, along with the participating bank, will require complete financial disclosure on the BESt Company in order to evaluate a loan request. As you have seen, with respect to rules established by the SBA, there are several issues regarding eligibility. The bank will use the information provided by the BESt CEO to determine whether or not the company meets those eligibility requirements.

Following is a checklist of documentation typically required when an SBA loan guarantee is requested. Please note that "Exhibit A," "Exhibit B," and so forth are listed in the order the information is requested on the Business Loan Application form.

Checklist of SBA Forms

❐ 1. Business loan application. (SBA Form 4)

❐ 2. Exhibit A: Schedule of collateral. (SBA Form 4 Schedule A)

❐ 3. Exhibit B: Personal financial statement. (SBA Form 413)

❐ 4. Exhibit C: Business financial statements. (no preprinted form)

❐ 5. Exhibit D: Business history. (no preprinted form)

❐ 6. Exhibit E: Resumes (management only). (no preprinted form)

❐ 7. Exhibit F: List of co-signors and/or guarantors. (no preprinted form)

❐ 8. Exhibit G: List of equipment to be purchased with loan proceeds and seller information. (no preprinted form)

❐ 9. Exhibit H: Details of bankruptcy of company officer, if applicable. (no preprinted form)

❐ 10. Exhibit I: Details of pending lawsuits, if applicable. (no preprinted form)

❐ 11. Exhibit J: Name and address of any related party who works for the SBA, any federal agency, or the participating lender. (no preprinted form)

❐ 12. Exhibit K: Details of affiliated interests. (no preprinted form)

❐ 13. Exhibit L: Details of related party transactions. (no preprinted form)

❐ 14. Exhibit M: Copy of the franchise agreement and the FTC disclosure statement, if applicable. (no preprinted form)

☐ 15. Exhibit N: Estimated project cost and a statement of the source of additional funds. (no preprinted form)

☐ 16. Exhibit O: Preliminary construction plans and specifications, if applicable. (no preprinted form)

☐ 17. Bank declination letter. A bank should state in a formal letter why it declined a loan request. (no preprinted form)

☐ 18. Statement of personal history. (SBA Form 912)

☐ 19. Compensation Agreement for Services in Connection with Application and Loan From (or in Participation with) Small Business Administration. This document is required to disclose any professional fees paid by the borrower for services related to the SBA loan. (SBA Form 159)

☐ 20. Assurance of Compliance for Nondiscrimination. Borrower attests to comply with SBA regulations pertaining to discrimination. (SBA Form 652)

☐ 21. Certification Regarding Disbarment, Suspension, Ineligibility, and Voluntary Exclusion Lower Tier Covered Transactions. The borrower attests that neither the BESt Company nor the owner has been debarred from doing business with the federal government. (SBA Form 1624)

Chapter 8

SBA's 8(a) Program

I always wanted to be somebody. If I made it, it's half because I was game enough to take a lot of punishment along the way and half because there were a lot of people who cared enough to help me.

—Althea Gibson

8.1 What Is 8(a)?

The 8(a) program is so called because it was authorized in 1968 by Section 8(a) of the Small Business Act. It was created to help minority and disadvantaged companies grow and prosper through a program of federal contracting that includes preferences and set-asides. Once certified as an 8(a), a participating company has the ability to receive government contracts up to $3 million on a non-competitive basis. If the contract is for manufacturing, then that limit is increased to $5 million. In addition to non-competitive (or sole-sourced) contracts, the federal government also sets aside a certain number of contracts and awards them strictly to 8(a) firms that compete only among themselves (and, in so doing, do not have to contend with competition from the "big boys").

The 8(a) program, or "8a" as it is commonly called, is a great deal for small minority businesses, if worked properly. More than 7,000 companies participate in the 8(a) program, but a significant number will never receive a federal contract. Despite this lucrative opportunity, many fail to take advantage because of myths and misconceptions about how the program is administered. (In Section 8.5 we'll debunk some of these myths.)

Even though it seems an 8(a) company is almost a "shoe-in" for 8(a) contracts, nothing could be further from the truth. It requires much hard work and persistence to secure an 8(a) contract. First, the 8(a) company must market itself relentlessly, and then it must prove that it has the technical ability and the financial wherewithal to fulfill the contract's requirements.

Being awarded a contract is only the beginning. The contract must then be satisfactorily performed. The old saying "it might not be good enough for the private sector, but it's good enough for government work" is not right thinking. Admittedly, the bureaucracy of some governmental agencies is very heavy and cumbersome. Many agencies, however, are very efficient and very demanding—especially on small business. The small size of most 8(a) contracts allows them to be easily monitored; there is no convoluted corporate structure to hide behind. If performance is not proceeding satisfactorily, the contract can be easily terminated.

The goal of the 8(a) program is to give viable small businesses a foothold in the federal procurement market so that they can grow their business and become stronger and more competitive in a relatively short period of time. A business may remain in the 8(a) program for nine years. By the time it "graduates" from the program, the company should be able to compete successfully in the open market without the benefit of set-asides. The time that a company spends in the 8(a) program is divided into two phases:

➤ **Development stage (four years):** [The company uses the program to open doors to business opportunities it might not otherwise have.

➤ **Transition stage (five years):** The company works feverishly to revert the business mix from mostly government contracts, to a balanced mix consisting of both government (public) sector and private sector business. This mix will allow a graduating 8(a) company to stay competitive and thrive after the set-aside business is no longer available.

Federally Speaking, Disadvantaged Means What, Exactly?

To qualify as an 8(a) business, the owner of the business must demonstrate social and economic disadvantage. The burden to demonstrate *social* disadvantage is lifted from African-Americans and other minorities due to the fact that, by definition, being a minority in America puts one in a socially disadvantaged situation. Consequently, over the years, most 8(a) companies have been owned by African, Hispanic, Asian, and Native Americans.

In order to meet the *economic* disadvantaged test, at the time an 8(a) application is prepared, the individual upon whom eligibility is based must have a net worth less than $250,000. This amount excludes the combined value of the business and the applicant's personal residence.

8.2 Eligibility Requirements

To qualify as an 8(a) company, a small business must pass several tests:

➤ The business must be 51-percent owned and controlled by a socially disadvantaged individual. That doesn't mean puppet ownership. Fifty-one percent of the stock must be owned by the individual upon whom eligibility is based, *and* that person must exercise control over the company. In other words, the owner must not only own the company but also make all the significant managerial decisions; in effect, he or she must also "run" the company.

Note: *As mentioned, certain groups, including African-Americans, Hispanic Americans, Asian Americans, and Native Americans are presumed socially disadvantaged. Others individuals not in these specific groups can also be deemed socially disadvantaged. However, they must be able to demonstrate, through a preponderance of the evidence, that they are disadvantaged because of race, ethnicity, gender, or handicap, or due to the fact that their residence is in an environment isolated from the mainstream American society. I will not focus on this exception because it does not apply to the typical reader of this book.*

➤ In order to meet the economic disadvantaged test, all individuals must have a net worth less than $250,000, excluding the value of the business and personal residence.

➤ Successful applicants must also meet applicable size standards.

➤ The company must have been in business for at least two years (this requirement can be waived).

➤ The company must display reasonable success potential. (Your business plan has to be reasonable.)

➤ The business owner should display good character.

8.3 8(a) Contract Awards

There are two basic ways that a government agency awards a contract to an 8(a) contractor:

▷ Single source awards: The government agency directly chooses the 8(a) company that it has deemed capable of satisfying its purchase requirements.

▷ 8(a) competition: The process is very similar to an "open bid" opportunity, except that the competing firms are all 8(a) firms.

The advantage that the government maintains for single sourcing a contract is that the products or services are delivered faster. No competition shortens the purchase cycle. Also, singling out a source early on in the purchasing process allows for more interaction with the 8(a) company, which increases the likelihood that the agency will get exactly what it wants. Single source contracts, however, have a $3 million cap for service contracts and a $5 million cap for contracts producing manufactured products. Any contract for more than the $3 and $5 million limit must undergo a competitive bid process.

Note: *8(a) firms may bid on any government work at any time, whether it's 8(a) set-aside or not. Sometimes the CEOs of prospective 8(a) companies wonder whether or not their public sector (government) work will be limited to only 8(a) contracts. Again, the answer is no. If you can find the work, go after it.*

8.4 Competition: One Pie, Many Tiny Pieces

Many minority business owners who are 8(a) participants eagerly endorse the program. In addition to the obvious competitive benefits, they claim that small disadvantaged businesses can leverage business contacts and a history of successful performance into substantial future business. And to a large extent, that's true. That's why a large number of prospective 8(a)s are applying for certification. But increasing participation is a double-edged sword. As more minority companies continue to enter the program, the 8(a) field is getting more and more crowded. There is legitimate concern that the contracting pie is being divided into smaller and smaller pieces. Some believe that the intense competition among the 8(a)s themselves is good for the government but counterproductive to the most viable of 8(a)s. The opportunity for the talented, well-managed companies to succeed and thrive is lessened. Others believe that the competition among "equals" is good and that the strongest of the 8(a)s will not only survive, but develop cutting-edge technology and foster more creative entrepreneurial thinking.

In my experience, those CEOs with the greatest understanding of the program, who understand its opportunities and limitations, are best suited to reap the most benefit. If your expectations are unrealistic, too much time and resources will be poured into a bottomless pit that yields no return. For example, I have seen businessmen spend a small fortune on travel expenses, running to and from Washington D.C. (where the action is!) in pursuit of opportunities that just don't pan out. They have endless meetings with congressional aids and liaison officers whose jobs are to glad-hand constituents and to put a positive spin on their proposals. In the end, they always make the same request: Prepare a proposal and send it to the appropriate agency. Money would be much better spent developing relationships with the purchasing agents and contract officers who work for the agencies that are soliciting the products and services of small businesses.

8.5 Four 8(a) Myths Debunked

In an effort to avoid unrealistic expectations, let's address four myths about the 8(a) program.

1. *Knowing your congressmen gives you a lock on available work.*

   False. Although such associations are generally positive and increase your comfort level with the federal bureaucracy, you must still respond to solicitations by creating a competitive offer and wait for a decision at the agency level—that is, the agency that is actually doing the buying, such as NASA, the U.S. Army, the IRS, the Department of Transportation, and so forth.

2. *The 8(a) program guarantees contracts to all 8(a) contractors.*

   False. Although the SBA 8(a) program does, in fact, set aside contracts for small 8(a) contractors, your ability to obtain these contracts is based on what you're selling, your pricing structure, and your active promotion of your company. There are no guarantees to specific companies.

3. *Competing against other 8(a)s is easy because they are poorly managed.*

   False. As with any population of competing firms in the public or private sectors, you'll have both poorly managed and well-managed companies. Many 8(a) firms are blessed with very dynamic and extremely talented management. Don't let an assumption of mediocrity forestall your efforts to compete at the highest level.

4. *Being an 8(a) contractor guarantees business success.*

   False. As I've said repeatedly, there are no guarantees—just opportunities. Many 8(a) firms spend the entire nine years in the program and are never awarded even a single contract. Why? Not because the opportunities aren't available, but because they are waiting for something to happen.

8.6 Certification: A Test in Paperwork Management

The most overwhelming aspect of applying for an 8(a) certification is simply the sheer amount of documentation that needs to be pulled together. There is nothing really difficult about the actual contents of the documentation required, but if you've not compiled such a package before, it can appear daunting and become quite confusing. If you are inexperienced with compiling and reviewing a large number of documents, my advice is to engage the services of an experienced consultant. (Even then, though, there is still quite a bit of work that only you will be able to perform.)

Let's take a look at the steps involved in obtaining an 8(a) certification and then you can decide whether or not to involve a consultant.

Step 1: **Make initial contact.** This step must be taken by the individual upon whom 8(a) certification will ultimately be based (usually the owner). In your case, as the CEO of your company, you must place a call to the local SBA office to let them know your intent and to sign up for an 8(a) orientation. Generally, the office sets aside several orientation dates each month to accommodate potential applicants.

Step 2: **Attend orientation.** This session is usually held in a conference room at your local SBA office. The 8(a) program is introduced, followed by a question and answer session. It is during this orientation that business owners either decide to go forward with the process or to stop the process. Also, the more armed you are with questions, the more productive the orientation.

Step 3: **Complete the application package.** The operative word here is *package*. This is the step where the bulk of the work is accomplished. Approximately 40 documents must be compiled in this phase. (See Appendix E for a summary of documents that are included in the final package.)

Step 4: **Review the package.** Even if your package is prepared by an outside consultant (including your CPA or attorney), it's always a good idea to have someone other than the person who compiled the package review it. If an outside consultant prepared the package, you should review the completed document. If you, as the BESt CEO, compiled the package, have your consultant review the package for errors and omissions.

Step 5: **Mail the package and wait.** Depending on your location, the package should be sent either to Philadelphia or San Francisco. Application packages are received on an ongoing basis. Waiting for a response could take as long as 90 days (or maybe longer).

Step 6: **Await final decision or reconsideration.** If the decision is an approval, you will get a congratulatory letter from the SBA that welcomes your business into the program. **Or** a letter will come with a list of deficiencies that prevents the Division of Program Certification and Eligibility from making a final approval. You are given 60 days to correct the list of problems or deficiencies. Don't panic! Receiving a letter of this sort is not unusual and certainly not a deal-breaker. Many packages have issues or conflicts that need to be reviewed and "fixed." It's just a matter of course, and if you respond within the appropriate time, that list of issues can be resolved relatively quickly. Alternatively, if the 60 days pass without a response, the entire package must be resubmitted and re-evaluated.

Step 7: Await decision after reconsideration. If all the deficient issues are addressed satisfactorily, the Division of Program Certification and Eligibility will then send a welcome letter. The date in the Letter of Acceptance marks your company's official entry date into the 8(a) program. The clock starts ticking and you have nine years of eligibility—nine years to take your BESt Company to the next level.

Step 8: Receive a Business Opportunity Specialist (BOS). A BOS is an SBA representative that is assigned to each 8(a) company. The BOS's job is to guide the 8(a) company through the program to ensure that the company complies with all SBA requirements and positions itself to take advantage of available opportunities. **Note:** Although the BOS will assist the BESt Company with a broad range of business development issues, including procurement, it is not the BOS's responsibility to "get contracts" for the BESt Company. That responsibly is a function of your marketing and sales efforts. As the CEO of your BESt Company, if you don't make it happen, it won't happen.

Step 9: Submit a comprehensive business plan. You should already have a comprehensive business plan in place. Make needed modifications as required by the SBA and submit to your BOS.

Step 10: Complete a Pro-Net profile. Pro-Net is an SBA-sponsored Internet-based database of information on approximately 290,000 small, disadvantaged, 8(a), HUBZone, and women-owned businesses. It is a free resource that federal and state government agencies, prime contractors, and other private-sector contractors use to get general information about small businesses that might be available to bid on a specific opportunity or go straight to work on a specific job. If you will, think of Pro-Net as the "yellow pages" of small businesses.

www.fedbizops.gov

BESt Websites ▐▐▐▶ This site provides a daily list of U.S. government procurement invitations, contract agreement awards, subcontracting leads, sales surplus property, and foreign business opportunities. This information can be delivered to your e-mail address. In short, this site is a daily list of items and services the federal government wants to purchase. Every listing has basic purchase specifications leading ultimately to the awarding of a contact.

pro-net.sba.gov or *www.ccr.gov*

Pro-Net provides 8(a) companies with an opportunity to market their businesses in a controlled manner. Companies can link their Websites to their Pro-Net profile and create a very powerful marketing tool. (See Step 10 in Section 8.6.)

Chapter 9

Setting Up the Books

CPAs can be a pain, but the IRS is a bigger pain.

—Bill Boudreaux

9.1 Your CPA: A Close Ally

Tiger Woods and Oprah Winfrey are not the only people who need the services of a certified public accountant (CPA). As I have been emphasizing throughout this book, a competent CPA is essential to a new business. Unless your spouse is a CPA, you should arrange to put one on your team. Having the ability to pick up the phone and call a CPA about unfamiliar or complicated matters is a great comfort and a worthwhile investment.

For example, you might be obligated to collect sales taxes on the sales your company makes. If you've never done this before, you'll have questions. You may be able to get someone from the sales tax office on the phone to trudge through the regulations and procedures with you, but he or she will only be able to view your company's transactions through a broad lens. It is much better to place a quick call to a CPA who has been working with you and who better understands the dynamics of your company and its operating environment. A CPA will put you on the right track in no time. That's not to say that you should pick up the phone and call several times a day. Although some are on retainer, most CPAs charge according to the amount of time they spend working for you. Having a CPA at your beck and call is comforting, but you should use him or her prudently. Besides, once you have a system in place, routines become quite familiar. As time goes on, you'll find yourself making fewer and fewer calls about day-to-day bookkeeping routines. Calls will gradually become more concerned with issues that deal with taxation, financial reporting, management advisory services, and a wide range of other financial matters.

How Do You Find a CPA?

Some CEOs may already have a CPA/tax preparer. Others may have their taxes prepared by a tax service; H&R Block, Jackson Hewitt, and other such firms are primarily tax-preparers. They are **not** CPA firms. They do an excellent job preparing taxes, but they do not provide the broad scope of services that a CPA provides and a BESt Company requires.

Most BESt CEOs will connect with a CPA through word of mouth via a recommendation from a friend or business associate. If these sources don't have any suggestions, a good place to start your search is with a call to the CPA Society of your state. Each state has a Society of CPAs. For example, the name of the society in Louisiana is the Louisiana Society of CPAs. Generally, each state's society offers a CPA referral service to help bring businesses together with the right CPA.

What Qualifications Should You Look For?

Licensed to practice. All CPAs are accountants, but not all accountants are CPAs. CPAs are distinguished from other accountants by stringent state licensing requirements. Most states require CPAs to have at least a college degree or its equivalent. Several states also require post-graduate work. All CPAs are licensed to practice by a specific state or states. For example, a CPA licensed in Florida may not necessarily be licensed to practice in Georgia. A license to practice generally means that the CPA has the appropriate education and technical expertise.

Competent in your industry. As with all professions, some CPAs are more talented and competent than others. Some are excellent auditors; others great tax advisors. If your industry is relatively complicated, you should find a CPA who understands it. For example, if your BESt Company develops software, it would be a coup to find a CPA that understands the ins and outs of the software industry.

Membership in professional organizations. Membership in professional organizations is an important qualification to consider. For example, more than 310,000 CPAs belong to the American Institute of Certified Public Accountants (AICPA). AICPA members must satisfy extensive continuing education requirements that keep them up to date on evolving accounting issues. Also, since the year 2000, new members are required to have completed 150 semester hours of higher education prior to joining the AICPA.

Compatibility. This qualification is often overlooked. It is harder to define but just as important as technical proficiency. Make sure that the CPA's personality and expertise match your needs. Keep in mind that a long-term working relationship between you and your CPA can help you take an informed, consistent approach to the financial problems of your business. You don't need the hassle of hiring and firing CPAs.

What Do CPAs Charge?

Normally, CPAs base their fees on the time required to perform the services requested. There are no "fee schedules" common to the profession. Fees depend on the type of services you require, the prevailing costs in the community, the CPA's level of expertise, and the complexity of your work. Talk frankly with your CPA about fees. More than likely, you will choose a CPA that is a sole practitioner or associated with a small firm. Their prices tend to be pretty reasonable. In some cases, the CPA will assign the work to a staff member who is under his or her immediate supervision, and the cost comes down even more.

As a guide, be prepared to spend somewhere in the neighborhood of approximately $200 to $300 per month. Obviously, you may spend much more, and in some cases perhaps even a few dollars less. Remember: A CPA's fees are directly related to the amount of work he or she does. If you require your CPA to spend a lot of time on your account, this generally means that business is good. In that case, a CPA's fee is a small investment to be able to sleep at night, knowing the experienced eyes of a competent professional are reviewing your business transactions.

What About All the Accounting Scandals?

The American Institute of CPAs is running an interesting promotional campaign: ***Don't underestimate the importance of the CPA designation***. Remember: Those three letters are awarded only to those individuals who have passed a rigorous uniform national examination. As a CPA, I agree with the campaign statement. You, on the other hand, might not, especially in light of all the alleged corruption from a slew of high-profile cases (for example, Enron, Global Crossing, and others). In these cases, CPA firms were allegedly complicit in the underhandedness that scandalized these behemoths. On many fronts, the accounting profession as a whole received a black eye. Was it deserved? In some cases, probably, and hopefully any offending accounting firm will be chastised accordingly. For the most part, however, CPAs are hardworking professionals who provide invaluable service to BESt Companies. Don't be prejudiced against CPAs because of a few high-profile cases.

How Do You Get the Most Value From Your CPA?

CPAs themselves have some suggestions on how to make the best use of accounting services and get the most value for your money. Here are just a few:

➤ Be prepared to discuss your plans and objectives. CPAs are in the best position to advise when they understand the goals you've set.

➤ Gather information about business decisions under consideration so you can ask specific questions.

➤ Clearly explain what you expect from the CPA's services.

➤ Save yourself unnecessary fees by keeping good records and not using a CPA's time for routine work.

➤ Keep your CPA informed of changes in your personal life. A recent marriage, divorce, or the birth of a child can all have a significant impact on your tax liability and company goals.

Here are just a few of the services a CPA may be able to offer you:

(Check off the items for which you think you may need a CPA's help. Bring the list with you when you have your first meeting with the CPA of your choice.)

❐ Setting up a bookkeeping system.

❐ Helping secure financing.

❐ Analyzing operating results.

❐ Providing management consulting services on such subjects as data processing systems.

❐ Developing budgets and business forecasts.

❐ Preparing tax returns.

❐ Auditing, reviewing, or compiling financial statements.

❐ Suggesting tax strategies.

❐ Minimizing tax liability.

❐ Representing you before tax authorities.

❐ Developing a personal financial plan.

❐ Assessing insurance needs.

❐ Devising savings and investment strategies.

❐ Other _____

❐ Other _____

❐ Other _____

Note: *This is only a partial list of the many services CPA firms offer. As you can see, there are many technical areas that the average person simply cannot handle on his or her own.*

9.2 Accounting Software Is Power

Today's accounting software packages have revolutionized the way BESt CEOs manage their affairs. Even though you'll probably let your CPA handle the monthly or quarterly write-up work (preparing financial statements and filing certain tax returns), you still have to prepare invoices, manage accounts receivable, and write checks. Installing good accounting software will almost always save time and place excellent management tools in your hands.

Buying Accounting Software

There was a time when keeping up with the accounting was nearly impossible without having an accountant on staff to do the invoicing, prepare checks, enter invoices, and create various management reports. There was a time when a section pertaining to setting up your own set of books would not have been included in an entrepreneurial guide; it would have been too technical for most. Today, however, with powerful and economical accounting software available at every large office supply store, you should not hesitate to make a choice of accounting software for your BESt Company.

If you were to enter "accounting software" in your Internet browser, the number of sites returned would be overwhelming. It is extremely difficult to itemize the pros and cons of each software title, and—frankly—who cares? All you need is something that is mature (has been around a few years), reliable, and cheap. And, as is the case with accounting software, cheap does not necessarily imply inferior. The peculiar thing about software is this: The more popular it is and the more licenses (the right to use the software) the developer sells, the quicker and more substantially the price comes down. Software that once cost tens of thousands of dollars can now be picked up for a few hundred!

You may think that you don't need accounting software, but you do. BESt CEOs do not purchase accounting software just to compile information for their accountants to do taxes. Today's software titles for small businesses are used to create invoices for customers, fax, or e-mail invoices to customers, pay bills online, track receivables and inventory, communicate with vendors, and keep track of payroll. In addition to keeping track of transactions, today's accounting software is an all-around, excellent management tool. These capabilities, available with the click of a mouse, will give you the ability to make faster, more informed decisions.

What to Consider Before Deciding About Software

Purchasing software for your BESt Company is actually a simple process. Larger companies might take weeks, even months, to make a proper decision. They have to deal with issues that do not concern you, at least not at the moment.

Accounting software is essentially categorized into three general groups. I share this information with you so you will have an appreciation for the capacity, scope, and price range of available software. It will allow you to appreciate the deal you're getting when paying $100 to $500 for software to run your BESt Company. The groups are:

- Low-end accounting software (companies with up to $5 million in revenue). **Cost range: $100 to $4,500+**

- Middle market (companies with $2 million to $50 million in revenue). **Cost range: $3,000 to $100,000+**

- Beginning Enterprise Resource Planning (ERP) (companies with revenues of $25 million and up). **Cost range: $10,000 to $300,000+**

BESt Principle # 6 ⅠⅠⅠ➡

LEARN AS MUCH AS POSSIBLE ABOUT
THE SOFTWARE YOU USE.
THE MORE YOU KNOW, THE HARDER YOU CAN
MAKE SOFTWARE WORK TO ACCOMPLISH
YOUR BESt COMPANY'S OBJECTIVES.

Peachtree and Quickbooks

Obviously, our attention will be focused on low-end accounting software packages. The goal is to match your business needs with the capabilities of the software. Although no single product is the end-all be-all for every business, allow me to save you a bunch of time and trouble by making a general recommendation. Based on my experience, of the top 10 accounting software products in the low-end market, Peachtree and Quickbooks are usually quite adequate for most BESt Companies. Unless you are involved in some intricate manufacturing or distribution process, either package will be well suited for your needs.

Software Company	Website	Phone Number (to order)
Intuit, Inc.	*www.quickbooks.com*	800–433–8810
Best Software SB, Inc.	*www.peachtree.com*	770–724–4000

 CAUTION ⅠⅠⅠ➡ Unless you have some accounting background, allow your CPA or someone with accounting experience to install the accounting application you choose—or at least guide you though the process.

Software Support

Before making a final software selection, ask your software vendor questions about the level of support that comes with the accounting package. For example, many software companies will give at least 30 days' support with each package that is registered. Thirty days might be enough time to install the accounting package and work through whatever installation issues you encounter. However, you may need more time. If you think you will, contact the software supplier's sales or customer service department and ask for a quote for an extended maintenance contract. *An extended maintenance contract is an agreement with the software vendor to continue to provide software support service beyond an initial maintenance period.* This contract will give you the ability to call the vendor whenever you encounter a software-related problem that you can't fix.

9.3 Entering Transactions

The first step in setting up an accounting system is to understand why such a system is necessary. Here are a few reasons:

➔ **Running your business through your personal checkbook is a recipe for immeasurable complexity**—not to mention the exposure to which you subject your personal records in the event the IRS ever audits your business's tax returns. Audits can be incredibly unpleasant. However, if your accounting records are in top shape, an audit can be no more bothersome than an overdue receivable—in other words, just another thing to deal with.

 **BESt Principle #7 ▐▐▶**

KEEP BUSINESS AND PERSONAL TRANSACTIONS SEPARATE.

EVEN THE SMALLEST BESt COMPANY SHOULD ABSOLUTELY AVOID COMMINGLING PERSONAL TRANSACTIONS WITH BUSINESS TRANSACTIONS.

➔ **You need to know exactly how your business is performing and the financial position of your company at any given point of time.** The two financial statements that present that type of financial information are the *balance sheet* and *income statement*. In order to properly prepare these statements, you must have a system that allows you to account for all sales and to capture all costs.

Both Quickbooks and Peachtree have a tutorial that leads you through the process of setting up accounting records (also called "setting up a set of books"). Both programs solicit information in an interview format. That is, a number of screens walk you through the process of choosing and setting up various bookkeeping options that will best serve your unique set of circumstances. The screens are easy to follow, and detailed instructions show exactly how to navigate around the system. The interview is divided into major sections, each dealing with topics that must be addressed (for example, setting up customer records, vendor records, inventory items, invoice terms, and so on). Most times, there is a ***help screen*** available for each topic.

The first phase of the interview process deals with general company information, such as:

- Name, address, phone and fax numbers, e-mail address, and Website.
- Business structure (sole proprietor, partnership, corporation, or limited liability company).
- Federal tax ID number (your social security number or employer's identification number (EIN), depending on legal structure).
- Tax year. A business tax year is a 12-month taxation period. Many businesses choose a tax year that starts in January, but January may not necessarily be the best choice for you. (See our previous discussion on tax year in Chapter 3.)

As I mentioned, you'll probably require the watchful eye of a CPA to help with the installation, but then you're off to the races.

Is Accounting Knowledge Necessary to Use Accounting Software?

No. Your CPA may want to give you an accounting tutorial to increase your accounting knowledge, but that's not necessary. There really is no need for you to understand double-entry bookkeeping or the mechanics of making journal entries (debits and credits) in order to fully utilize today's accounting software applications. For the most part, data input screens are fashioned to look like documents that you see every day, such as checks, delivery tickets, invoices, and payroll time sheets. You will become very comfortable entering data once you get familiar with the screens. Even preparing income statements and balance sheets is virtually automatic; all the required accounting is done behind the scenes.

Periodically, your CPA will want to reconcile certain accounts or propose journal entries to adjust various balances. That is common and normal, and not anything you need to learn.

Major Accounts to Keep a Handle On

Cash. You may have several cash accounts. You must know what's in the bank at all times. Managing cash will help you manage cash flow, and cash flow is the lifeblood of your company.

Don't forget about the petty cash kept in the desk drawer. It may not be much, but you still need to account for it.

Accounts Receivable. Virtually all accounting software allows you to maintain an accounts receivable aging. An A/R aging is a detailed listing showing customer name, a detailed listing of invoices, and the length of time each invoice has been outstanding. This report will become one of your most useful management tools. It is used to determine whether or not customers are paying according to terms, whether or not they are entitled to take discounts, and how much credit they still have available.

Inventory. If your BESt Company maintains inventory, you will need to know exactly what is on hand and available for sale. A stock status report will help you respond to customers' calls for price and availability. Again, this report is readily available with most accounting software packages.

Accounts Payable. This represents what is owed to vendors from whom you purchase equipment, supplies, and inventory. As with accounts receivable, it is a detailed listing and a very useful management tool. Not only does it allow you to effectively manage cash paid out, but it also serves as a handy report to catch vendors who may inadvertently invoice your BESt Company twice for the same merchandise.

Sales. This figure is one of the most closely watched by all business managers; it represents the amount of revenue your company is invoicing out. In the beginning, sales revenue may fluctuate somewhat, but once your *customer base* is established it tends to become more predictable. In addition to tracking sales, it is also useful to track the cost associated with those sales. Monitoring sales and their attendant cost reveals whether gross profit margins are being maintained. (For a discussion of gross profit margins, see Section 11.4.)

General Ledger

The general ledger is the basis for the company's financial statements. Your general ledger should include accounts that reflect the nature of your business. Recent versions of Peachtree and Quickbooks will give you the opportunity to choose a pre-designed chart of accounts that is similar to your business. Once selected, it can be used as a starting point for your final chart of accounts. To make the chart of accounts specific to your operations, simply add and delete accounts as needed.

Be sure to spend adequate time in selecting the expense accounts you will ultimately decide upon. Financial statement analysis will generally center on expense accounts. The more meaningful the account titles, the better. For example, don't just clump various types of supplies into an account titled "Supplies." You may find that two supply accounts present a clearer picture of what's going on, for example, "Office Supplies" and "Shop Supplies." It's easy to see how two separate supply accounts give more visibility and permit more precise analysis. The same goes for many other expense categories.

Hard Copies and Backups

Computers are wonderful until they go wacky. Whenever they go haywire, it's always at the most inconvenient time. Regular backups will protect your computer system from potential data loss due to damaged hardware, viruses, newly installed software, upgrades, and user errors. I back up my important files on a daily basis. The most I could ever lose is one day of work. I know you intend to be careful, but many times, in a rush, things get neglected. Don't get careless with your data.

It is also in your best interest to keep a hard-copy printout of reports you use on a regular basis (for example, accounts receivable aging, stock status, and accounts payable aging). If the system goes down for any reason at all (even a power outage), you won't have to operate completely in the dark, so to speak. You can still make collection calls from your accounts receivable aging and sell inventory from a printed stock status report.

BESt Principle #8 ⅢⅢ➡

BACK UP YOUR RECORDS ROUTINELY.
A FEW MINUTES A DAY CAN PROTECT YOU FROM HAVING TO REDO A MOUNTAIN OF WORK AT THE MOST INCONVENIENT TIME.

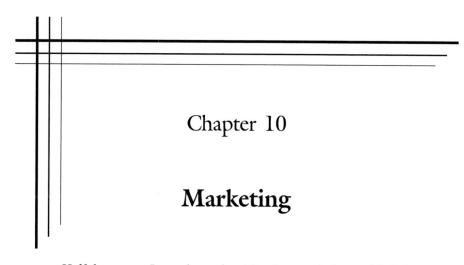

Chapter 10

Marketing

Half the money I spend on advertising is wasted; the trouble is I don't know which half.

—John Wanamaker

10.1 Marketing Plans

Marketing is definitely more art than science. It takes lots of imagination and creativity. I enjoy it immensely. It's quite a challenge to introduce and expose your product to as many people as possible, for as little money as possible—and that's the key.

Apart from the fact that advertising increases sales, there is really not much more than can be considered axiomatic. In other words, there are very few hard and fast rules when it comes to *getting the word out.* An advertising campaign in the local newspaper might elicit an overwhelming response one week and absolutely bomb the next week. Or a small ad in a free community paper might bring a very unexpected and welcomed response. Marketing is very complex with a whole host of variables—many of which are simply beyond your control.

The key to maximizing marketing effectiveness is to know your customer as well as possible and to target your marketing to those potential customers. It does no good to market to the entire planet. Some people will buy your product, and some will not. It's not personal; that's just Economics 101, where people make choices on the basis of their limited income.

The dynamic interaction between the BESt Company and its customers is highlighted in what is called the ***marketing concept.*** So far, we have successfully avoided such talk about "concepts," "principles," and other academic jargon. I don't intend to start now. But I do need to mention the marketing concept because it is so central to your ultimate success out there in the marketplace.

*The **marketing concept** is concerned with selling products and services that customers demand through a plan that takes into consideration sales goals and overall company objectives, especially profitability.* The marketing concept includes the following elements:

➤ **Market research.**

1. Identify your customers.

2. Determine what they want to buy.

3. Estimate potential sales volume of products and/or services.

   Note: *Generally, companies use past sales history to predict future sales. Because you probably will not have history to call upon, you could get a sense of potential sales by reviewing industry statistics. Several sites on the Internet publish industry stats, but most will cost you. At this point, I would recommend relying on your experience and informal surveys of prospective customers to estimate your BESt Company's potential sales.*

➤ **Market strategy.** Realizing you can't be all things to all people, how will you best satisfy the needs of your customers? What will you do to distinguish yourself from your competition?

➤ **Target market.** Focus your efforts on a limited number of key market segments. For example, some lawncare companies will only maintain residential customers, whereas others have chosen to concentrate on business customers. Remember BESt Principle #2: Focus!

➤ **Market mix.** Provide customers with the best value for their money by carefully considering the 4 "Ps" of marketing: **Products** (and services), **Promotion, Place** (distribution), and **Price.** We will take a closer look at the first two of the four Ps in the sections that follow. (We will save our discussion of place and pricing for Chapters 11 and 12, respectively.)

Put Yourself in Your Customers' Shoes

Let's talk a bit about how to put yourself in your customers' shoes. First, ask this question: *What would it take for you to buy from you?* Because you do not have a high-powered and expensive marketing research team, you must begin to think the way your customer does. The key here is to be realistic. Responses such as, *I would buy from me because I'm just so wonderful* or *I'm the only game in town* are a bit presumptuous, don't you think? Consumers always have alternatives, especially with the widespread appeal and ease of use of the Internet.

Look at each product or service separately. Do not employ a "catch-all" strategy for all your products or services. For example, if your business involves renting sports equipment such as bicycles and canoes, your strategy to position your bicycles might be totally different than your strategy to position canoes. You may be able to effectively market both products in a local health magazine, but posting a flyer for bicycle supplies at the trailhead of a bicycle trail could bring sizzling results. The simple business card of a fitness trainer pinned to the bulletin board in a health club could totally inundate that business with calls.

10.2 Product Mix (the First "P")

An effective product mix answers this question: *Which products will you decide to handle, or which services will you provide for customers?* Here's a quick story that deals with this issue.

Recently, I went canoeing with friends. The week had been pretty hectic leading up to the departure date. I didn't have enough time to make sure I had everything I needed before heading to the backcountry for several days of peace and quiet. Of course, once I had canoed several hours and pitched a tent on a sand bar, I would be miles away from a store. Being prepared is a necessity. Usually, I would run down a checklist to make sure I had everything in tow (quick-dry clothes, food, ice, tent, raingear, etc.) This time, however, I didn't have a real opportunity to thoroughly check my gear until I was in line waiting to sign out a canoe. Luckily, the company that rented the canoes also operated an adventure supply store. Very conveniently the few items I'd neglected to pack were right there on the store shelves, ready to be picked up by half-packed canoeists like me—and not at a cheap price!

The store owners did not sell boxes of detergent, staplers, toasters, or roach spray. But they did sell mosquito repellent, and there was an ample supply of bottled water, bungee cords, cameras, butane, matches, canoe paddles (imagine that!), and almost any emergency item a canoeist might need before shoving off on a two- or three-day trip. The product mix was well defined and made the most efficient use of the tiny store's available shelf space. In essence, product mix is about having the right items for sale when the customer comes calling.

10.3 Positioning

It is extremely noisy out there. Every product and service is screaming for attention and recognition. Think about toothpaste. How many different brands bombard you as you pass down the personal hygiene aisle at the local supermarket or drugstore? Different brands claim they will give you a sexier smile, a whiter smile, a more dazzling smile; others claim to remove plaque or give you longer-lasting fresh breath. Every brand must provide some unique benefit for its customers, and it must drive that point home 24/7/365. This pithy message is called a ***unique selling proposition (USP)***.

Your USP is a phrase explaining why a potential customer should do business with you rather than your competitor. A USP gives a business its winning edge. You want to incorporate your USP in advertisement copy, on business cards, on letterhead, and on your Website's home page.

The pithy message conveyed in your USP has to be something that your customers will remember. It should:

▷ Be one sentence or phrase.

▷ Be clear and straight to the point.

▷ Be easy to understand by all readers (or listeners).

▷ Separate you from the competition. Without a good USP, you are in the middle of a herd without an identity. Even if you have the best products and services, your customer won't know what to think about you or what you think about them.

Here are a few ideas that can be incorporated in your USP:

1. Low prices.

2. Great customer service.

3. High quality.

4. Great selection.

Unique Selling Propositions	
USP Example	**USP Idea**
"Always on the job. 24/7/365."	Great customer service
"You won't find a lower price. We guarantee."	Low prices
"When you've shopped the rest, come to the best."	High quality
"If we don't stock it, you won't need it."	Great selection
"All you need—and more."	Value-added service

Table 10-A

Without a USP, your BESt Company can be perceived as just another "also-ran." Also-ran is a term often used to describe a politician's unsuccessful bid for office. Soon after the election, everyone remembers the victor, but hardly anyone remembers the losers. On one hand is the grand; on the other is the "also-ran." Avoid being just another "me too" business, doing just enough to get by. You promise no great service, no great value—just an unenthusiastic plead to "buy from me" without giving the potential customer any compelling reason.

Think hard and come up with a pithy USP, then integrate it into every contact with customers. Remember: Never lose sight of the fact that your USP is your word. And your word is your bond. In other words, if you say it, do it.

10.4 Advertising (the Second "P")

Through the course of this book we've talked about some pretty important topics, but none is more vital than letting people know that you're in business and that you have something they need. Indeed, once you have a quality product or service for sale, advertising is *the* key to business success.

There are many ways to get the word out, including radio, newspapers, the Internet, business cards, placards, and signage; each has its own pros and cons. One might think that it would be nice to just blitz potential customers from each of these media—preferably all at once. That, however, is very unlikely. It's also very impractical and nowhere near the best strategy. As I mentioned, not everybody is interested in buying what you're selling, so why waste resources?

The first, and most significant, limitation in your advertising campaign is the advertising budget. And even if resources were unlimited (which is hardly the case in any situation—ever!), you still wouldn't want to spend more on advertising than potential sales revenue to be derived from a particular group of potential buyers (market segment). To do so would not make economic sense. You would have a dollar chasing a dime! But enough talk about unlimited budgets; let's get back to the real world.

As a newly formed business, you will have a very limited advertising budget. You must get the most advertising bang for your advertising buck. "Build it and they will come" is true. But only if two other conditions are met:

1. You get their attention and tell that you've built it.

2. They want and/or need what you've built.

There has to be a meeting of the minds: *"You inform"* and *"they want."* These two conditions are achieved through effective advertising. Quite literally, thousands of books have been written on the most effective ways to get the message out. Let's boil all those millions of words down into a simple statement: *Advertising is a dynamic, ongoing communication effort designed to get the attention of potential customers and persuade them to purchase products or services.* You will never stop conveying information about your products. The minute you do, air leaves the room and your business suffocates.

Paul H. is a friend and an avid skin diver. A few years ago, he made a critical error that almost cost his life: He miscalculated the amount of oxygen in his scuba tank before an extended dive. About 40 feet beneath the water off the coast of Grand Cayman, he tried to draw a breath and there was nothing there. He thought there were another 30 minutes of air in his tank. He described that moment as being akin to trying to suck air out of your thumb. That is a vivid picture of the desperate situation he faced. It also describes your sales effort without an advertising campaign: Sales suffocate.

10.5 What Are Some Advertising Options?

As essential as advertising is to overall company success, BESt CEOs readily admit to being overwhelmed by the many possible ways to spend advertising dollars. Quite literally, the choices range from A to Z and everything in between, from airplane placards to mass mailing campaigns that target specific zip codes. As overwhelming as it might be, deciding on the media is relatively easy compared to developing a message that will get potential customers to notice and hopefully respond. Before working on a message, let's first examine some of the more appropriate media alternatives for a BESt Company.

Television

Advertising on television tends to be a budget-breaker. But even here there are exceptions. There are time slots and channels that can be quite affordable, even for a small upstart. The commercial might run at 2 a.m., but for some companies such a time frame may be ideal. That being said, let's examine a few options that tend to be favored by BESt Companies—both in affordability and reach.

Direct Mail

I like direct mail, especially if you already have a mailing list to work with. Depending on the size of the list, direct mail is fairly expensive due to the low response rate. It does, however, provide a personal touch. For example, you can send a flyer or catalog to the exact person you have in mind (for example, a maintenance supervisor or a purchasing agent). Out of every 100 pieces sent, expect two or three responses. Such a low rate might be a bit discouraging, but don't give up. There is another important benefit. Not only are you getting sales you may not otherwise get, but you are also telling your potential customers you're in the game and that you're working for their business. The name grows with each mass mailing.

Newspapers

Just be prepared for the jumble of competing ads due to the general nature of a newspaper. Local papers are a favorite of many diverse businesses, including local grocers, department stores, banks, discount stores, thrift shops, garage sales, beauty shops, and so on. If your community has a newspaper that offers free advertising, consider creating copy for it. After all, it has the right price: free! But, as with most things, you get what you pay for. Still, you're getting the word out. By the way, ***advertising copy*** *means the* ***persuasive words*** *you write to encourage your targeted customer to visit your business.* Some people have a real flair for writing copy. Ask around, because you may have a talented writer closer than you think.

Website

If you have an Internet connection via an Internet service provider ("ISP"), the subscription cost probably includes Website space. The challenge, however, is that you'll need to learn to create a Website. Of course, these days, that is a whole less difficult than it use to be. Many Websites are created from templates that have already been developed. It can be as simple as answering a series of questions, and—viola!—a Website in 30 minutes! But that's just the beginning. If you're not experienced, the site will be plain and uninspiring. Rather than just throwing something together, get a little help. Don't be shy to ask for assistance. Many people would be willing to give you a hand without charging an arm and a leg. One of the best sources of Website talent is your local high school. Many high schools have computer clubs with technology-savvy students eager to make a few extra dollars.

If the Internet is an effective medium for your particular product or service, promote the site by submitting it to several search engines. Getting a high listing on the search engines can be a fairly complex task. Unless you understand the dynamics of submitting to a search engine, you will need help here as well. Search engine optimization is beyond the scope of this book, but those same students can probably help here as well.

Also, examine the possibility of listing your Website with a few of the more popular online malls and e-zines. E-zine is short for electronic magazine. It is a publication that is delivered periodically via e-mail to those specifically requesting a subscription. Each time the e-zine is delivered, the recipient has the option to continue or discontinue receiving the publication. One of the best deals on the Internet is the information contained in well-written, information-packed e-zines.

Internet

Your business Website is a specific site, but there are many other possibilities for getting the word out over the Internet. This is where your creativity and hard work can pay huge dividends. As I mentioned, usually you get what you pay for. If it's free, don't expect much. That is not necessarily true with the Internet, though. It is truly unbelievable how much free information and access the Internet has made available to small businesses.

Since 1994, the Internet has continued to gain prominence as an advertising medium. The most significant difference between the Internet and other advertising media is how it is used. Not only is it a medium to *convey information,* but customers can also ***make purchases and payments*** online. No other medium can accomplish these three functions instantly. Without doubt, the Internet can be a very effective selling tool. If you view the World Wide Web as a viable means of getting the word out, consider this Internet "to do" list:

1. Register a URL that is loaded with key words. For example, my URL is *www.blackhomebusiness.com*, which are all key words for my Website.

2. Put your URL everywhere: on letterhead, business cards, promotional items, e-mail, and so forth.

3. Keep expectations realistic. There are billions of Web pages in cyberspace. Don't get anchored to your computer trying to promote your business, using every available avenue. Choose a few approaches and budget time wisely.

4. Develop an Internet promotion budget and stick to it. There are thousands upon thousands of marketing companies trying to separate you from your advertising dollars. Ask for references before cutting a check.

5. Unlike any other medium, some of the Internet's best promotional opportunities are free.

Always keep in mind that a well-designed home page can be as important to a business as a clean, orderly storefront. Ask yourself: *Would I find a shabby, unpainted grocery store with broken windows, scraggly shrubbery, peeling paint, and an unswept entrance an inviting place to shop?* Probably not. In the same way you would bypass such a place, visitors to a poorly designed Website move on just as fast.

Business Cards

There was a time when having a box of business cards was the sum total of a small business advertising effort. The importance of business cards still cannot be overstated. Fortunately, in-house, desktop publishing gives you the capacity to create well-designed business cards in a matter of minutes. There is no reason to be without a fresh supply.

When you consider how many business cards you hand out, it's easy to see how useful they can be as a significant means to convey information about your BESt Company. In addition to the demographic information, such as name and address, the business card can be designed to include your USP, Website URL, memorable logo, and any other information pertinent to your company.

A "Packet"

A "packet" is a collection of various documents prepared to convey a substantial amount of information about the company. A packet gives more information than is contained in a typical advertising spot. A packet is sent to those companies that you have identified as being imminently interested in doing business with your company. It generally includes the following documents:

1. Letter of introduction with contact information.

2. Statement of capabilities (services provided or products sold).

3. Catalog or line sheet that describes the features of the products or services.

4. Price list.

5. Copy from a recent advertising campaign, if available.

6. Credit application.

To keep the information together, it should be placed in some sort of binder, either a pocket folder or a low-capacity ring binder. Using desktop publishing software, you should be able to create an impressive cover sheet.

Trade Shows

Doing a trade show can be a hectic experience—to say the very least. *A trade show is a large collection of vendors under one roof. These vendors disseminate information about their particular company and demonstrate their products or educate prospective customers about their services.* Trade shows are generally industry-specific, but not always. According to estimates from *www.tradeshowtraining.com,* there are approximately 175,000 shows in the United States annually. Trade shows are powerful vehicles to get the word out, but they require a significant investment of both resources and time. Also, they tend to be fairly contained. In other words, those who learn about your company tend to be only those in attendance.

As a small BESt Company, participating in a trade show might be an ambitious undertaking for the first year or so. Nevertheless, if you can attend one without incurring too much cost, it might be worth checking out. Much can be learned simply by milling around, picking up brochures and questioning exhibitors.

Here are a few issues that must be dealt with **before** exhibiting and participating in a trade show:

1. *How will I display my goods and/or services?* Your display should look professional. Quality banners, table coverings, and a colorful backdrop make a great impact on those strolling by.

2. *Who should I invite?* There are many sources to tap, but one often-overlooked source is referrals from existing customers.

3. *Do I have time and funding to train assistants, if required?* Depending on your product or service, you may need help to exhibit and educate effectively. Visitors will only wait a few minutes for you to finish talking with others before they move on. Remember to have your assistant dress appropriately. This is a business setting. Professional dress always works best, although, in recent years, golf shirts with an embroidered logo are becoming very popular.

4. *How will I follow up with visitors who visit my booth?* Without effective follow-up, much of the good accomplished goes right down the drain. From a profitability perspective, this is probably the most important function. This may be an occasion to pass out a "packet" to those prospective customers who demonstrate significant interest.

Most times, trade shows are held in large metropolitan areas, such as New Orleans, Houston, and New York. The simple reason is that these cities have hotels, restaurants, and other facilities that can accommodate large gatherings. On occasion, however, some organizers will sponsor smaller, local trade shows. These are generally less expensive and do not require a significant investment in travel and accommodations. To find out if there is a local show in your community, ask around. Ask clients, friends, representatives of the local chamber of commerce, public relations officials with the local university, or the local business press.

These are all general guidelines. Depending on your particular product or service, participating in a trade show might be the most costly way to spend your advertising dollars. If you do decide to participate in a trade show, my three words of advice are: Prepare, prepare, prepare! Only when you are adequately prepared will the show have a chance to be successful.

Flyers/Brochures

Desktop publishing allows you to create flyers and brochures effortlessly. Keep in mind that your message must be pithy (brief, forceful, and meaningful) and your document must not be cluttered and confusing. Think URL and USP.

Radio

I spend hours each day either actively or passively listening to the radio. I'm sure my listening habits are typical. Now, think of the way you listen to the radio. One of the great strengths of advertising on the radio is the large blocks of time during which the target audience listens—in some cases hours upon end. The key to effective radio advertising is repetition. If this is the medium of choice, make sure your budget is sufficient enough to allow the ad to run repetitiously, ideally in the same time slot.

There is a significant difference in advertising cost among various radio stations. It is advisable to contact the sales department of the station that appeals to your targeted audience and just ask a lot of questions. The advertising manager of each station will gladly answer all your questions and give you a price quote.

Magnetic Signs

Easy-to-apply magnetic signs can turn your vehicle into a moving advertisement. Today's signs are portable, are lightweight, and adhere to vehicles even when traveling at high speeds. These signs are an especially convenient and effective way to turn a truck or van into a delivery vehicle/moving billboard.

Letterhead

Well-designed letterhead can contain the same pithy information that is contained on your business cards. Letterhead is not an effective method of advertising, but, if it is not well designed, it can work against company image.

10.6 Summary

Without proper planning, advertising can be costly and unfocused, likened to pitching money into a bottomless pit. Even the largest advertising budgets can't guarantee cost-effectiveness, but the more you plan your advertising strategy the more likely you are to have positive results.

In summary, effective advertising addresses the following questions:

1. *Who comprises your market?* Decide who your primary customers are. What are their characteristics?

2. *How do your primary customers get their information?* Do your homework to find out what they read, listen to, and watch.

3. *Are you spreading your advertising budget over an extended period of time?* Spending your advertising dollars over an extended period of time allows your message to be delivered consistently. Don't blow your entire budget in a one-shot media blitz. For example, don't take out a full-page ad when 12 smaller ads, taken weekly or every other week, could be purchased for the same money.

4. *Are you measuring the effectiveness of your advertising campaign?* Don't be afraid to move on if you are not getting acceptable results.

The key to a home-based business advertising success is to think big but cut small checks—to get the most for your advertising buck. There are no two ways about it: Effective advertising strategy requires thorough planning and quite a bit of creativity.

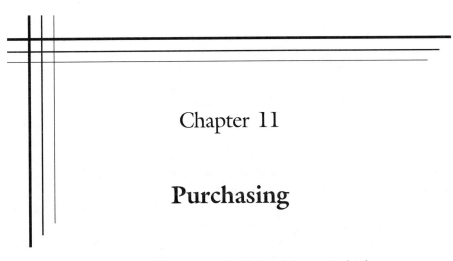

Chapter 11

Purchasing

A wise man should have money in his head, but not in his heart.

—Jonathan Swift

You would think the easiest thing in the world is to buy merchandise when you have the money or credit to do so. Not so fast! For a business, purchasing is not a single, impulsive act. Purchasing is an ongoing process.

In large organizations, the purchasing process can be very complicated and involve many people. Large companies want to make sure that no one is buying merchandise without proper authorization. Because you are going to do most (if not all) the buying, theft is not an issue. Purchasing for your home-based BESt Company is a fairly straightforward process, but it is nonetheless a process.

Purchasing is not simply buying things. Purchasing is about buying **right**—the **right** merchandise, at the **right** price, at the **right** time. For a BESt Company, the definition of ***purchasing*** *is the process of determining the specifications of what to buy and who to buy it from, soliciting prices (or bids), comparing prices, placing the order, and receiving the order.* Purchasing pits you against your vendors. Their goal is to sell as high as they can, and your goal is to buy as low as possible.

You may think that you'll be able to purchase with a freshly sharpened #2 pencil and a few names written on the backs of business cards. Such thinking is fatal and will not work in today's ultra-competitive environment.

 **BESt Principle #9** ➠

SHOP AROUND AND NEGOTIATE.

YOU HAVE TO GET THE BEST DEAL ON THE MERCHANDISE THAT YOU PURCHASE, EVEN WHEN DEALING WITH CLOSE FRIENDS.

Just keep in mind that the difference between your purchase price (cost) of an item and its selling price is *your gross profit margin.* Translation: Lower cost sends more money heading toward the bottom line. For example, purchased goods might represent as much as 60 percent (or more) of a particular business's cost. Invariably, the less paid for merchandise, the greater the gross profit and the more money available to pay expenses.

You can bet your competition is putting a great deal of thought into every purchase decision. If you intend to be around for the long haul, you must do so as well. You simply cannot afford to purchase from a guy because you've known him a long time or because he's your next-door neighbor's best friend. Your purchasing decision has to be based on investigation and sound economics, not friendship. If your purchase decisions are based on friendships, the following progression is inevitable: first friendship, then hardship, and finally receivership (a condition of bankruptcy). That's not saying that business associates can't also be your friends—on the contrary: Dealing with friends is an added plus to being in business for yourself. I'm simply saying that your purchase decisions have to be prudent and based on a good deal.

Monitoring Gross Profit Margins in the Purchasing Process

Before proceeding much further in understanding the purchasing process, it is essential that you get a firm grip on the concept of *gross profit margin* (also called gross margin or just margin). Gross profit margin is the percentage computed by dividing the *cost of sales (which includes purchases) by total sales.* Gross profit margin is *inversely* related to the prices you pay when purchasing inventory or paying for the labor that goes into the cost of manufacturing items for resale. With this inverse relationship, the more you pay for merchandise or direct labor, the lower the gross profit margin. And, of course, the reverse is also true: The less you pay for merchandise or direct labor, the higher the gross profit margin.

Then, we need to consider the relationship between **gross** profit margin and **net** profit. Gross profit margin has a *direct* relationship to net profit. Higher margins translate into higher net profits. Lower margins mean lower profits. Because gross margins have such an immediate and direct impact on net profit, it is important to understand the computation that is used to determine gross margin. It is also important to understand how our purchasing effort affects gross margin, which in turn directly affects bottom-line profits.

Finally, in this semi-technical area, I want to caution you not to confuse gross profit margin percentage with percentage markup. Many times new CEOs do. To minimize this confusion, I will show you how to compute each percentage in the next section.

11.1 Gross Profit Percentage vs. Percentage Markup

Many business owners have a very difficult time understanding the difference between these two computations. The reason for this difficulty is that both deal with the same variables: *selling price* and *cost*. Watch out, now! Just the mention of the word variable reminds you of algebra class and old Miss What's-her-name. I see your mind getting a bit hazy, but stay with me.

First, let's review the difference. *Gross profit margin* is computed as a percentage of the **selling price,** whereas *markup* is computed as a percentage of the **seller's cost.** Understanding the difference between margin and markup is crucial when it comes to determining how much you can afford to pay for the items that are purchased for resale and how much to charge for those items when they are actually sold. Thinking that your markup is one thing when it is actually something else could prove devastating to your business.

To get a good look at the difference, let's look over Jamaica Thorn's shoulder as she makes the computations.

Example: *If Jamaica Thorn buys a set of cosmetic brushes for $30 and sells them for $75, she computes **gross profit margin** and **markup** as follows:*

Gross Profit Margin.

1. Compute the gross profit margin **dollars** as follows:

Selling Price	$75
Your Cost	$30
Gross Profit Margin ($)	$45

    Note: *It is not necessary to compute gross profit margin dollars before computing gross profit margin percentage. This step was included so you could see the numbers that go into the computation of gross margin percentage.*

2. To compute a gross margin **percentage**, use the following formula:

    (Selling Price − Cost) / Selling Price = Gross Profit Margin Percentage

    ($75 − $30) / $75 = Gross Profit Margin Percentage

    ($45) / $75 = .60 or 60%

Markup is a different computation. When Jamaica decides to mark up an item, the following computation is made:

(Selling Price − Cost) / Cost = Markup %

Again, using the same illustration of Jamaica Thorn's purchase, the percentage markup would be calculated as follows:

($75 − $30) / $30 = Markup %

($45) / $30 = 1.50 or 150%

Note: So many people are confused by this simple computation that they would be willing to spend the cost of this book just to have someone explain it as simply as illustrated here. I can't tell you how many clients have called in exasperation, trying to understand this difference. It's a simple concept, but it's still very easy to get the two computations totally confused.

 Imagine needing to mark up an item 150 percent and only marking up 60 percent because you are not clear about the difference between markup and margin. As you can see, not understanding this difference can be disastrous to your business.

1.2 A Few Purchasing Guidelines

Your accounting software will probably have a purchasing module. In addition to the purchasing options offered by Peachtree, Quickbooks, or whichever accounting software application you choose, let me offer five guidelines that will help you purchase efficiently and save money in the process.

1. **Develop a list of preferred suppliers.** Keep a list of suppliers that you prefer, but also shop around for acceptable alternative suppliers. This will accomplish two goals: helping you get the best price and giving you an alternative in the event availability becomes an issue with your preferred supplier.

2. **Shop around for prices.** Unless you're sure you have the best price, make two calls to your supplier. In the first call, ask for pricing. Then call back a bit later and place the order. This puts your supplier on notice that you are checking prices and determining what the competition has to offer. **Price is important, but not everything.** Also look for service, consistency, and quality.

3. **Be mindful of your suppliers' delivery costs.** Try to order in quantities that will not only allow them to give you a volume discount, but that will allow them to pass the savings in freight costs to you as well.

4. **Negotiate terms.** Try to get the highest discount the supplier offers. (See Section 11.6 for a discussion of discount.)

5. **Separate purchasing decisions from friendships.** As I said, it's okay to do business with your friends, but do not let your friendship impede your ability to get the best deal.

11.3 How to Find Suppliers

If you've been around and involved in the industry in which you're now building your business, chances are you know the suppliers—both those with good reputations and those whose reputations are tarnished. You may have already begun to cultivate relationships with the reputable suppliers. If you have, that's great. You probably already have a sense of their ability to satisfy your purchasing requirements. Better yet, you may have already dealt with these suppliers in your former job, in which case you know their capabilities. But if you haven't, let me give you a few pointers that will help you find the right supplier for your business:

1. **Internet research.** Use the Internet to search on your specific purchase requirements. To limit the number of returns, try to be as specific as possible in your search request. For example, if you're in business to resell pipeline flanges, your search should request *stainless steel, high pressure flanges* and not simply *oilfield supplies*.

2. **Word of mouth.** Listen to the testimonies of business acquaintances. But you will have to listen carefully. Don't be too quick to write off a vendor due to a customer's single bad experience, nor be too quick to accept a recommendation on the basis of one testimony.

3. **Read trade journals.** Trade journals are filled with ads from suppliers.

4. **Manufacturers directory.** The Thomas Register of American Manufacturers is a comprehensive directory for finding companies and products manufactured in North America. You can register for a free online membership at *www.thomasregister.com*. This is an outstanding service, especially for wholesalers.

5. **Trade shows.** Find out which trade shows cater to your particular industry. If it is within your budget, make it a point to attend. Not only will you pick up information about suppliers, but an amazing amount of other helpful information.

6. **References.** Once you identify potential suppliers, don't just assume they are who they claim to be. Ask for two or three current references—and check them out.

 **BESt Websites**⟫

www.tradeshows.com
Many potential suppliers may have conventions scheduled for your area.

www.thomasregister.com
This comprehensive onine resource allows you to find companies and products manufactured in North America.

11.4 Company Information Sheet

As you begin to acquire suppliers, they will all require certain information about your company, including customer references, mailing address, and ship-to address. Some of the information will be used to evaluate your credit worthiness; other information is used to set up your account. Unless you create a company information sheet (see Figure 11-A), you'll find yourself re-creating the same letter or e-mail over and over. To avoid this endless repetition, prepare a single document with essential information about your BESt Company. This single document can be copied and mailed, faxed, or attached to an e-mail. You can edit the document to add or delete information depending on the user's needs.

Let's take a look at the company information sheet for our friends at Jamaica-Max Tropical Cosmetics on page 139. First, I want you to notice how they used their letterhead. It has the company's slogan, a pithy USP, and their Website address. These guys are always advertising. Even when they're sleeping, their copy is circulating—always on the job.

11.5 Inventory

Inventory represents a significant investment. Obviously, if you are a service company, inventory (or stock) is not an issue. Manufacturers, wholesalers, and retailers, however, do have to be concerned about how much to invest in inventory. If this section applies to your company, you'll quickly find out how important it is to manage inventory. A substantial amount of your company's value will be tied up in inventory. In some cases as much as 40 to 50 percent of a company's value is in inventory. Inventory is money on the shelf. Controlling inventory is essential to controlling overall cost.

How Much Inventory Should Be Carried?

Inventory is carried to provide your customers with the convenience of getting the products they want when they want them—period. Enough should be carried to meet customer needs, but not so much that it overwhelms operating capital. I've heard some say that the best inventory is no inventory at all. Many reasons are given for such a claim: Inventory ties up capital. Some jurisdictions assess *ad valorem* or inventory taxes at the end of each year. Inventory requires a considerable amount of time to manage—time to order, receive, stock, count, reorder, and so forth.

In spite of its burden, it is nonetheless indispensable to some businesses. There is no easier way to get a bad reputation for service than to be out of stock on a certain item when a customer comes calling. Here are a few guidelines to help manage inventory and keep each stock item at an acceptable level:

➤ **Find out which items move.** Your accounting software will help you determine the real movers and provide the information necessary to compute inventory turnover factor. *Inventory turnover measures how quickly a company sells its products.* To judge the effectiveness of inventory turnover, compare it to the industry average. Determine through research the average inventory turnover for your particular industry, and try to stay within that range.

Jamaica-Max Tropical Cosmetics, LLC
Every Color Under the Sun

555 Main Street, Suite 200
New Orleans, Louisiana 70821
Phone: 985–555–1212
Fax: 985–555–1213

Company Information Sheet

Company Name	Jamaica-Max Tropical Cosmetics, LLC
Mailing Address	P.O. Box 555, New Orleans, LA 70821
Shipping/Physical Address	555 Main Street, Suite 200 New Orleans, LA 70821
Phone	985–555–1212
Fax	985–555–1213
Contact	Ms. Jamaica Thorn
Federal ID#	72-1234567
State Sales Tax Exemption #	99-9999999
Parish/County Sales Tax Exemption#	88-8888888
Bank	First Bank of New Orleans
Bank Contact	John A. Banker
Trade References	Acme Supply 123 Main Street, New Orleans, LA 71234 Phone 985–555–1234 Fax 985–555–1235

BLJ Trucking 123 Elm Road, New Orleans, LA 70123 Phone 985–555–7522 Fax 985–555–9998

LEN, Inc. 500 Price St., New Orleans, LA 70123 Phone 985–555–9874 Fax 985–555–3738 |
| Notes: | |

Visit Our Website: *www.jamaicamax.com*
Every Color Under the Sun

Figure 11-A

Trade associations (such as, for our Jamaica-Max example, the Beauty and Barber Supply Institute) are the best source for financial statistics. They usually offer trade publications that report operating statistics on the entire industry as a benchmarking service to their individual members. A quick search on the Web will help you locate your particular trade association.

➤ **Sell off slow-moving or "dead stock."** If an item sits too long, sell it at a discounted price. (In other words, have a sale.)

➤ **Survey your largest customers.** Ask them what they would like you to stock. This technique is especially powerful for home-based businesses for two reasons: The number of customers is relatively small, and the product lines are relatively limited. For example, with 50 or 100 customers it is a fairly simple matter to contact each one and poll them on their requirements. Or if your product mix consists of 100 different items, it should be relatively easy to determine which are the real movers. *Product mix is the specific assortment of products a BESt Company offers for sale to its customers.*

➤ **Never stock anything that you can get in time to satisfy your customers needs.** For example, if you have a supplier across town, do not stock items that can be picked up in a few minutes.

➤ **Be careful stocking items that cannot be returned.** The exception here would be if the customer pays in advance.

➤ **Be mindful of restocking charges.** Even if your supplier allows returns, you may be charged a 15- to 25-percent fee.

11.6 Dealing With Suppliers

Establishing Credit

Once you have identified your suppliers, the next step is to apply for a credit line and negotiate terms for payment. Unlike banks and professional lenders, suppliers usually don't have to meet with a lending board and go through elaborate formalities to set you up with a credit limit in order to buy their merchandise. *Credit limit is the amount of purchasing power a company is willing to extend to a customer so that merchandise can be conveniently ordered without having to pay before shipment is made.*

Of course, credit policy varies widely among different companies. But to open an account, most companies will simply require that you complete a credit application. The amount of credit a company will be willing to extend will be determined by the length of time you've been in business and your payment history.

Because you have a new company, do not expect extravagant credit limits. Most will start you off small and allow you build a credit history before bumping your account higher. Take whatever credit limit the company is willing to extend. Usually, it will be enough to serve your needs. If not, you may need to negotiate for a larger credit limit. The supplier may ask for concessions, such as a deposit. Try to avoid giving such concessions. You should be able to find an ample number of suppliers who are willing to do business with you without requiring such concessions.

Negotiating Cash Discounts

The next challenge is to negotiate cash discounts, if available. *A cash discount is an amount that a firm allows a customer to deduct from an invoice as an inducement for prompt payment.* The terms of a cash discount look like this: **"2%/10, net/30 days."** This notation means that a discount of 2 percent can be knocked off the invoice amount (before taxes and freight) if payment is made within 10 days from the date of the invoice. For example, assume a $400 invoice is dated August 5th. If the BESt CEO cuts a check and has it postmarked by August 15th, $8 ($400 × .02) can be deducted from the invoice amount. The BESt CEO will only need to remit $392 to totally satisfy the payable.

The 2-percent discount may not seem to be a significant savings, but, when viewed as a finance charge to use money for a 20-day period, the 2 percent actually represents an annual interest rate of approximately 37 percent to the seller (and a substantial savings to you!). If at all possible, negotiate a discount as large as the company is willing to give, and then be sure to take advantage of it.

One last point: Some companies will not offer a cash discount unless you ask. Also, rarely will they offer more than 2 percent.

11.7 Freight and Shipping Cost

If you purchase merchandise from vendors, freight expense can become a very significant cost of doing business. *Freight cost is the cost of getting purchased goods from your vendors to your BESt Location. Shipping cost, on the other hand, is the cost of getting your product to your customers.*

Sometimes vendors will ship goods as *freight collect, where carriers will collect shipping and handling charges at the time of delivery.* As with cash discounts, freight discounts can often be negotiated with the shipping company, especially over-the-road carriers. Over-the-road carriers are the trucking companies and highway freight haulers. Again, you won't know unless you ask.

There are several Web-based services that allow BESt CEOs to compare shipping rates of various companies, purchase shipping services, schedule pickups, and even print shipping labels for parcel. I've found *www.iship.com/*

default.htm to be one of the best. According to iShip's mission statement, the company gives its customers Shipping Insight through Internet-based, multi-carrier shipping services that allow all individuals and companies to conveniently make the smartest shipping decisions. The comprehensive iShip service makes it possible for anyone to price, ship, track, and manage shipments over the Internet.

The iShip service also allows shippers to easily compare rates and services among multiple carriers, including UPS, DHL, FedEx Express, FedEx Ground, Airborne Express, and the U.S. Postal Service. iShip delivers precise and detailed shipping information, all in one easy-to-access, hosted service. The iShip service empowers CEOs to make the best shipping decision for their customers. This resource can help save a small fortune.

The Big 3 Shippers

In terms of national shippers, you'll be hard-pressed to find any shipping company that could out perform UPS, FedEx, or the U.S. Postal Service. According to information from its Website, UPS delivers nearly 13 million packages and documents each **day** and spends more than $1 billion a year on information technology to improve package handling.

These shippers have harnessed the power of the Internet to provide fast, easy, and convenient service to their customers. The downside to the "big three" is that historically they have not handled large, bulky shipments. As of late, though, that limitation is being overcome. Depending on the nature of your products, this may or may not be an issue.

 BESt Websitelllll▶

www.iship.com/default.htm

iShip allows shippers to easily compare rates and services among multiple carriers, including UPS, DHL, FedEx Express, FedEx Ground, Airborne Express, and the U.S. Postal Service.

11.8 Expediting Merchandise

Whenever you place an order with your suppliers, you agree on a delivery date. Sometimes the agreed-to delivery date is so crucial that you need to make sure it will not be delayed. *Expediting is the process of contacting your supplier to determine where the order is in the delivery process and moving the process along if it has stalled.*

Years ago, this was a constant and time-consuming task. As we just discussed, shippers have placed great expediting power in your hands, but only after the shipment is en route. If the order has not left the factory, you'll have to speak directly to the vendor to find out why the order has not shipped.

When expediting a particular order, you will need a *work order number,* an *authorization number,* a *confirmation number,* or some other number that is associated with your order. Have that number available when contacting the supplier. It will greatly expedite the process of expediting, so to speak. You could probably still expedite the order without this number, but the process is quicker and more accurate if you have one.

11.9 Receiving Merchandise

BESt Companies often wonder if they should use a purchase order system to track purchases and to facilitate the receiving process. The question is often asked because the amount of purchasing volume is relatively small and easy to control. Some BESt CEOS ask, "Can't I just keep track of what I buy in my head?" The answer is: Why should you keep anything in your head that can be tracked much more efficiently by your computer? Regardless of the volume, small home businesses should definitely use purchase orders ("POs") when ordering merchandise from vendors. Most accounting software will allow you to create purchase orders very easily. Plus, you'll find that POs are invaluable in the receiving process. By using a purchasing order, you'll have a document in hand to determine if what you ordered matches what you receive. Using POs will help you minimize the chances of receiving the wrong color, style, or size.

Even though each company establishes its own business rules, there are three basic steps in the receiving process:

1. **Inspect incoming shipment against the purchase order.** Your inspection should verify that the quantity of all items ordered are included in the shipment and that the merchandise is not damaged. Note any discrepancy on the PO.

2. **Accept the order.** Once the PO has been checked, the merchandise should be accepted. If something was overlooked and a discrepancy is later found, call the supplier immediately. Most will resolve the problem without a hassle.

3. **Compare the purchase order to the invoice (when it comes in).** Make sure the invoice reflects what was actually received. Note any discrepancy on the invoice, then immediately call the supplier to rectify the discrepancy.

Don't assume that invoices received from vendors are correct. Errors are made all the time. Your vigilance in the receiving process will go a long way in minimizing errors and the possibility of being overcharged.

11.10 In Closing

Let me again remind you to always view purchasing as an opportunity to increase profits. The better you buy, the higher your profits. Unless you know you're getting the best price, shop around—even with small purchases, excluding items such as office supplies.

Remember: Don't hesitate to call your salesperson whenever you have a problem. Most vendors are interested in building long-term relationships and want to keep all their customers as happy as possible.

Chapter 12

Management

Business is like an automobile. It won't run by itself, except downhill.

—Henry Ford

Effective leadership is putting first things first. Effective management is discipline, carrying it out.

—Stephen R. Covey

12.1 Management

The classical business school definition of management is "getting things done through the efforts of other people." As you look around the office, there is a fax machine, a computer, a telephone, but probably no people—not yet. It would be deadly to think that you could do all that is required to operate a successful business by yourself. Even though you may not have employees, you still will require the services of many other people to accomplish your BESt Company's goals. Some of the services will come with a price, but it is surprising how many services are available without a price tag. Of course, someone, somewhere, is paying, but that someone, in many cases, does not have to be you.

Value-Added Service

A few of the many business associates who will provide effort to make your business a success are your banker, CPA, attorney, vendors, printers, Internet service provider, and creditors. As you look at the list, you may think, *But, I pay these people!* Of course, but only for **specific** goods and services they provide. In their efforts to attract customers and clients, most businesses offer value-added services. *Value-added services are the freebies that your "business associates" are willing to give away at no additional cost in order to build goodwill with you and the rest of their customers.* In other words, these businessmen and women have customers that they want to keep happy and for whom they are willing to go the extra mile. For example, banks may offer free checking, certain vendors might track purchase history to give you a better picture of your purchasing habits, and others might offer free delivery. Each of these freebies has real economic value.

"Business Associates"

Although none of these people (vendors, bankers, CPAs, attorneys, and so on) are under your direct control, you still must be able to manage their efforts as they relate to your business. You must let them know that you will not be satisfied with mediocre or inferior service and that you expect to take advantage of all they have to offer. You've heard the old adage, *a squeaking wheel gets the oil.* If your business associates don't hear from you, they will think you're totally satisfied—whether you are or not. Certainly, they will take the path of least resistance and deal with the clients who are ringing their phone. They may not ignore you entirely, but you will not have their full attention unless you demand it.

When I use the word *demand*, I'm not talking about obnoxious behavior filled with presumptuous requests. What I'm suggesting is to make them aware of your *high expectations*—that is, letting business associates know that you expect prompt attention and value-added service. Please understand that you can only demand immediate and first-rate attention if you pay your bills in a timely manner. No one is willing to continually provide value-added services to a customer who is a consistently late-payer.

When communicating with business associates, your view should always be directed toward *specific outcomes* or meeting *specific objectives.* For example, telling your vendors you want increased profitability is pointless (doesn't everyone?). But if you express that your objective is to reduce shipping costs, then you have given your vendor an objective that has concrete meaning with a measurable outcome.

After identifying such objectives, call in the business associate that can help you accomplish those goals. Let your objective become their objective; let your problem become their problem. You can't control this group of people or the way they operate, but you can effectively communicate your objectives. Then watch with amazement how much effort they are willing to put forth to benefit your company.

 Don't adopt the "Tom Sawyer" principle, where once you give a business associate the problem, you watch him do all the work (in other words, don't sit in the shade while your friends whitewash the fence). On the contrary, stay proactive and manage their efforts until the desired result is achieved. Otherwise, they will eventually see through your insincere and unethical intention.

Things Don't Just Happen!

Managing your BESt Company is not much different from what you've been doing to get to this point. Management is a process. It is the process of using your resources to achieve company goals in an efficient and effective manner. Effective management is essential to the health and growth of your business. It's one thing to get things going, but it's quite another to keep them going. Some managers tend to get caught up in that *oh well, things will somehow just work out* fantasy. And, from time to time, things may, in fact, *just work out.* But simply waiting for things to work out is not a way to effectively manage a business. Think back on the last time you saw a house being built. Five concrete workers didn't all wake up one morning and independently decide to just show up and pour a foundation. Obviously, there was a general contractor coordinating the entire effort. For your business, you are that general contractor.

12.2 Time Management

Effective management starts with the appropriate use of resources, and, without question, your most important resource is time. Let's take a look at time management.

Set Regular Hours

You have the luxury of setting your own schedule. That is one of the main reasons you've decided to become your own boss. As tempting as it might be, especially when you first start, do not make a habit of sleeping in or doing laundry for the first half of the day. Set regular work hours—especially if you have a steady flow of customers coming and going.

As a graduate student at the University of New Orleans, I once worked on a research paper that explored the question of why there were so few African-American businesses in a mid-sized town right outside New Orleans. During the course of conducting field research, I posed the following question to the black entrepreneurs I interviewed: *What is the greatest image problem that black businesses have to overcome when viewed by the general public?* The top two answers were keeping regular business hours and incompetence. I knew that perception of incompetence was alive and well, but the "keeping regular business hours" came as somewhat of a surprise.

If you have a business that requires customers to come to you, the expectation in many communities is that you will not **physically** be there in the clutch. Your customers come to you because they have needs. If you're not there, they will quickly find an alternative source, and your competition is only too glad to take your business.

Your greatest challenge is to attract customers. To keep the customers you do attract is a no-brainer. To establish your reputation as a dependable business, you simply must be *open for business* during regularly scheduled hours.

Every business, of course, has to do the same. Not every business, however, has to overcome the possible negative perception that you must. But, hey—we've been down that road before, and proving yourself is a well-worn path.

With your customers in mind, select business hours on a practical basis. For example, if you have a medical records transcription business, regular 8-to-5 hours will probably suffice. If you prepare income tax returns, don't expect to close the doors before 10 p.m. during the busy tax season.

Highly Organized People Make Work Look Easy

Poor time management is characterized by a desk cluttered with sticky notes, unanswered phone calls, and moving from one crisis to another—just to mention a few symptoms. To the uninitiated eye this constant shuffling and movement may seem to be signs of success, but the converse is probably more accurate. They are signs of a business owner who is inefficient and perhaps unnecessarily stressed. Lots of action, but little forward progress—or, to quote best-selling author H. Jackson Brown, Jr., *"like an octopus on roller skates."*

Every day you are called on to be a salesman, cashier, accountant, delivery-man, and customer service representative. You may have to run to the post office, the bank, and Office Depot all before lunch. You may not have the luxury of a "gopher" (someone to "go for" this or "go for" that). Perhaps someday you will, but not now. When something needs to get done, you're the "go-to" guy!

What's the first thing you notice when watching Tiger Woods hit a drive from the tee box? Or Michael Jordan (in his heyday) take it to the hoop? Or Oprah chatting it up with guests? You hear folks say, "Look how easy Tiger makes that look," or "Michael's move left his defender flat-footed!," or "Oprah looks like she's just visiting with guests in her living room." These talented professionals are so efficient and effective in their work that they make you feel (until reason sets in) that you could do what they do. They have honed their actions until their work appears relatively effortless. Likewise, when a manager is in command of his day, he handles his workload in a similarly efficient manner. As I mentioned previously, time is your most valuable asset. You cannot afford to waste it surfing aimlessly through the Internet or shuffling through the same stack of papers 10 times in one day. You have to make the most of every waking moment in order to maintain normal rest and recreation hours.

How Far Into the Future Should You Plan?

Effective time management involves planning for some period of time. The length of that period is different for different people. A week might be sufficient for some; for others, planning a month at a time might be more effective. If you don't know what works best for you then start by planning one week at a time. You can schedule events in your organizer for months in advance, but effective planning has a more definite focus than simple scheduling. Effective planning is more about completing tasks than avoiding scheduling conflicts.

Effective time management will allow you to:

▹ Maintain regular business hours.

▹ Accurately allocate time to each task.

▹ Sell proactively by reviewing customers' records before meetings.

▹ Enhance goodwill by returning phone calls on a timely basis.

▹ Keep the ball in the other person's court (for example, expedite outstanding purchase orders).

▹ Meet deadlines.

▹ Take guiltless lunch breaks.

▹ Manage stress.

You may not have had to manage your time effectively on the last job you held. You got paid a straight eight hours regardless. That was then; this is a different ball game. Your success is directly related to your ability to accomplish daily tasks in an efficient way. Every dollar that comes in is attributable to your effort. The minutes that you once squandered throughout the day has to stop. Those lost minutes represent lost productivity, which translates into lost sales or increased costs.

Electronic Organizers

Not very long ago some business owners were reluctant to organize their data in electronic devices. The chief complaint was that it took more time than it saved to maintain the data. That may have been true then, but not now. Once the bulk of data is entered, it only takes a few seconds or so per entry to maintain data or make new entries. For example, if you make 30 entries a day, which is probably on the high side, that's approximately 15 minutes of updating time. Once the appointment or meeting is in the device, it keeps track of your day—pretty much as a secretary would. In fact, I think of my device as an electronic secretary. The time necessary to update an electronic organizer is well worth the effort. I've seem some business owners give up after spending 15 minutes rifling through stacks of files in search of a scrap of paper with an important phone number. Now that's wasted time!

**BESt Website** ▐▐▐▶   ***www.handheldcomputerdepot.com***
This site allows you to compare the prices and features of various brands of electronic organizers.

Time-Management Strategies

Time management is being aware of time and developing commonsense strategies to make the most of every *working minute*. Notice, I said every **working** minute. You will find that as a business owner, you're never fully off the clock. By learning to apply effective time-management techniques, though, you'll discover a direct relationship between effective time management and quality family/recreational time.

Time management keeps your organized. It gives you the ability to control time rather than respond to it in a random fashion. Once you begin to see the benefits of effective time management, you will quickly realize just how much capacity you have—that is, how much work you can accomplish in a day and still catch your son's basketball game.

Remember: A cluttered desk is a symptom of poor time management. Here are a few strategies that will help you keep your desk (and your day) manageable:

➤ **Organize files in way that is meaningful to you.** Every time something important hits your desk, either deal with it immediately, file it in your current files, or file it in your permanent files. *Current files* are those that contain documents that must be reviewed periodically, perhaps daily or weekly (open purchase orders or unanswered correspondence, for example). *Permanent files* are files that contain documents that do not have to be viewed or handled frequently (including old bank statements, paid bills, and tax records).

Keep a box of file folders and a permanent, felt-tip marker nearby. Use it to label the folders. Just write right on the tab—forget file labels. (Using file tab labels generally requires you to change the paper on the printer, which tends to be a hassle and tends to break workflow. Using a felt marker is much easier and just as effective.)

➤ **Keep a trash can on hand.** Don't be afraid to use it. The amount of junk mail you will get on a weekly basis can be mind-boggling. If you don't get rid of unsolicited mail and other correspondence, over time they will develop a kind of importance in your mind. Your thought processes will go something like this: *This mail has been around a long time. It must be something important; I'd better hold on to it.* Generally, it isn't important at all. When you get unsolicited mail, immediately determine whether it is something you want to respond to; otherwise, toss it.

➤ **Make a point to clear your desk routinely.** Don't get in the habit of viewing the process of clearing your desk as some sort of ritual, or "that time to clean my desk," or that thing that has to be done before a big client comes in. Such thinking leads to procrastination and a perpetually cluttered desk.

➤ **Decide which items will be visible on your desktop.** Store everything else. I keep the following items on my desk: computer monitor, notepad (one at a time), a pencil holder with a few pens, calculator, tape dispenser, a few envelopes, a filled paper-clip dispenser, and a letter opener. To further minimize desktop clutter, I invested in a wireless keyboard and mouse. I paid a total of $80 for the pair of devices. This was an excellent investment, as my desk is virtually free of the spaghetti jumble of wires.

Going Paperless

I once had intentions of going paperless. Although it sounds like a great idea (and it is), it is still a bit difficult to achieve. You'll find yourself printing a fair number of the documents: contracts, proposals, financial statements, invoices, purchase orders, flyers, pamphlets, line sheets, and so forth. With so much printing going on, being organized is more important than trying to go entirely paperless. Although running an entirely paperless office may be difficult to achieve, you should make a conscious effort to reduce the amount of paper and printouts generated. Keep addresses and phone numbers in your organizer rather than on slips of paper. Update customer and vendor records immediately when there is a change. Question why you keep four copies of an invoice instead of one. Seek to minimize the volume of paper, but don't try to run your office without keeping a hard copy of your most vital documents.

12.3 Going to the Bank and Post Office

To save time (and a few bucks), avoid renting a post office box. Using your home address allows the mail to be delivered straight to your home office. (Besides, freight companies such as UPS won't deliver to a PO box.) If for some reason your mail is being delivered to a PO box, going to the post office will be a necessary errand. In fact, your cash flow depends on it! After dunning customers (calling to determine when payment can be expected), you'll have an idea of receivable payments that are en route. When a check is expected, going to the post office can take the highest priority of the day. Regardless of this, though, it's important to develop a routine to take care of this simple errand. To save time, try to combine the post office and bank into one trip. One day you'll have someone to run these errands for you, but for now you'll need to budget the time and go yourself.

12.4 Setting Prices for Services

The key to setting prices is to find that delicate balance where you don't price your merchandise out of the market nor do you leave money on the table. The old adage, *sell at a price that the market will bear* is still the best guide. But exactly what is that price? Figure 12-A gives you a step-by-step guide to decide what to charge for your services. It is a bad practice to just "spout off" prices for your services without some underlying logic. What invariably happens is that you give one price to Customer A and another price to Customer B, who both have sons in the same biddy basketball league. At halftime they talk and discover that your pricing is arbitrary and inconsistent. *How do you think the customer who was charged the higher price feels about this revelation?* Remember to put yourself in your customers' shoes. He's *not* a happy camper! (You wouldn't be either!)

To avoid such a problem and to develop consistent pricing, Figure 12-A on page 153 will help you determine an hourly rate for your services.

12.5 Pricing for Products in Inventory (Items for Resale)

Setting prices for products involves a different analysis. You must find the price that includes your cost and also reflects the value that your customers place on your products.

In my years of experience, when I did some work for a wholesaler/distributor, a 30-percent markup allowed for a comfortable existence. In some industries, such a markup might be possible; in others, it might be totally unreasonable. There is no rule of thumb in price setting. One client gave me his thoughts: *If you apply a 40-percent markup, you'll do fine—no matter the product.* I've had another say, *I wouldn't touch those products unless I could double the price.* Don't pay too much attention to such dogmatic statements. To find the price level for your products, consider the following steps:

1. Analyze your costs, including the cost of the product and all the costs necessary to get the product to the customer. Don't forget to add a factor for overhead. Then, include a profit margin.

2. Find out what the competition is charging. Your prices should be close to theirs. You can charge a higher price if your customers feel they get superior service.

3. Evaluate the degree of competition. If your product has little competition because of its uniqueness, customers will be willing to pay more. If there is a close alternative, your prices will have to stay close to your competition. Customers are not willing to pay substantially more for a product when a close alternative can be purchased.

4. Review pricing data from your particular industry.

 If you price much lower than your competition, potential customers might be spooked. They might think that because your products cost less, they are inferior.

 Don't get in pricing wars with Wal-Mart or any store that sells greater volume. As a small, home-based BESt Company, your volume will probably be relatively small. You will not have huge volume discounts when purchasing, nor can you offer huge discounts when selling.

Assigning a Value to Your Services

I. Estimated Salary

Decide on how much salary you would like to earn (before taxes) for the year. Enter that amount here: _____

II. Administrative/Indirect Costs

CEO Desk Days ("DDs"): Number of days you plan to spend behind the desk attending to administrative and selling tasks. Typically, this will account for 30–40 percent of your time. Fill in the following blank with the number of DDs per week _____, then multiply by 52 (weeks per year). Enter that total here _____

Personal Days ("PDs"): Number of days off for family activities, voluntary work, weekends, church, vacation, etc. Weekend days off (_____ × 52 =) _____ + vacation days _____ + official holidays_____ = _____total PDs.

Sick Days ("SDs"): Anticipated number of sick days. (Be conservative!) The higher this number, the higher your billing rate. A billing rate that is too high will decrease your competitiveness. Enter SDs here_____

Now compute your billable days:

Add: DDs + PDs + SDs = _____ (total indirect days)

Subtract:

365 – _____ total indirect days (from previous line) =_____ Billable Days

III. Hourly Rate:

Divide: Estimated Salary/Billable Days =_____Daily Rate

And, of course, to find your hourly rate, divide the above daily rate by eight.

Example: *Malik Jamison is a full time Website developer. He decided that he would like to make $60,000 per year. He plans to spend one day a week doing all his administrative tasks (1 day each week x 52 weeks = 52 DDs), and he plans to take off every Sunday (52 days off). He also plans to take a 5-day vacation, to not work on eight federal holidays, and to budget five sick days. Malik's hourly rate will be computed as follows:*

I.   Estimated salary: $60,000

II. Administration/Indirect Costs:

52 DDs + 65 PDs + 5 SDs =   122 days

365 total days - 122 indirect days =   243 billable days

III. Hourly rate: $60,000/243 days = $246.91 per day

$246.91 / 8 hours = $30.86 per hour

Note: *I would round the $30.86 to the nearest quarter, making the billing rate equal to $30.75/hr. Charging a client $30.86 per hour gives the impression that you're "pennying" the client, which, in turn, makes him or her feel like a meal ticket rather than a person.*

Figure 12–A

12.6 Analyzing Financial Information

You should have a good CPA on your management team, but you do not have to be a CPA to understand and analyze your own financial statements. Understand me well: *If you are not an accountant, I'm not trying to make you an accountant.* The intent of this guide is to provide a basic understanding of financial statements. That should be enough to supply you with the tools needed to analyze the financial well-being of your BESt Company and to engage in effective, daily fiscal management. To get more proficient in analyzing financial statements, you should take advantage of the many resources geared to giving small business owners more detailed information about this topic, including workshops and training seminars offered by the Small Business Administration and local universities. For now, let's just break the ice.

Why Concern Yourself With the Financials?

Why should you concern yourself with reading and analyzing financials in the first place? It's simple. Financial statements contain huge amounts of information that is of great value in running your BESt Company. You should do all that is humanly possible to provide excellent products and deliver first-rate service to your customers. But don't neglect the responsibility of keeping your own company fiscally sound and running as the proverbial "well-oiled machine." Financial statement analysis helps determine if a company is fiscally sound.

There is no secret formula to understanding financial statements and, fortunately, you do not have to be a financial guru to analyze the content. You must learn a few concepts, however. Master those concepts and your comfort level will shoot through the roof! Let's explore the two statements that you'll spend the most time reviewing.

Balance Sheet

The balance sheet is designed to show what the business owns (assets), what is owed to outsiders (liabilities), and what it owes its owner (equity or net worth). It gives a snapshot of the business on a specific date (for example, March 31, 2004). If a balance sheet is prepared for the same company a day later (on April 1, 2004), many account balances may have changed. Typically, however, balance sheets are prepared only once a month (or in some cases less frequently, perhaps quarterly or semi-annually, depending on the needs of the company).

The balance sheet is, in accordance with its name, to always be in balance. The relationship among assets, liabilities, and net worth (or owner's equity) is represented in the **accounting equation,** which is represented as follows:

Assets = Liabilities + Net Worth

The accounting equation shows the financial position of a company at all times. The notion of equality says that regardless of the type of business transaction, the balance sheet stays in balance. Essentially, for every action, there is an equal reaction. For example, buying an asset will increase an asset account, but it might simultaneously increase a liability account as well. Or if you buy an asset, you might reduce other assets. In all cases, the net effect is that nothing happens without affecting something else.

Liabilities and net worth represent the sources of funds for your BESt Company. Liabilities represent funding from outside sources, and net worth represents funding provided by you. Assets, on the other hand, represent how you are using the funds. Either you are leaving the money in the bank in the form of cash, you are acquiring inventory or equipment, or you are prepaying expenses (such as insurance).

How often should the balance sheet be prepared? The balance sheet is usually prepared on a monthly or quarterly basis. In all cases, however, a balance sheet must be prepared at least on an annual basis. This annual accounting becomes the basis for federal and state income tax returns.

Accounting applications such as Peachtree and Quickbooks make creating a balance sheet a cinch. Once these applications are installed and operational, you could literally run financial statements each day, several times a day if you wanted to. (I'm not saying you should, just that you could.) In spite of the ease provided by these software applications of creating a balance sheet on demand, running a daily balance sheet is hardly practical. Circumstances typically do not change enough from one day to the next to justify the time required to print and analyze daily financial statements—regardless of the fact that they could be created with just a few clicks of the mouse.

Income Statement

The income statement shows your BESt Company's revenue and expenses; it is this statement that gives the "bottom line." The bottom line is the number that tells whether the business made a profit or incurred a loss for a specific accounting period (a month, quarter, or year). The income statement is read from the top down and is designed to allow you to monitor your income and expenses from one accounting period to the next.

The Key to Understanding Financial Statements

There are other statements, but these two are the most common and the two with which you need to become most familiar. The key to understanding financial statements is to ask yourself two questions:

1. Does the transaction in question affect an expense or income account?

2. Does the transaction affect something I own or owe?

If you answer yes to the first question, you should look to the income statement for the answer. If you answer yes to the second question, the answer probably lies in the balance sheet.

Another helpful way to familiarize yourself with financial statements is to get involved in their design. Hold on—stay cool! Your CPA will still guide you through the process, but your input could be invaluable to your analysis later. (This is yet another reason to have a good working relationship with your CPA.) You should weigh in on the decisions regarding the account titles that will be used in statements; assign account titles that are meaningful to you.

Let's look at an example regarding account titles. Of the two financial statements we'll examine, let's consider the income statement first. Ask yourself the following questions: *What expenses will my business incur, and how do I best monitor them?* For example, instead of viewing all telecommunications lumped together as "telephone expense," you may want to differentiate between the various types of telephone expense (cell phone, pager, office telephone) and show each separately on the statement. Or, rather than seeing an expense item titled "insurance expense," you may want to monitor a breakdown here as well (for example, "medical insurance," "general liability insurance, and/or "auto insurance"). Of course there are generally accepted rules on how to format information on the financial statements and how to determine what goes where, so you don't want to get carried away with minute detail. But the more input your have in the up-front design, the more intuitive your analysis. In other words, your analysis will be easier and make more sense if the account titles being used make sense to you.

Financial Statement Analysis: A Case Study

To continue breaking the ice surrounding financial statement analysis, I have prepared a fictitious income statement and balance sheet for you to examine and analyze—based on our Jamaica-Max example. Remember: You will not have to understand the mechanics of preparing financial statements. Leave that to the accountants. Your job is to read the statements and make some sense of what's behind the numbers.

12.7 Example: Analyzing the Income Statement

One more time—for the sake of emphasis: We will not perform any complicated financial statement analysis. It's just not necessary. Our analysis of the income statement will involve scanning account balances and a technique called vertical analysis. (More on that later.)

The income statement for Jamaica-Max Tropical Cosmetics, LLC for 12 months ended December 31, Year 1 is shown on page 157. Study it closely.

Jamaica-Max Tropical Cosmetics, LLC
Income Statement
For 12 months ended December 31, Year 1

	Current Month		Year-to-Date	
	Amount	Ratio	Amount	Ratio
Sales	14,320	100.00%	140,720	100.00%
Total Cost of Sales	6,195	43.26%	59,505	42.29%
Gross Margin	8,125	56.74%	81,215	57.71%
Expenses				
Advertising	125	.87%	1,450	1.03%
Auto	74	.52%	822	.58%
Bank Charges	10	.07%	75	.05%
Depreciation	650	4.54%	8,000	5.69%
Insurance—Auto	250	1.75%	3,005	2.14%
Insurance—Liability	64	.45%	760	.54%
Insurance—Health	215	1.50%	2,490	1.77%
Interest	315	2.20%	3,660	2.60%
Legal and Accounting	120	.84%	1,500	1.07%
Office Supplies	155	1.08%	1,620	1.15%
Promotional Samples	72	.50%	825	.59%
Repairs and Maintenance	60	.42%	1,610	1.14%
Supplies	922	6.44%	2,580	1.83%
Telephone	275	1.92%	3,120	2.22%
Utilities	52	.36%	740	.53%
Total Expenses	3,359	23.46%	32,257	22.93%
Net income	4,766	33.28%	48,958	34.78%

Exhibit 12–A

Analyzing sales. Many business owners consider the income statement the most important financial report. Its purpose is to measure whether or not a business achieved or failed to achieve its primary objective of earning an acceptable income and profit. CEOs generally set goals for accounts such as sales and net income. In this exhibit, Jamaica-Max Tropical Cosmetics annual sales totalled $140,720. If Jamaica-Max's sales goal was $500,000, the company did miserably. If the goal was $150,000, it did much better. If the goal was

$100,000, the company excelled. The key to sales analysis is to establish an annual sales goal that is realistic. In this case, take a minute to review the sales projections made by Jamaica-Max in the original business plan back in Chapter 5. The company projected sales of $137,000 for the first year. Actual results show that the company posted revenues in the amount of $140,720. Looking at the company from strictly a sales perspective, the company did very well. It not only met its sales goals, but it exceeded projected sales by $3,720, or 2.7 percent.

More sales analysis. Here is another analytical question that gives insight: *How were the current month's sales in comparison to the year's average?* In the current month, December of Year 1, sales were $14,320. December sales seem to be higher than the monthly average of $11,727 ($140,720 divided by 12 months). There are several possible causes for this variance. For example, monthly sales are trending upward, or there is a temporary spike in sales, or sales are cyclical (maybe there is some holiday shopping going on). Your job is to determine exactly what's what. Such investigation can take you down many paths. And this is just the beginning of breaking down the statements to determine the meaning behind the numbers.

Gross margin and net profit. Gross margin and net profit are two percentages you definitely want to track. Analyzing gross margin and net profit involves essentially the same logic, so let's look at both simultaneously.

Gross margin for Year 1 is 57.71 percent, with a net profit of 34.78 percent. It would appear that the Thorns are managing their costs and expenses quite well, but it's hard to truly say without comparing the results of their operations against statistics from the cosmetic industry or some other useful standard. If the industry's gross margin averages 50 percent, then the Jamaica-Max star is shinning brightly. If the industry's gross margin averages 65 percent, then management has some tweaking to do—perhaps finding cheaper supply lines or buying in greater volume. Whatever the solution, this type of analysis gives the first indication that some action needs to be taken.

Vertical analysis (ratio analysis). Hang in there. You're doing fabulously. *Vertical analysis, sometimes referred to as common-size analysis, is a technique that expresses each item within a financial statement in terms of a percent of a base amount or designated total.* More simply, a ratio is the percentage a particular expense account is of sales. For example, in the current month, the ratio of health insurance expense is 1.5 percent. That ratio is computed as follows:

HEALTH INSURANCE EXPENSE / TOTAL SALES
$215 / $14,320 which is 1.5%

Examining the year-to-date column, we could say that *advertising expense* is 1.03 percent of sales, *auto expense* is .58 percent of sales, and so on. I know this sounds a little vague, but hang with me. The *base* for vertical analysis on the income statement is the amount of *total sales*. By expressing the ratio of each expense as a percentage of total sales, we can easily monitor each line item from month to month, irrespective of total dollars paid out for that expense or the total dollar value of monthly sales. Vertical analysis keeps all analysis relative to 100 percent. As a result, from month to month, the percentages always yield valuable information when compared.

For example, if advertising expense shoots up to 5.7 percent in January of Year 2 (a month later), it would be a good idea to find the reason for such a large increase. Vertical analysis sends up a red flag for any account that deviates from a normal percentage. When BESt CEOs see these red flags, they should begin to investigate the reasons behind the deviations.

Carefully study the ratios in the income statement. If you compare the current month's ratios with the year-to-date ratios, most expense items seem to match fairly closely. There are a couple of exceptions, however. Current month *supplies expense* ratio is 6.44 percent. When compared to the year-to-date supplies ratio of 1.83 percent (which is more typical of the percentage the business owner should expect to spend as a percent of sales), current supplies expense is 4.61 percent higher than the year-to-date ratio. That seems very high and should set off some alarms. It would definitely be a good idea to thoroughly investigate such a large variance.

Repairs and maintenance expense, on the other hand, is approximately .72 percent lower than the year-to-date ratio. That's a good deal lower than the average, but repairs and maintenance is the type of account that can typically experience rather wide fluctuations. It may just have been a good month. Nothing broke down, and less maintenance was done. Even though there is a downward tick in the repairs and maintenance ratio, it doesn't necessary point to any abnormal activity.

As you can see, there is much information that can be gleaned from these percentage ratios. The most important component of financial analysis is experience and knowledge of industry. After a while you will get a feel for what's normal and what's not. The final point is this: When a fluctuation seems out of line, it should be investigated thoroughly.

Subcategories. Finally, as I mentioned earlier, subcategories allow for more intuitive analysis. In our example, *insurance expense* is broken down into subcategories: auto, liability, and health. Subcategories give greater visibility to sensitive expense items. Without these subcategories, the expenses would be lumped into one account called *"Insurance."* It would be difficult to determine how much was spent during the year on, say, auto insurance expense, without going back to the original documents and paging through checks and invoices that are probably already filed away.

12.8 Example: Analyzing the Balance Sheet

As with the income statement, complicated financial statement analysis of the balance sheet isn't necessary. Our analysis of this statement will involve scanning account balances and computing four ratios (*working capital ratio, days in accounts receivable ratio, days in inventory ratio,* and *inventory turnover;* the last two only apply if you handle inventory). Sure, a tremendous amount of scrutiny can be performed on the statement, but this simple analysis is a great start.

Scanning the accounts. In Exhibit 12-B, Jamaica-Max's balance sheet has several categories of assets that total $81,548. These assets equal the total liabilities of $53,616 and members' equity of $27,932. When analyzing the balance sheet of your BESt Company, it is a good idea to scan all accounts to make sure that no account has a balance that is significantly different from what you think it should be.

Jamaica-Max Tropical Cosmetics, LLC
Balance Sheet
December 31, Year 1

Assets		Liabilities and Members' Equity	
Current Assets		**Current Liabilities**	
Petty Cash	200	Accounts Payable	12,102
Cash in Bank	18,418	Current Maturities	9,200
Accounts Receivable	15,700	Total Current Liabilities	21,302
Inventory	12,110		
Prepaid Expenses	3,120		
Total Current Assets	49,548		
Fixed Assets		**Long-term Liabilities**	
Furniture and Fixtures	32,000	Notes Payable—FirstBank	41,514
Equipment	8,000	Less: Current Maturities	(9,200)
Less: Accumulated Depreciation	(8,000)	Total Long-term Liabilities	32,314
Total Fixed Assets	32,000	Total Liabilities	53,616
		Members' Equity	
		Members' Equity	19,500
		Member's Draw	(40,526)
		Current Earnings	48,958
		Total Members' Equity	27,932
		Total Liabilities and Members'	
Total Assets	81,548	Equity	81,548

Exhibit 12–B

Working capital ratio. *Working capital is the relationship between current assets and current liabilities. It is also a measure of your BESt Company's ability to meets its obligations as they become due.* In our example, the working capital ratio for Jamaica-Max is computed as follows:

WORKING CAPITAL RATIO = CURRENT ASSETS / CURRENT LIABILITIES

For this example: working capital ratio = $49,548 / $21,302

working capital ratio = 2.32

Translation: For each $1.00 in bills coming due, Jamaica-Max has $2.32 available to pay those bills. An old rule of thumb is that any ratio that is 2:1 or better is generally considered good. Of course, it is always advisable to compare your ratios to industry standards.

Number of days' sales in accounts receivable. The number of days' sales in accounts receivable shows the average age of accounts receivable. This measure is important because it shows the effectiveness of the company's ability to collect its receivables. Accounts receivables that are collected timely enhance cash flow, and good cash flow keeps the doors open. It's just as simple as that!

Let's do the computation using figures from Jamaica-Max's balance sheet. First, compute the average day's sales:

average day's sales   = annual sales / 365

= $140,720 / 365

= $385.53

Then, compute the number of days' sales in accounts receivable:

number of days' sales
in accounts receivables   = accounts receivable /average day's sales

= $15,700 / 385.53

= 41 days (rounded)

Hmmm…this number is suspect. If the management of Jamaica-Max gives its customers 30 days to pay invoices, it seems as if their customers are not paying according to terms. Industry averages will give an indication of what to expect, but your terms should be adhered to as closely as possible.

Number of days' sales in inventory. Number of days' sales in inventory shows the number of days that sales could be made from the inventory you have on hand. This measure is important because it shows the effectiveness of the company's ability to control inventory cost as well as the efficiency of the purchasing process.

First, compute the average day's cost of goods sold:

average day's cost of goods sold = cost of goods sold / 365

= $59,505 / 365

= $163.03

Then, compute the number of days' sales in inventory:

number of days' sales
in inventory = inventory / average day's cost of goods sold

= $12,110 / $163.03

= 74 days (rounded)

What does this measurement tell us? It tells us that there is enough stock on the shelf to sell customers for 74 days, assuming customers want to buy what's on the shelf and that they do not want any special orders. This number seems high. High inventory levels are unhealthy, because they represent an investment with a rate of return of zero. Also, if prices begin to fall, it might leave the company vulnerable to a sustained period of lower profitability. Even though this number seems high, industry standards would give a better indication than just "gut feel."

Inventory turnover. I will keep this as simple as possible:

INVENTORY TURNOVER = NET SALES / AVERAGE INVENTORY (AT RETAIL)

Example: *After 12 months of operations, Jamaica-Max had sales of $140,720 and average inventory of $14,450. (Average inventory is computed from the general ledger. For our example, the amount is given.) Inventory turnover would be computed as follows:*

inventory turnover = $140,720 / $14,450 = 9.7 times

The key is to have inventory turn quickly, but not too quickly. Inventory that is turning too rapidly might indicate several problems. First, we will consider the advantages of quick inventory turnover, then we will list the possible problems associated with exceptionally high turnover.

Quick turnover usually means:

▷ Higher sales volume and profit.

▷ Fresh or up-to-date inventory.

▷ An effective advertising strategy.

Exceptionally high turnover could mean:

▷ Lost sales due to frequent stock outs.

▷ Profit being adversely or negatively affected. (As you scramble for merchandise, you may not receive volume discounts, the best selection, or the best price.)

Inventory that is turning over 9.7 times per year might be acceptable. Of course, once you have some history, you will ultimately be the best judge of how many times inventory should turn each year.

Final Note on Analyzing Financial Statements

Financial statement analysis will assist you in evaluating the financial health of your company and your managerial effectiveness. Be aware, however, that an analysis of your company is based on historical data—on events that have already happened. Although analyzing your financial statements is important, you should not make financial decisions solely on the basis of what your analysis reveals. Give adequate consideration to all factors that are at your disposal.

Concepts of financial management are not difficult, just unfamiliar. Understanding these concepts and using them effectively to control your business will enhance the likelihood of your success as a BESt CEO. It is vitally important that you select a CPA who has a reputation for customer service, someone who will take the time to thoroughly answer questions that arise. I have a philosophy: Educate the BESt CEO, and it will save both the CEO and the CPA time. An educated CEO will minimize expending useless energy on guesswork and duplication of effort.

I'm Making Money, So Why Can't I Pay My Bills?

If cash is not flowing, there may be profits at the bottom line but not enough money in the bank to pay bills. Such a business is cash-starved. This condition is more common than you might think. CEOs must employ effective cash-management strategies to avoid being in a cash-starved position. Late-paying customers are the primary reason for this condition. Instead of paying within terms, say 30 days, they might hold you out for 75 days. When customers pay late it starts a domino effect. First, vendors start calling, looking for payment. If they are not paid according to their terms, your company will be placed on a "cash on delivery" (COD) basis, which intensifies the cash-tight position. Then, payroll taxes are paid late, which invariably leads to penalties, interest, and all sorts of time wasted corresponding with the IRS and other taxing authorities. Also, purchasing becomes inefficient. Instead of buying to take advantage of the best deals, you buy when the money is available—which can have a disastrous effect on gross margin. These are just a few consequences to poor cash flow (or, worse yet, negative cash flow).

As we consider cash flow, the balance sheet accounts listed here are often associated with "flowing capital." There are certain questions about each account that the BESt CEOs must consider. If the answer to any of these questions reveals a problem, the CEO must manage that account to correct the deficiency. Any one of these situations has the potential to send a profitable company into financial distress.

> **Cash (and cash equivalents such as CDs).** Is there enough cash on hand to meet obligations as they become due?

> **Accounts receivable.** Are my receivables being collected quickly enough? Do I have a plan to deal with slow payers? What will I do with customers who refuse to pay?

> **Inventory.** Am I losing sales because I do not stock what my customers want? Am I turning over my inventory at a rate comparable to other companies in my industry? What can I do about slow-moving inventory or dead stock?

> **Accounts payable.** Am I paying my bills in such a way as to not undermine my credit rating? Am I taking available discounts?

> **Notes payable.** Can I meet the principal and interest payments as they come due?

> **Labor cost and owners' draw.** Can I draw a paycheck routinely?

12.8 Understanding Cash Flow

To compete successfully in the marketplace, home-based businesses must be prepared for all contingencies. The lifeblood of a business is its cash flow. If cash stops flowing, the company cannot meet its obligations, and failure is inevitable. Trying to operate a business without positive cash flow can be likened to trying to win a war without ammunition: It simply can't be done.

Using a different analogy, a healthy body not only has blood, but the blood must continually flow throughout the human system, bringing nutrients to each organ and removing waste. If that flow ceases, death would occur immediately. In a similar fashion, positive cash flow allows a business to maintain a healthy, vigorous existence.

Cash flows through a time frame called an operating cycle. *An **operating cycle** covers the time span between the purchasing of inventory through the collection of receivables.* The cash-flow cycle begins with the cash in your bank accounts that is then used to purchase inventory. At this point, you have changed the character of your asset from one form to another: You have changed cash into inventory. As inventory is sold, the character of your assets changes yet again from inventory to receivables. Receivables are then collected and the asset once again becomes cash, thus completing the operating cycle. (See Figure 12-C.)

Cash Flow Cycle

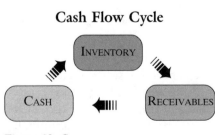

Figure 12–C

It is important that this flow continues unimpeded. A cash-flow analysis should reveal whether inflows and outflows from your business combine to result in either a positive cash flow or a negative cash drain—more simply, whether or not daily operations generate enough cash to meet your obligation. Preparing a full cash-flow analysis is beyond the scope of this book. We will, however, review strategies to enhance cash flow for a BESt Business.

Strategies to Enhance Cash Flow

Collect receivables. It's okay to be a nice guy, but not at the expense of letting your customers' invoices "grow a beard." Actively manage accounts receivables and aggressively collect overdue accounts. Remember: An overdue account is any invoice that goes beyond its terms. If you decide to give your customers 30 days to pay, on the 31st day you should have an action plan: to either place a call or send a statement of account. The longer a customer's balance remains unpaid, the less likely it is that you will receive full payment.

Sell on a COD basis. As credit terms become more stringent, more customers will be placed on COD. In the short run, this will infuse cash into the business. In the long run however, many customers may seek to buy from a company that will extend liberal credit. There is a push/pull dynamic between sales and the amount of credit extended to customers.

Of course, if your investigation of a potential customer reveals that it is a poor credit risk, always require full payment before shipment.

Tap the credit line. Establishing a credit line with a financial institution will ensure that you'll have the ability to draw against the line to cover short-term cash-flow problems. Most banks will set up credits lines in such a way that you draw down only what you need to cover the checks that hit the bank each day. This convenience provides only the cash you need and keeps interest expense at a minimum.

Increase sales? Increasing sales may seem to be an obvious strategy to increase cash flow. However, if large portions of your sales are made on account, increasing sales will only increase accounts receivables, not cash. Meanwhile, depleted inventory must be replaced. Because receivables usually will not be collected until 30 days after sales, a substantial increase in sales can work against positive cash flow.

Use a personal computer. Most readily available and comparatively inexpensive accounting software give the added advantage of quick cash-flow projections. These applications will enable you to review projected cash inflows and outflows from month to month. By analyzing these projections, BESt CEOs can "predict" fluctuations in cash flow and avoid potential shortfalls.

Control expenses. In the 1990s, the economy was exploding. Home businesses were likewise experiencing double-digit increases in sales volume.

When sales are increasing and business is on the move, there is a tendency for the uninitiated to allow expenses to grow out of proportion. Fortunately, out-of-control spending can be stopped at the drop of a hat for home-based companies. BESt CEOs can make a decision today that can be implemented today and yield results today. As Benjamin Franklin said, "A penny saved is a penny earned." Every decision that saves a dollar in operating expenses is a dollar that falls directly to the bottom line on a dollar-for-dollar basis. As A. Thibodaux, a friend and colleague, once said, "Cutting cost and increasing cash flow are different sides of the same coin." Well said.

Accept debit cards (check cards). Debit cards continue to increase in popularity, which is great for the BESt Company. This payment method is convenient for customers and eliminates the problem of overdrafts. Unlike checks, money is drawn directly and virtually instantaneously from your customers' bank accounts. In additional to convenience, debit cards also provide customers with several other benefits: They're more easily accepted by merchants than checks, cash can be withdrawn from automated teller machines, and they are generally easier to obtain than credit cards for smaller, more recently formed companies.

12.9 Extending Credit

You didn't start a home-based business just to sell to relatives. So banish the thought that a successful business can be grown selling only to Uncle Jacob and Granny Frye. You will have to sell to people you don't know—obviously. Not so obvious is the fact that you'll need to develop a credit policy, especially if you sell to other companies, because most companies buy on credit.

In a perfect world, you would collect monies at the time of sale. Generally, that is not likely. To protect yourself from frauds that have no intention of paying and companies with a delinquent pay history, you will have to investigate credit requests. This investigation begins with a credit application.

In short, when selling on account, *you* are the one extending credit. Do you recall the third degree you were subject to when you approached the bank for a loan? Well, forget trying to subject customers to that same degree of screening to open a trade account. Nevertheless, you can employ a number of safeguards and techniques to help screen potential creditors and identify the slow payers and deadbeats.

Credit Application

Credit applications are a way of life in Corporate America. Purchasing agents and buyers expect to be asked to complete them, so you won't offend them by asking. In fact, most companies anticipate the type of information requested and develop their own "Information Sheet" similar to the one shown in Figure 12-D. Whenever you require credit information, they'll simply fax the information sheet to you. It's up to you to apply "due diligence" to make sure the applicant is a worthwhile credit risk. You should call at least three references to get a third-party assessment of the applicant's payment habits and history.

Let's review the type of information Jamaica-Max sends to its vendors. It is very similar to the Company Information Sheet in Chapter 11 (Figure 11-A). This is the type of information you can expect to receive from your potential customers.

Jamaica-Max Tropical Cosmetics, LLC *Every Color Under the Sun* 555 Main Street, Suite 200 New Orleans, Louisiana 70821 Phone: 985–555–1212 Fax 985–555–1213	
Trade References	
Mailing Address	P.O. Box 9999, New Orleans, LA 99999
Phone	985–555–9999
Fax	985–555–9998
Contact	Jamaica Thorn
Federal ID#	72-9999999
Shipping Address	9999 Main Street, New Orleans, LA 99999
Trade References	Acme Supply, 123 Main Street, New Orleans, LA Phone 985–555–1234 Fax 985–555–1235 BLJ Trucking, 123 Industrial Road, New Orleans, LA Phone 985–555–7522 Fax 985–555–9998 Lindy Repairs, Inc., 500 Price Drive, New Orleans, LA Phone 985–555–9874 Fax 985–555–3738
Visit Our Website: *www.jamaicamax.com* *Every Color Under the Sun*	

Figure 12-D

Dun & Bradstreet (D&B) and Others

In addition to your own investigation, you might consider using a commercial credit rating service such as D&B or credit bureaus (Experian, Equifax, or TransUnion) to help evaluate the creditworthiness of potential customers. D&B, for example, maintains an abridged history of trade transactions, bank transactions, bankruptcy filings, and so forth on approximately 13 million U.S. businesses. For more information on these services, see their Websites.

Service	URL
Dun & Bradstreet	*sbs.dnb.com*
Experian	*www.experian.com*
Equifax	*www.equifax.com*
TransUnion	*www.tuc.com*

Collection Policy

There is a delicate balance between giving credit to every business that makes a request and being too restrictive. By setting your credit policy too loosely, your receivables will skyrocket, but the likelihood that some customers will not pay is greatly increased. On the other hand, if your policy is too restrictive, potential customers will simply find a competitor that isn't quite so restrictive. Result: lost sales.

Finding the balance is crucial. Taking a few precautions before opening a credit account could save thousands of dollars down the road. As tempting as it might be, don't do credit business with poor credit risks! Down the road, it could be extremely costly and you will be sorry. Consider this: How many dollars are you willing to toss out the window to let the wind blow down the street? Exactly—none! But without an effective credit policy in place, the effect is the same.

 Actively manage receivables! Customers will push the envelope if they sense you're lax in collecting. Use an accounts receivable aging and, when making collection calls, be cordial but firm.

Encouraging Prompt Payment

To encourage prompt payment after you have extended credit, there are a number of measures that can be employed.

➤ **Send invoices immediately.** The clock usually starts when a customer receives your invoice. The sooner you get it into the customer's hands, the sooner it gets paid. If a lack of urgency is shown in invoicing, the customer may reciprocate by showing a lack of interest in paying.

➤ **Spell out the terms of sale on each invoice.** Because the terms of sale might be different for each customer or for each sale, spell out the terms on each invoice. While you're at it, ask the customer if any other information on the invoice would be helpful and would expedite the payment process.

➤ **Assess a finance charge on delinquent accounts.** For example, charge 18 percent per year (or whatever the law allows) on all unpaid balances beyond 30 days, or whatever terms you allow.

➤ **Dun accounts promptly.** Don't wait until an account is 60 days old before calling. Start calling immediately after the terms expire. Some businessmen are content to allow their customers to drag out their receivables to whatever is typical in the industry. I have clients in the oilfield industry who give 30-day terms on their invoices, yet make comments along the lines of, *"I'm happy if I get paid in 60–90 days. Oh, by all means, I would like my money sooner; but that's just how the industry pays."* That is tantamount to training your customers to ignore your terms. Hold to your terms, and discontinue working for someone who is stringing you out.

Prompt Communication With Customers Is Vital

It is mandatory that you communicate with customers who are going beyond established payment terms for several reasons: First, the squeaky wheel gets the oil, and second, in some cases, the invoice you are calling about might not be in their payables system. The mail may have gotten diverted, or the invoice could have been mishandled (filed in the wrong place). At any rate, you're waiting for the payable department to pay an invoice that might not be in their possession. Faxing a second copy usually resolves the problem. Be aware, however, that some companies don't consider the discount terms to start until the invoice is received. This is yet another good reason to send the invoice as soon as possible. Ideally, you should send the invoice the same day the services were provided or the goods were shipped. By no means should you delay longer than a day or two after the sale.

Supposing Customers Don't Pay According to Terms

Determine a course of action to be taken whenever a customer goes beyond terms and apply it consistently. Some BESt Companies engage in a lengthy letter-writing procedure. A BESt CEO should only write a *collection letter* after placing a courtesy *collection call.* Before calling, make sure you are up to speed on the account. Have a statement that shows all activity on the account, including invoice numbers and their purchase order numbers. If the customer tells you that the check is processed (or in the mail), ask for the check number. If they give you a check number, you'll probably get your money within a few days.

If a quick phone call doesn't product payment, you will have to write a series of letters. If the customer does not respond to a friendly reminder, the correspondence has to become increasingly stronger, leading finally to a demand letter. A typical progression of correspondence might proceed as follows:

Type of Collection Letter	Approximate Date Sent
First Reminder	0–2 days past due
Gentle Warning	10–30 days past due
Stronger Warning	31–60 days past due
Demand Letter	After 60 days past due

This schedule is not absolute. It is an example of when collection letters could be sent; each BESt CEO will have to develop his or her own policy.

Engaging in a lengthy letter-writing campaign can easily add another 30 to 45 days to an already delinquent account, and the longer an invoice is outstanding, the less likely it is to be paid. This long time frame yet again emphasizes the need to actively manage accounts receivable and to check them out in the first place.

When the Letter-Writing Stops

Letter-writing is generally effective with those who want to maintain a trusting and courteous relationship. But for those who are not so concerned—deadbeats, for example—writing a series of letters might not produce any results. Then it's time to involve a collection agency or an attorney and draw a line in the sand.

Collection agencies usually take cases on a contingency basis, but carefully read the fine print on any contract or agreement. Many collection agencies will charge according to the age of an invoice. For example, E-Z Collection Agency might charge 20 percent to collect a receivable that is between 30 and 90 days old. If the receivable is 91 days old, however, the collection fee might jump to 30 percent. At 120 days, that same agency might charge as much as 50 percent of the invoice amount.

Collection agencies, by nature, are extremely aggressive. BESt Companies should only engage a collection agency when it's felt that there's no other alternative. Many times they are successful, which invariably emboldens them to ask for more business. Do not feel obligated. Regardless of how often the collection agency calls, only give them the business of invoices that you deem un-collectable. Hopefully, that will be very few. And hopefully, you'll only need the collection agency's services once every blue moon.

Chapter 13

Image and Etiquette

Honesty is the best image.

—Tom Wilson

*An **image**...is not simply a trademark, a design, a slogan, or an easily remembered picture. It is a studiously crafted personality profile of an individual, institution, corporation, product, or service.*

—Daniel J. Boorstin

13.1 Image and Business Etiquette

Today's business world is evolving at a dizzying speed. BESt CEOs must have the ability to present a professional image to all the diverse people with whom they come into contact. The goal of image and etiquette is to convey poise, understanding, and power. Good *business etiquette* begets *good business,* which begets *more business.*

BESt Principle #10 ▐▐▐➡ **PRACTICE GOOD BUSINESS ETIQUETTE.** GOOD BUSINESS ETIQUETTE BRINGS DOLLARS TO THE BOTTOM LINE.

When I mention the word *etiquette,* you probably conjure up all sorts of images about which fork to use for your salad, holding the door open for the person entering behind you, or just remembering to say thank you with a smile. Certainly, these chivalrous acts require understanding and social etiquette. Business etiquette, on the other hand, is a quite different. *Business etiquette is based on presenting and conducting oneself in a manner that is respectful of power, position, and authority. It is an awareness of superior and subordinate relationships and making members from either group comfortable in your presence.* Business etiquette deals with making introductions, shaking hands, using nametags, communicating by phone and e-mail, and handling general written and verbal communication. Forget that endless list of all those elaborate dos and don'ts. The points we discuss simply take good, common sense to effectively handle day-to-day situations. When you think business etiquette, think military, superior-subordinate relationships, and authority, not forks, in-laws, and driving in congested traffic.

Making introductions. You will be presented with many opportunities to make introductions. Gender is not regarded, rank is. The key point here is to remember to introduce the person of less rank or authority to the person of greater rank or authority. Also, mention the person of greater rank first. So, an introduction might be similar this: *Mr. or Ms. Higher Rank, I would like to introduce you to Mr. or Ms. Lower Rank.*

There is one exception to this general rule: The customer is always the most important person to your BESt Company. Always present your customers as having the greater importance. Accordingly, here's an introduction of one of your customers: *Mr. or Ms. Customer, I would like to introduce you to Mr. or Ms. Less Important.*

I know you may be a bit uncomfortable with situations where some people are designated to be "more" or "less" important than others. Remember: These introductions have nothing to do with human value. It's all about authority and power in a business setting.

Shaking hands. There are a lot of issues about shaking hands that, in my opinion, bring too much to bear on such a simple gesture. Should a woman extend her hand first? What about religious practices that prevent men touching women at certain times? In short, I have three guidelines for shaking hands:

1. It doesn't matter who initiates the handshake.

2. Deliver a firm handshake, not a crushing one.

3. Maintain eye contact during the handshake.

Case closed!

Using telephones. A significant portion of your day will be spent on the telephone. It's the most economical way to get most of your work done. Calls are made to customers, vendors, tax authorities, the bank, shippers, the post office, and so on. Via the computer (if you have a dial-up connection), you will use the telephone to check bank balances, make wire transfers, and send e-mails and faxes. The telephone is the single, most cost-effective piece of equipment you own.

Here are a few guidelines to bring a professional touch to telephone usage:

➤ **Dedicated line.** With so much benefit derived from the telephone, you must have at least one telephone line exclusively for business use. In other words, you must have a *dedicated line.* In the beginning, it's just too easy to use your personal telephone line for the business. But nothing yells "amateur" louder than having your son or daughter pick up a business call thinking it's for him or her. Quite frankly, a child answering a business call is the kiss of death for a business transaction.

➤ **Telephone greetings.** When you answer a business call, you should identify your BESt Company, identify yourself, and extend an offer of service. For example, you would say, "Good morning, Jamaica Thorn speaking. How may I help you?"

➤ **Answering machines/service.** Face it: We're all getting used to technology. We all know that we should wait for the "beep" before leaving a message. It does not have to be a part of your message. Use this example as a guide when deciding on a message for your answering machine.

   Example: *Hello. You have reached the office of Jamaica-Max. There is no one able to take this call at the moment. We are in constant contact with this machine, so if you please leave a message, we will return your call as soon as possible.*

13.2 Stationery and Logo

Your stationery is your calling card. I know this is a small detail, but it's a detail that speaks volumes about the quality of work that can be expected from you. Your customer wants to believe that you will be able to deliver top-quality products or services at a fair price. Until your potential customers actually do business with you, all they have to go on is image. A thoughtful logo helps to create a good, positive image. Use your creative abilities. If yours is somewhat lacking, ask a creative friend or family member to help create something that conveys the spirit of your business. Avoid using stock images from most publishing software. They are a last-ditch alternative. Your business is unique. Try to find your own unique voice.

Fonts

Use fonts that are crisp, balanced, and appropriate. Avoid using animated, playful fonts if your business is caring for the sick or elderly. On the other hand, playful fonts might be totally appropriate for a balloon delivery service, a birthday clown service, or dance classes for preschoolers.

13.3 Speaker Phones

People are getting a bit more relaxed about carrying on a business conversation on a speaker phone, but you should avoid doing so. You should only use a speaker phone if you are using your hands to do something related to that specific call. Even then, ask your caller for his or her permission to put the call on hands-free and turn on the speaker.

13.4 Summary

This is your company and the cold reality is that, from now on, all actions regarding how you conduct yourself in transacting business will convey a message. Business is being conducted all around you, but, in relative terms, your BESt Business is still a rarity. The perception is that small, home-based black businesses are generally limited to beauty parlors or barber shops. Although those are great businesses to run, we have a lot more to offer—a whole lot more. The image we convey speaks louder than any other thing we do.

Remember the question I posed back in Chapter 1? *Is there a difference between operating a black-owned, home-based business and a home-based business that is not black-owned?* I'll answer it again: Yes—especially in terms of perception. Although image is important to every business, it is especially important, almost critical, to your BESt Company. As CEO, the responsibility is all yours to create a positive image that can go a long way toward helping make your company as successful as possible.

Chapter 14

Eye to the Future

The future belongs to those who prepare for it today.

—Malcolm X

The future ain't what it used to be.

—Yogi Berra

Congratulations! You have reached another milestone in your life. You have seen the brass ring, you have gone for it, and you have grabbed it. Your dream of owning a business has become a reality. There are few things in life as sweet as the fruit of success brought about through smart work and persistent effort. You deserve this great moment to reflect on your accomplishment. Your efforts have been based in reality and not some get-rich-quick scheme. You've come a long way, and you have learned much in the process. Now here you are, reading a set of financial statements in your comfortable chair and thinking about the next few months. You're ecstatic about the progress you've made, but there is also a bit of concern on your face. Looking toward the future can be a little disconcerting, even a bit frightening, but at the same time, it's very necessary. You've birthed a business. Now what?

This epilogue is organized around bridging your past efforts with future opportunities and, above all, staying committed to the ongoing, daily processes and procedures that breed success. The common theme in all your efforts thus far has been the BESt Principles that we have discussed throughout the text. In summary, the BESt Principles are:

- ➡ **Work smart.** Leave the hard, unfocused work to those who don't do their homework.

- ➡ **Specialize.** Focus on your strengths. Don't try to be all things to all people.

➠ **Commit totally.** Once your mind is made up, don't look back and don't half-step.

➠ **Plan to stick to your plan.** Deviate only when it makes $ense.

➠ **Plan.** Or you'll go where you don't want to go, stay longer than you want to stay, and spend more than you need to spend.

➠ **Learn as much as possible about the software you use.** The more you know, the harder you can make software work to accomplish your BESt Company's objectives.

➠ **Keep business and personal transactions separate.** Even the smallest BESt Company should absolutely avoid commingling personal transactions with business transactions.

➠ **Back up your records routinely.** A few minutes a day can protect you from having to redo a mountain of work at the most inconvenient time.

➠ **Shop around and negotiate.** You have to get the best deal on the merchandise you purchase, even when dealing with close friends.

➠ **Practice good business etiquette.** Good business etiquette brings dollars to the bottom line.

Stepping Into Tomorrow

The future looks bright, but staying on top of your game in an ever-changing environment is quite a challenge. Well-known jazz trumpeter Donald Byrd released a song back in the day titled "Steppin' into Tomorrow." The lyrics speak of one who has set his sights on the future, with destiny in focus and both feet treading on firm ground as the journey is made. It is about being centered and levelheaded, not flighty and impulsive. You can be sure there are many who rush into a course of action without adequate deliberation. For those, I can almost guarantee the same scattered outcomes that result when entrepreneurs try to organize a business without a well-thought-out plan. They will be plagued by inefficient effort, unnecessary costs, and wasted time.

Moving toward opportunities that the future holds is not a mad rush into the dark unknown; instead, each step must be carefully thought out, methodical, and based on light gained from your growing experience. One of the chief functions of a CEO is to assess the strengths and weaknesses of the company, as well as to develop strategies that deal with threats to the company's health and to capitalize on opportunities that arise. The future success of your BESt Company depends on your ability to recognize and respond to trends as they begin to manifest. Even now, as you look toward the future, there are a number of trends coming into focus that represent both opportunities and challenges to your company. Your responsibility as the CEO of your BESt Company is to leverage these trends into opportunities that can take your company to the next level. Those who resist these trends and who refuse to think within the context of the big picture will find it harder and harder to hold their own, much less grow and prosper in the ever-evolving environment of the new economy.

Let's take a look at four easily observable trends that can have tremendous impact on your business if they are embraced and effectively integrated into your business strategy:

1. Continued contraction of time and distance in the information explosion.

2. Increased competition among small businesses.

3. Electronic shopping.

4. Customer service.

Continued Contraction of Time and Distance in the Information Explosion

It seems everybody wants everything yesterday. In the past, such responsiveness was difficult for BESt Companies. But in today's new economy, technology such as wireless communications, fax machines, the Internet, e-mail, and overnight shipping connect BESt Companies to business associates and customers in the most efficient ways possible. Using available technologies, such as computerized accounting and inventory handling, small companies have the ability to ship orders efficiently and insure next-day delivery. In short, technology gives BESt Companies the ability to provide many of the services previously provided only by larger companies. And guess what? Your customers expect it! It is critically important that you possess a commitment to lifelong learning, especially as it pertains to what technology can and cannot do. Such commitment is vital to maintain the skills necessary to accomplish your business's objectives in an ever-changing, technology-driven information age.

Without doubt, the world is becoming a smaller place—and it's all due to technology. To shy away from technology is the kiss of death to maintaining a competitive edge and thus business longevity. So rather than simply learning enough to be able to say, "at least I'm not computer illiterate," embrace technology and employ it as much as possible in solving everyday problems.

Increased Competition Among Small Businesses

Today's business environment is truly global in scope. Globalization is a word you are going to hear more and more. *Globalization is the expansion of economic opportunities made possible by technology and legislation that pulls down trade barriers. It spans borders and reduces or eliminates cultural barriers that tend to hinder competition. The result is increased consumer choice among competing products.* Globalization is a mouthful. It is also a double-edged sword. On the one hand, it allows BESt Companies to market more products to more customers. On the other hand, BESt CEOs need to fully analyze potential competition in an expanded marketplace before diving into new projects. Multinational companies are reaching into many cities and towns and are making alliances at the neighborhood level. CEOs need to assess whether potential opportunities are both realistic and achievable, given this expanded degree of competition from not only traditional small business, but larger businesses that are operating at the micro (or neighborhood) level.

Electronic Shopping

Consumers are becoming increasingly comfortable with Internet shopping. Brick-and-mortar storefronts just aren't as necessary as they once were. To optimally position your BESt business, aggressively engage the Internet in your marketing efforts.

The Internet is revolutionizing the way information is disseminated and transactions are carried out. Don't shy away from the Internet. Learn as much as you can, but realize that you will probably need some help to fully take advantage of its potential. Create those alliances early on so that you are able to include the Internet as a proactive component of your business strategy.

Customer Service

Customer service is proving to be the defining factor between good companies and great companies. As consumers become more and better informed, they tend to become more discriminating. What once sufficed or was merely adequate simply will no longer cut it. BESt Companies must be willing to invest in themselves in order to enhance customer service. Recall the discussion in Chapter 12 about value-added service. Just as you expect business associates to go beyond the call of duty on your behalf, so do your customers also expect that of you. Gone are the days of simply opening the door and selling. In addition to products and services, customers want information, attention, and cultural sensitivity. To maintain your market position and improve it, you must endeavor to keep customer needs on the front burner and adjust company goals to make sure they never lose touch with the people who keep the doors open.

Conclusion: Being the BESt Is Imperative for Success

The imperative for success, being the BESt, is at the same time both simple and complex. It is simple in that it is an easy concept to understand. To be the best means that you are willing to compare your products and processes to those of your competitor and, in an objective analysis, have outcomes that are superior to your competition. For example, your *product* tastes better, operates more efficiently, lasts longer, and so on. Or, if your *processes* are being compared to the competition, they yield faster delivery, less shipping errors, better service, and so forth. Objectively speaking, being the BESt is very simple to understand. Even the youngest children readily grasp it. Recall the arguments from the school's playground, where one kindergartener squares up to another and proclaims, "Yeah, well...my dad is stronger and smarter than yours."

Being the BESt is also complex. The complexity results because the mix of variables that bring about this condition of excellence is both numerous and dynamic. For example, some of the variables involved in managing excellent companies include customer service, productivity, managerial effectiveness, and a whole host of others, each multidimensional and dynamic. Imagine, for example, just trying to control all of the business processes that enhance customer satisfaction can be daunting. Even when BESt variables, such as customer service, are identified, the elements of customer service that satisfy one customer might not be the same elements that satisfy another customer. And even those elements can change from year to year.

Regardless of the challenge, it is important that the CEO recognizes and manages this mix of ever-changing variables, including future trends, to bring the BESt Company to the next level and to keep it functioning at the top of its game. By being the BESt at what you do, people take notice, a reputation is born, and goodwill is created. A reputation for excellence is virtually priceless in a herd of "also-rans."

Entrepreneurship is a different type of ship, but a ship nonetheless. Instead of oil, it feeds on opportunity. Instead of steering away from rocks, one has to deal with risks. But regardless of the type of ship, each needs a helmsman. You are that helmsman. You see the opportunities. You are willing to deal with the risks, and you understand that there are no guarantees. Seeing opportunities as they are forming on the horizon and steering your company away from threats and toward those opportunities are the hallmarks of an effective CEO—exactly what your BESt Company needs and deserves. There is much that can be done to encourage sales and develop your BESt Company's potential besides waiting for the phone to ring and orders to come in. Your greatest challenges are to keep a fresh perspective, to be proactive, to unleash your imagination. In essence, your mission, regardless of your business strategy, is to simply be the BESt each and every day and in everything that you do.

Appendix A

Business Plan Questionnaire

If they were graded, some business plans would receive average scores while others would excel. What moves a business plan from adequate to excellent? The answer is fairly straightforward—effective, comprehensive communication of your business ideas. This simple answer, however, belies the process. Develpoping a great business plan requires thinking, researching, writing, rethinking, editing, and finalizing. The questions in this appendix are designed to facilitate and organize your initial thinking process in order that you may effectively communicate your ideas. They are not by any means meant to be answered like high school history questions, stapled together, and presented as a business plan. Instead, use your computer's word processing program or a dedicated, spiral-bound composition book to capture your thoughts and begin the process.

Each section in the sample business plan is represented here. Each section's questions are representative of the type of information included in that section. Be ready and willing, however, to modify existing questions or to add questions to more accurately reflect the story you are interested in communicating.

Section I: Executive Summary
1. What is your overall business strategy? What are the immediate goals of the company? How does the company plan to achieve its goals?

2. Describe the current status of the business. When was it founded? Identify the management. Describe management's experience and capabilities.

3. What is the request the company is making? What amount of money is the company seeking?

Section II: Company Overview

1. What is the company's mission statement?

2. Provide the company's ID information: legal name, date founded, company address, phone number, fax number, and e-mail address.

3. Describe the company's legal structure (sole proprietorship, partnership, corporation, and so on). Describe ownership. If there is more than one owner, list all owners and give ownership percentages.

4. Give a brief overview of sales strategy. If applicable, describe the Website and how business will be conducted via the Internet.

Section III: Industry Analysis

1. Describe the industry. Provide general overview of products offered and/or services provided. How large is the potential market? Is the industry growing, declining, or steady?

2. Describe the local marketplace.

3. How much of the local market share can the company capture? What is the overall strategy that the company will use to capture market share?

Section IV: Products and Services

1. Briefly describe your products and services. Give a clear description of features and benefits.

Section V: Advertising and Promotion

1. Describe customers demographically and geographically. How much do customers spend locally? What are their purchasing habits?

2. Describe how customers get information to make purchasing decisions. How will you best convey the benefits and features of your products and/or services to potential customers?

3. Describe your proposed choice of advertising media (newspapers, radio, outdoor, etc.). Why do you think your choice will be effective? How do you plan to monitor the effectiveness of the advertising campaigns?

Section VI: Sales Strategy

1. What are your sales goals for Year 1? Year 2? Year 3?

2. What is your targeted gross margin? How do you plan to control costs?

3. Describe sales programs (direct sales, Internet sales, etc.).

4. What services are most important to the customers? How does the company plan to satisfy customers' requirements? How will the company monitor customer satisfaction?

5. Describe how you plan to keep the promises in your USP. How will your USP make customers' operations more efficient or effective (or make their lives easier)?

Section VII: Competition

1. Identify five immediate competitors. What are they doing that is successful? What practices do they employ that you want to avoid? How do you plan to adopt their successful practices or to improve them?

2. How much do your competitors charge for their products and/or services?

3. What barriers must be overcome to capture market share?

Section VIII: Management and Operations

1. Describe the professional history of the owner.

2. Describe specific accomplishments of management (owner) that will benefit the new BESt Company.

3. Describe duties and responsibilities.

Section IX: Finance

1. Compute start-up capital requirements. Itemize how the funds are to be spent.

2. How is the loan to be repaid? Project sales and expenses. Will the business enjoy a positive cash flow? (A complete set of projected financial statements must be developed.)

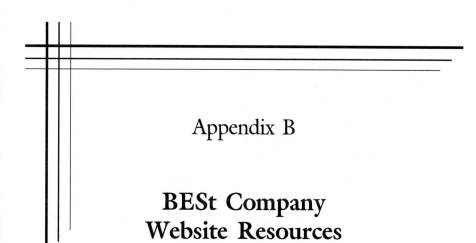

Appendix B

BESt Company
Website Resources

American Home Business Association: *www.homebusiness.com*
Provides valuable support and resources to home-based or small businesses.

Bplans.com: Business planning made easy: *www.bplan.com*
Owned and operated by Palo Alto Software, Inc. A resource to help entrepreneurs plan better businesses. Includes sample business plans for various industries.

BusinessFinance.com: *www.businessfinance.com*
Business loans and venture capital sources.

Business Start Page: *www.bspage.com*
Business tips and reviews of business books.

Concept Marketing Group, Inc.: *www.marketingsource.com/associations*
Comprehensive source of information on associations and professional societies, including business and trade associations.

Hoovers Online: The Business Information Authority: *www.hoovers.com*
Free newsletters and many articles on various business topics.

Inc.com: *www.inc.com*
Strategies for starting, growing, and running your business.

Internal Revenue Service: *www.irs.gov*
Provides tax forms and publications.

Minority Business Development Agency ("MBDA"): *www.mbda.gov*
An agency under the auspices of the U.S. Department of Commerce.
The only federal agency formed specifically to foster the creation,
growth, and expansion of minority-owned businesses in America.

Minority Business Entrepreneur: *www.mbemag.com*
Maintained by *Minority Business Entrepreneur Magazine.* The magazine
features articles that are concerned with minority enterprise
development.

morebusiness.com: *www.morebusiness.com*
Sample business plans, legal forms, contracts, newsletter, and more.

National Association of Home Based Business: *www.usahomebusiness.com*
An Intranet HomeSite System for home-managed businesses that give
members and subscribers a quick and reliable source of business, trade,
management, and direct and network marketing information.

National Minority Supplier Development Council—("NMSDC"):
www.nmsdcus.org
NMSDC acts as a liaison between corporate America and minority-
owned businesses. The goal is to match the purchase requirements of
3,500 corporate members with more than 15,000 minority companies
that seek to satisfy those purchase requirements. The NMSDC national
office is located in New York, and 39 regional councils are spread out
across the country.

U.S. Department of Labor: *www.dol.gov*
General information about federal labor laws, including those that
guarantee workers' rights to safe and healthful working conditions, a
minimum hourly wage and overtime pay, freedom from employment
discrimination, unemployment insurance, and son on.

United States Patents and Trademark Office: *www.uspto.gov*
Primary services include processing patents and trademarks and
disseminating patent and trademark information. Also promotes an
understanding of intellectual property protection.

Appendix C

Participating Intermediary Lenders

U.S. Small Business Administration MicroLoan Program

Alabama

Birmingham Business Resource Center
110 12th St. North
Birmingham, AL 35203
Phone: 205–250–6380 Fax: 205–250–6384
Service Area: Jefferson County

Alabama

Southeast Community Capital
1020 Commerce Park Dr.
Oak Ridge, TN 37830
Phone: 865–220–2020 Fax: 865–220–2030
Service Area: Bibb, Blount, Calhoun,
Chambers, Chilton, Colbert, Coosa, Cullman,
De Kalb, Elmore, Etowah, Fayette, Franklin,
Hale, Jackson, Lauderdale, Lawrence,
Limestone, Macon, Madison, Marion,
Marshall, Morgan, Pickens, Randolph,
St. Clair, Shelby, Talladega, Tallapoosa,
Tuscaloosa, Walker, and Winston

Community Equity Investments, Inc.
302 North Barcelona St.
Pensacola, FL 32501
Phone: 850–595–6234 Fax: 850–595–6264
Service Area: Baldwin, Mobile, Washington,
Clarke, Monroe, Escambia, Conecuh,
Covington, Geneva, Coffee, Dale, Henry, and
Houston counties

Arizona

Prestamos CDFI, LLC (*formerly Chicanos Por
La Causa, Inc.*)
1112 E. Buckeye Rd.
Phoenix, AZ 85034-4043
Phone: 602–252–0483 Fax: 602–252–0484
Service Area: Urban Maricopa and Pima
Counties, Graham and Gila Apache
Reservation, Coconino and Mohave Counties
(including the Kaibab, Havasupai, and
Hualapai Reservations and western portions
of the Navajo and Hopi Reservations),
Yavapai and La Paz Counties

PPEP Housing Development Co/Micro Ind.
Credit Rural Org.
901 East 46th St.
Tucson, AZ 85713
Phone: 520–806–9513 Fax: 520–806–9515
Service Area: Cochise, Santa Cruz, Pinal,
Yuma, rural Pima, and rural Maricopa
Counties, including the Fort Mcdowell, Gila
River, Maricopa, Papago, Salt River, and San
Xavier Indian Reservations

Self-Employment Loan Fund, Inc.
1601 North 7th St., Suite 340
Phoenix, AZ 85006
Phone: 602–340–8834 Fax: 602–340–8953
Service Area: Maricopa County

Arizona Council for Economic Conversion
10 East Broadway, Suite 210
P.O. Box 42108
Tucson, AZ 85701
Phone: 520–620–1241 Fax: n/a
Service Area: Tucson and Pima Counties

Arkansas
Southern Financial Partners
605 Main St.
Pine Bluff, AR 71923
Phone: 870–246–9739 Fax: 870–246–2182
Service Area: Southern and extreme northeast
areas of the state, including Arkansas,
Ashley, Bradley, Calhoun, Chicot, Clark,
Clay, Cleveland, Columbia, Craighead,
Dallas, Desha, Drew, Garland, Grant,
Greene, Hempstead, Hot Spring, Howard,
Jefferson Lafayette, Lawrence, Lincoln, Little
River, Lonoke, Miller, Mississippi,
Montgomery, Nevada, Ouachita, Phillips,
Pike, Poinsett, Polk, Prairie, Pulaski,
Randolph, Saline, Sevier, and Union
Counties

Forge-Financing Ozarks Rural Growth and
Economy
208 East Main, P.O. Box 1138
Huntsville, AR 72740
Phone: 501–738–1585 Fax: 501–738–6288
Service Area: Crawford, Baxter, Yell, Perry,
Conway, Boone, Madison, Marion, Carroll,
Franklin, Pope, Benton, Washington, Searcy,
and Newton

California
Arcata Economic Development Corporation
100 Ericson Court, Suite 100
Arcata, CA 95521
Phone: 707–822–4616 Fax: 707–822–8982
Service Area: Del Norte, Humboldt, Lake,
Mendocino, Siskiyou, and Trinity Counties

California Coastal Rural Development Corp.
221 Main St., Suite 300, P.O. Box 479
Salinas, CA 93906
Phone: 831–424–1099 Fax: 831–424–1094
Service Area: Santa Clara, Santa Cruz,
Monterey, San Benito, San Luis Obispo,
Santa Barbara, and Ventura Counties

CDC Small Business Finance Corp.
925 Ft. Stockton Dr.
San Diego, CA 92110
Phone: 619–291–3594 Fax: 619–291–6954
Service Area: San Diego

Oakland Business Development Corp.
519 17th St., Suite 100
Oakland, CA 94612
Phone: 510–763–4297, ext. 103
 Fax: 510–763–1273
Service Area: Alameda and Contra Costa
Counties

PCR Small Business Development
3255 Wilshire Blvd.
Los Angeles, CA 90010
Phone: 213–739–2999, ext. 222
 Fax: 213–739–0639
Service Area: South Los Angeles County

Sierra Economic Development District
560 Wall St., Suite F
Auburn, CA 95603
Phone: 530–823–4703 Fax: 530–823–4142
Service Area: Modoc, El Dorado, Lassen,
Nevada, Plumas, Sierra, and Placer Counties

Southeast Asian Community Center
875 O'Farrell St.
San Francisco, CA 94109
Phone: 415–885–2743 Fax: 415–885–3253
Service Area: Alameda, Contra Costa, Marin,
Merced, Sacramento, San Francisco, San
Joaquin, San Mateo, Santa Clara, and
Stanislaus Counties

Valley Economic Development Corp.
5121 Van Nuys Blvd., 3rd Floor
Van Nuys, CA 91403
Phone: 818–907–9977 Fax: 818–907–9720
Service Area: Los Angeles and Orange
Counties

Valley Small Business Development Corp.
3417 W. Shaw, Suite 100
Fresno, CA 93711
Phone: 559–438–9680 Fax: 559–438–9690
Service Area: Fresno, Kings, Kern, Stanislaus,
Madera, Mariposa, Merced, Tuolumne, and
Tulare Counties

Colorado
Colorado Enterprise Fund
1888 Sherman St., Suite 530
Denver, CO 80203
Phone: 303–860–0242 Fax: 303–860–0409
Service Area: City of Denver; Adams,
Arapahoe Boulder, Denver, and Jefferson
Counties; 10 counties in eastern Colorado

Region 10 LEAP for Economic Development
300 North Cascade St., Suite 1, P.O. Box 849
Montrose, CO 81401
Phone: 970–249–2436 Fax: 970–249–2488

Service Area: West central area, including Delta, Gunnison, Hinsdale, Montrose, Ouray, and San Miguel Counties

Connecticut
Community Economic Development Fund
50-G Weston St.
Hartford, CT 06120
Phone: 860–249–3800 Fax: 860–249–2500
Service Area: Statewide

Connecticut Community Investment Corp.
100 Crown St.
New Haven, CT 06510
Phone: 203–776–6172 Fax: 203–776–6837
Service Area: Statewide

Delaware
Wilmington Economic Development Corp.
100 W. 10th St., Suite 706
Wilmington, DE 19801
Phone: 302–571–9088 Fax: 302–652–5679
Service Area: New Castle County, in the cities of Wilmington, Newark, New Castle, Middletown, Odessa, and Townsend

District of Columbia
H Street Community Development Corp.
501 H St., NE
Washington, DC 20002
Phone: 202–544–8353 Fax: 202–544–3051
Service Area: West: the Anacostia River; East: 7th St., NW; North: Benning Road to K St.; South: the Southeast/Southwest Freeway

Florida
Central Florida Community Development Corp.
P.O. Box 15065
Daytona Beach, FL 32115
Phone: 368–258–7520 Fax: 368–238–3428
Service Area: Brevard, Flagler, St. Johns, and Volusia Counties

Clearwater Neighborhood Housing Services, Inc.
608 North Garden Ave.
Clearwater, FL 33755
Phone: 727–442–4155 Fax: 727–446–4911
Service Area: City of Clearwater and Pinellas County

Community Enterprise Investments, Inc.
302 North Barcelona St.
Pensacola, FL 32501
Phone: 850–595–6234 Fax: 850–595–6264
Service Area: Florida Panhandle including Bay, Calhoun, Escambia, Gadsden, Gulf, Jackson, Holmes, Liberty, Leon, Franklin, Wakulla, Walton, Washington, Okaloosa, and Santa Rosa Counties

Minority/Women Business Ent. Alliance, Inc.
625 E. Colonial Dr.
Orlando, FL 32803
Phone: 407–428–5860 Fax: 407–428–5869
Service Area: Orange, Osceola, Lake, Seminole, Polk, Hillsborough, Sumter, Brevard, Volusia, and Marion Counties

Partners for Self-Employment, Inc./ d.b.a./ Micro-Business, USA
3000 Biscayne Blvd., Suite 102
Miami, FL 33137
Phone: 877–722–4505 Fax: 305–438–1411
Service Area: Miami-Dade, Broward, Palm Beach, and Pinellas Counties

Tampa Bay Economic Development Corp.
2105 N. Nebraska Ave., 2nd Floor
Tampa, FL 33602
Phone: 813–274–7969 Fax: 813–274–7551
Service Area: Hillsborough County

The Business Loan Fund of the Palm Beaches
1016 North Dixie Hwy., 2nd Floor
West Palm Beach, FL 33401
Phone: 561–838–9027 Fax: 561–838–9029
Service Area: Palm Beach County, Hendry, Indian River, Martin, Palm Beach County Development Regions, and St. Lucie

United Gainesville Community Dev. Corp., Inc.
505 2nd Ave. NW, P.O. Box 2518
Gainesville, FL 32602
Phone: 352–334–0943 Fax: 352–334–0947
Service Area: Alachua and Marion Counties

Georgia
Enterprise Funding Corp/GRASP Enterprises
241 Peachtree St., Suite 200
Atlanta, GA 30303
Phone: 404–659–5955 Fax: 404–880–9561
Service Area: Fulton, Dekalb, Cobb, Gwinnett, Fayette, Clayton, Henry, Douglas, and Rockdale Counties

Small Business Assistance Corporation
111 E. Liberty St., Suite 100, P.O. Box 10750
Savannah, GA 31412-0950
Phone: 912–232–4700 Fax: 912–232–0385
Service Area: Appling, Atkinson, Brooks, Bacon, Berrien, Ben Hill, Bryan, Bulloch, Bleckley, Brantley, Coffee, Charlton, Camden, Clinch, Candler, Cook, Chatham, Dodge, Emanuel, Echols, Effingham, Evans, Glynn, Irwin, Johnson, Jeff Davis, Laurens, Liberty, Long, Lowndes, Lanier, McIntosh, Montgomery, Pierce, Tift, Turner, Telfair, Truetlen, Toombs, Tattnall, Ware, Wilcox, Wayne, and Wheeler Counties

Southeast Community Capital
1020 Commerce Park Dr.
Oak Ridge, TN 37830
Phone:865–220–2020 Fax:865–220–2030
Service Area: Barrow, Bartow, Carroll,
Cherokee, Dade, Elbert, Fannin, Floyd,
Franklin, Gordon, Gwinnett, Hall, Hart,
Heard, Paulding, Pickens, Polk, Stephens,
Union, Walker, and Whitfield

Hawaii
Pacific Gateway Center
720 North King St.
Honolulu, HI 96817
Phone: 808–845–3918 Fax: 808–842–1962
Service Area: Statewide

Idaho
Sage Community Resources (*formerly Ida-Ore
Planning and Development Association, Inc.*)
10624 W. Executive Dr.
Boise, ID 83713
Phone: 208–322–7033 Fax: 208–322–3569
Service Area: Payette, Washington, Adams,
Valley, Gem, Boise, Elmore, Ada, Canyon,
and Owyhee Counties

Panhandle Area Council
11100 Airport Dr.
Hayden, ID 83835-9743
Phone: 208–772–0584 Fax: 208–772–6196
Service Area: Northern Panhandle, including
Benewah, Bonner, Boundary, Kotenai, and
Shoshone Counties

Illinois
Accion Chicago, Inc.
3245 W. 26th
Chicago, IL 60623
Phone: 773–376–9004 Fax: 773–376–9048
Service Area: Cook County (including parts of
Chicago); Lake, McHenry, Dekalb, Kane,
Dupage, Kendall, Grundy, Kankanee, Will,
and Lasalle Counties

Justine Petersen Housing & Reinvestment Corp.
5031 Northrup Ave.
St. Louis, MO 63110
Phone: 314–664–5051, ext. 117
Fax: 314–644–5364
Service Area: Clinton, Jersey, Madison, and St.
Clair Counties

Indiana
Bloomington Area Microenterprise Initiative
216 W. Allen St.
Bloomington, IN 47403
Phone: 812–339–8937 Fax: 812–335–7352

Service Area: Morgan, Owen, Greene,
Lawrence, Monroe, Brown, and Jackson
Bartholomew, Decatur, and Jennings
Counties

Iowa
Siouxland Economic Development Corp.
428 Insurance Center, 507 7th St.,
P.O. Box 447
Sioux City, IA 51102
Phone: 712–279–6286 Fax: 712–279–6920
Service Area: Cherokee, Ida, Monona,
Plymouth, Sioux, and Woodbury Counties

Kansas
South Central Kansas Economic Dev. Dist. Inc.
209 East William St., Suite 300
Wichita, KS 67214
Phone: 316–262–7035 Fax: 316–262–7062
Service Area: Butler, Chautauqua, Cowley,
Elk, Greenwood, Harper, Harvey, Kingman,
Marion, McPherson, Reno, Rice, Sedgwick,
and Sumner Counties

Growth Opportunity Connection
(Go Connection)
4747 Troost Ave.
Kansas City, MO 64110
Phone: 816–235–6146 Fax: 816–756–1530
Service Area: Wyandotte, Johnson, Douglas,
and Leavenworth Counties

Kentucky
Community Ventures Corp.
1450 North Broadway
Lexington, KY 40505
Phone: 859–231–0054 Fax: 859–231–0261
Service Area: Anderson, Bourbon, Boyle,
Clark, Estill, Fayette, Franklin, Garrard,
Harrison, Jessamine, Lincoln, Madison,
Mercer, Nicholas, Powell, Scott, and
Woodford Counties

Kentucky Highlands Investment Corp.
362 Old Whitley Rd., P.O. Box 1738
London, KY 40743-1738
Phone: 606–864–5175 Fax: 606–864–5194
Service Area: Bell, Clay, Clinton, Harlan,
Jackson, McCreary, Rockcastle, Wayne, and
Whitley Counties

Louisville Central Dev. Corp./Business Plus
1407 West Jefferson St., Ste. 200
Louisville, KY 40203
Phone: 502–583–8821 Fax: 502–589–1173
Service Area: Jefferson County (primary focus
Enterprise Impowerment Zone)

Purchase Area Development District
1002 Medical Dr., P.O. Box 588
Mayfield, KY 42066
Phone: 270–247–7171 Fax: 270–251–6110
Service Area: Ballard, Calloway, Carlisle, Fulton, Graves, Hickman, McCracken, and Marshall Counties

Louisiana
NewCorp Business Assistance Center
1600 Canal St., Suite 601
New Orleans, LA 70112
Phone: 504–539–9340 Fax: 504–539–9343
Service Area: State of Louisiana

Maine
Androscoggin Valley Council of Government
125 Manley Rd.
Auburn, ME 04210
Phone: 207–783–9186 Fax: 207–783–5211
Service Area: Androscoggin, Franklin, and Oxford counties

Coastal Enterprises Inc.
36 Water St., P.O. Box 268
Wiscasset, ME 04578
Phone: 207–882–7552 Fax: 207–882–7308
Service Area: Statewide excluding Aroostock, Piscataquis, Washington, Oxford, Penobscot, and Hancock Counties

Community Concepts Inc.
19 Market Square, P.O. Box 278
South Paris, ME 04281
Phone: 207–743–7716 Fax: 207–743–6513
Service Area: Oxford County

Northern Maine Development Commission
302 South Main St., P.O. Box 779
Caribou; Bangor, ME 04736
Phone: 207–498–8736 Fax: 207–493–3108
Service Area: Aroostook

Eastern Maine Development Corporation
One Cumberland Pl., Suite 300
Bangor, ME 04401
Phone: 207–942–6389 Fax: 207–942–3548
Service Area: Hancock, Penobscot, Piscataquis, and Washington Counties

Maryland
The Development Credit Fund
2526 N. Charles St., Suite 200
Baltimore, MD 21218
Phone: 410–235–8100 Fax: 410–235–5899
Service Area: Statewide Maryland, excluding Montgomery and Prince George's Counties

H Street Community Development Corp.
501 H St., NE
Washington, DC 20002
Phone: 202–544–8353 Fax: 202–544–3051
Service Area: Montgomery and Prince George's Counties

Massachusetts
Community Development Transportation Lending Services
1341 G St., NW, Suite 600
Washington, DC 20005
Phone: 202–661–0210 Fax: 202–737–9197
Service Area: North central Massachusetts; county subdivisions of Athol, Winchendon, Gardner, Templeton, Phillipston, Orange, Erving, Wendell, Montague, Gill, and Greenfield Counties

Economic Dev. Industrial Corp. of Lynn
37 Central Square, 3rd Floor
Lynn, MA 01901
Phone: 781–581–9399 Fax: 781–581–9731
Service Area: City of Lynn

Greater Springfield Entrepreneurial Fund
1441 Main St.
Springfield, MA 01103
Phone: 413–755–1318 Fax: 413–731–8530
Service Area: Hampden County, excluding the towns of Chester and Chicopes

Jewish Vocational Service Inc.
105 Chauncey St., 6th Floor
Boston, MA 02111
Phone: 617–451–8147 Fax: 617–451–9973
Service Area: Greater Boston, with special emphasis on businesses in the Boston Enterprise Zone / Boston Empowerment Zone, and businesses in Mattapan, Dorchester Roxbury, Hyde Park, and Jamaica Plain

Jobs for Fall River Inc.
1 Government Center
Fall River, MA 02722
Phone: 508–324–2620 Fax: 508–677–2840
Service Area: City of Fall River

South Eastern Economic Development Corp/ SEED
80 Dean St.
Taunton, MA 02780
Phone: 508–822–1020 Fax: 508–880–7869
Service Area: SE Massachusetts; Norfolk, Bristol, Plymouth, Barnstable, Dukes, and Nantucket Counties

Western Massachusetts Enterprise Fund
P.O Box 1077
Greenfield, MA 01302
Phone: 413–774–4033 Fax: 413–774–3673
Service Area: Berkshire and Franklin Counties;
the towns of Chester and Chicopes within
Hampden County; Springfield; the towns of
Athol, Petersham, Phillipston, and Royalston
within Worcester County; Hampshire County

Michigan
Center for Empowerment and Economic
Development (CEED)
2002 Hogback Rd., Suite 12
Ann Arbor, MI 48105
Phone: 734–677–1400 Fax: 734–677–1465
Service Area: Washtenaw, Oakland, Wayne,
and Livingston Counties

Community Capital and Development Corp.
The Walter Reuther Center
316 West Water St.
Flint, MI 48503
Phone: 810–239–5847 Fax: 810–239–5575
Service Area: Genesee County

Kent Area MicroBusiness Loan Services
233 East Fulton St., Suite 101
Grand Rapids, MI 49503
Phone: 616–771–6880 Fax: 616–771–8021
Service Area: Kent County

Northern Economic Initiative Corp.
228 W. Washington St.
Marquette, MI 49855
Phone: 906–226–1662 Fax: n/a
Service Area: Upper Peninsula of Michigan

Rural Michigan Intermediary Relending
Program, Inc.
121 East Front St., Suite 201
Traverse City, MI 49686
Phone: 231–941–5858 Fax: 231–941–4616
Service Area: Emmet, Charlevoix, Antrim,
Leelanau, Benzie, Grand, Traverse, Kalkaska,
Manistee, Wexford, Missaukee, Cheboygan,
Presque Isle, Otsego, Montmorency, Alpena,
Crawford, Oscoda, Alcona, Roscommon,
Ogemaw, Iosco, Osceola, Mason, and Lake
Counties

Saginaw Economic Development Corp.
301 E. Genesee, 3rd Floor
Saginaw, MI 48607
Phone: 989–759–1395 Fax: 989–754–1715
Service Area: Saginaw County

Minnesota
Minnesota Minneapolis Consortium of
Community Developers
2308 Central Ave., N.E.
Minneapolis, MN 55418-3710
Phone: 612–789–7337 Fax: 612–789–8448
Service Area: Portions of the city of Minneapolis

Southern Minnesota Initiative Foundation
525 Florence Ave.
P.O. Box 695
Owatonna, MN 55060
Phone: 507–455–3215 Fax: 507–455–2098
Service Area: Sibley, Nicollett, LeSueur, Rice,
Wabasha, Brown, Watonwan, Blue Earth,
Waseca, Dodge, Olmsted, Winona, Martin,
Faribault, Freeborn, Mower, Fillmore, and
Houston Counties

Southwest Minnesota Foundation
1390 Hwy. 15 South
P.O. Box 428
Hutchinson, MN 55350
Phone: 320–587–4848 Fax: 320–587–3838
Service Area: 18 counties of southwest MN
(Big Stone, Chippewa, Cottonwood, Jackson,
Kandiyphi, Lac qui Parle, Lincoln, Lyon,
McLeod, Meeker, Murray, Nobles, Pipestone,
Redwood, Renville, Rock, Swift, and Yellow
Medicine)

Northeast Entrepreneur Fund, Inc.
820 Ninth St. North, Suite 200
Virginia, MN 55792
Phone: 218–749–4191/800–422–0374
Fax: 218–749–5213
Service Area: Aitkin, Carlton, Cook, Itasca,
Koochiching, Lake, Cass, Pine, and St. Louis
Counties

Northwest Minnesota Foundation
4225 Technology Dr., NW
Bemidji, MN 56601
Phone: 218–759–2057 Fax: 218–759–2328
Service Area: Beltrami, Clearwater, Hubbard,
Kittsson, Lake of the Woods, Mahnomen,
Marshall, Norman, Pennington, Polk, Red
Lake, and Rousseau Counties

WomenVenture
2324 University Ave., Suite 200
St. Paul, MN 55112
Phone: 651–646–3808 Fax: 651–641–7223
Service Area: Cities of Minneapolis and St.
Paul; Anoka, Carver, Chisago, Dakota,
Hennepin, Isanti, Ramsey, Scott,
Washington, Steele, and Wright Counties

Mississippi
Friends of Children of Mississippi, Inc.
939 North President St.
Jackson, MS 39202
Phone: 601–353–3264 Fax: 601–714–4278
Service Area: Statewide

Missouri
Growth Opportunity Connection
(Go Connection)
4747 Troost Ave.
Kansas City, MO 64110
Phone: 816–561–8567 Fax: 816–756–1530
Service Area: Platte, Jackson, Clay, and Cass
Counties

Justine Petersen Housing & Reinvestment Corp.
5031 Northrup Ave.
St. Louis, MO 63110
Phone: 314–664–5051, ext. 117
Fax: 314–664–5364
Service Area: Counties of Franklin, Jefferson,
Lincoln, St. Charles, St. Louis, and Warren;
the City of St. Louis

Rural Missouri, Inc.
1014 Northeast Dr.
Jefferson City, MO 65109
Phone: 573–635–0136 Fax: 573–635–5636
Service Area: Statewide, excluding Platte,
Jackson, Clay, and Cass Counties

Montana
Capital Opportunities/District IX HRDC, Inc
321 East Main St., Suite 300
Bozeman, MT 59715
Phone: 406–587–5444 Fax: 406–585–3538
Service Area: Gallatin, Park, and Meagher
Counties

Montana Community Development Corp.
110 East Broadway, 2nd Floor
Missoula, MT 59802
Phone: 406–728–9234 Fax: 406–542–6671
Service Area: Lake, Mineral, Missoula, Ravalli,
and Sanders Counties

Nebraska
Rural Enterprise Assistance Project-Center for
Rural Affairs
101 South Tallman St., P.O. Box 406
Walthill, NE 68067
Phone: 402–846–5428 Fax: 402–846–5420
Service Area: Adams, Antelope, Banner,
Blaine, Boone, Box Butte, Boyd, Brown,
Buffalo, Burt, Butler, Cass, Cedar, Cherry,
Cheyenne, Clay, Colfax, Cuming, Custer,
Dakota, Dawes, Deuel, Dixon, Dodge,
Fillmore, Franklin, Gage, Garden, Garfield,
Greeley, Hall, Hamilton, Harlan, Holt,
Howard, Jefferson, Johnson, Kearney, Keya
Paha, Kimball, Knox, Lancaster, Loup,
Madison, McPherson, Merrick, Morrill,
Nance, Nemaha, Nuckolls, Otoe, Pawnee,
Phelps, Pierce, Platte, Polk, Richardson,
Rock, Saline, Saunders, Scottsbluff, Seward,
Sheridan, Sherman, Sioux, Stanton, Thayer,
Thurston, Valley, Washington, Wayne,
Webster, Wheeler, and York Counties

West Central Nebraska Dev. District, Inc.
201 East 2nd St., Suite C, P.O. Box 599
Ogallala, NE 69153
Phone: 308–284–6077 Fax: 308–284–6070
Service Area: Arthur, Chase, Dawson, Dundy,
Frontier, Furnas, Gosper, Grant, Hayes,
Hitchcock, Hooker, Keith, Lincoln, Logan,
Perkins, Red Willow, Thomas, and
McPherson Counties

Self Employment Loan Fund of Lincoln
1135 M St.
Lincoln, NE 68508-3169
Phone: 402–436–2386 Fax: 402–436–2360
Service Area: Lancaster and Lincoln Counties

Nevada
Nevada Microenterprise Initiative
113 West Plumb Ln.
Reno, NV 89509
Phone: 702–734–3555 Fax: 702–734–3530
Service Area: Statewide

New Hampshire
Northern Community Investment Corp.
347 Portland St., P.O. Box 904
St. Johnsbury, VT 05819
Phone: 802–748–5101 Fax: 802–748–1884
Service Area: Grafton, Carol, and Coos
Counties

New Jersey
Community Lending and Investment Corp. of
Jersey City
30 Montgomery St.
Jersey City, NJ 07302
Phone: 201–333–7797 Fax: 201–946–9367
Service Area: City of Jersey City

Cooperative Business Assistance Corp.
433 Market St., 2nd Floor, Suite 201
Camden, NJ 08102
Phone: 856–966–8181 Fax: 856–966–0036
Service Area: Camden, Gloucester, Atlantic,
Cape May, Cumberland, and Salem Counties

Greater Newark Business Dev. Consortium
744 Broad St., 26th Floor
Newark, NJ 07102
Phone: 973–242–5563 Fax: 973–242–0485
Service Area: Bergen, Essex, Hudson,
  Middlesex, Monmouth, Morris, Passaic,
  Sussex, and Ocean Counties

Regional Business Assistance Corp.
247 East Front St.
Trenton, NJ 08611
Phone: 609–396–2595 Fax: 609–396–2598
Service Area: Portions of the city of Trenton;
  Mercer, Burlington, Hunterdon, and Warren
  Counties

Union County Economic Development Corp.
Liberty Hall Corporate Center
1085 Morris Ave., Suite 531
Union, NJ 07083
Phone: 908–527–1166 Fax: 908–527–1207
Service Area: Union and Somerset Counties

New Mexico
Women's Economic Self Sufficiency Team
414 Silver SW
Albuquerque, NM 87102-3239
Phone: 505–241–4760 Fax: 505–241–4766
Service Area: Statewide

New York
Adirondack Economic Development Corp.
60 Main St., Suite 200, P.O. Box 747
Saranac Lake, NY 12983
Phone: 518–891–5523 Fax: 518–891–9820
Service Area: Clinton, Essex, Franklin, Fulton,
  Hamilton, Herkimer, Jefferson, Lewis,
  Oneida, Oswego, St. Lawrence, Saratoga,
  Warren, and Washington Counties

Alternatives Federal Credit Union
125 N. Fulton St.
Ithaca, NY 14850
Phone: 607–273–3582 Fax: 607–277–6391
Service Area: Schuyler, Tompkins, Tioga,
  Cortland, Chemung, and Broome Counties

Buffalo Economic Renaissance Corp.(BERC)
617 Main St.
Buffalo, NY 14203
Phone: 716–842–6923 Fax: 716–842–6942
Service Area: City of Buffalo

Buffalo and Erie County Industrial Land
  Development Corp.
275 Oak St.
Buffalo, NY 14203
Phone: 716–856–6525 Fax: 716–856–6754
Service Area: Erie County

Hudson Development Company (*formerly
  Columbia Hudson Partnership*)
444 Warren St.
Hudson, NY 12534-2415
Phone: 518–828–4718 Fax: 518–828–0901
Service Area: Columbia and Green Counties

Community Development Corp. of Long Island
2100 Middle Country Rd., Suite 300
Centereach, NY 11720
Phone: 631–471–1215 Fax: 631–471–1210
Service Area: Suffolk and Nassau Counties

Manhattan Borough Development Corp.
55 John St., 17th Floor
New York, NY 10038
Phone: 212–791–3660 Fax: 212–571–0873
Service Area: Borough of Manhattan

Albany-Colonie Reg. Chamber of Commerce
1 Computer Dr. South
Albany, NY 12205
Phone: 518–453–5223 Fax: 518–453–5220
Service Area: Albany, Rensselaer, Saratoga,
  Schenectady, Schoharie, Greene, Fulton, and
  Montgomery Counties

NY Assoc. for New Americans, Inc.
17 Battery Pl.
New York, NY 10004
Phone: 212–425–5051 Fax: 212–425–7260
Service Area: Boroughs of Queens, Manhattan,
  the Bronx, Brooklyn, and Staten Island

Renaissance Economic Development Corp.
1 Pike St.
New York, NY 10002
Phone: 212–964–6002 Fax: 212–964–6181
Service Area: Boroughs of Brooklyn,
  Manhattan, and Queens

Rural Opportunities Enterprise Center, Inc.
400 East Ave.
Rochester, NY 14607
Phone: 585–340–3387 Fax: 585–340–3326
Service Area: Onandaga, Ulster, Monroe,
  Schuyler, Chemung, Allegheny, Cattaraugus,
  Cayuga, Chatauqua, Dutchess, Erie,
  Genessee, Greene, Livingston, Niagara,
  Ontario, Orange, Orleans, Putnam, Seneca,
  Steuben, Sullivan, Wayne, Wyoming, and
  Yates Counties

North Carolina
Neuse River Development Authority, Inc.
233 Middle St., 2nd Floor
New Bern, NC 28563
Phone: 252–638–6724, ext. 3032
  Fax: 252–638–1819

Service Area: Carteret, Craven, Duplin, Greene, Jones, Johnston, Lenoir, Onslow, Pamlico, and Wayne Counties

Self-Help Ventures Fund
301 West Main St., P.O. Box 3619
Durham, NC 27701
Phone: 919–956–4400 Fax: 919–956–4600
Service Area: Statewide, excluding Watauga, Avery, Mitchell, and Yancey Counties

W.A.M.Y. Community Action
152 Southgate Dr., Suite 2, P.O. Box 2688
Boone, NC 28607
Phone: 828–264–2421 Fax: 828–264–0952
Service Area: Watauga, Avery, Mitchell, and Yancey Counties

North Dakota

Dakota Certified Development Corp.
51 Broadway, Suite 500
Fargo, ND 58102
Phone: 701–293–8892 Fax: 701–293–7819
Service Area: Grand Forks, Devils Lake, Minot, Williston, and Dickinson Counties

Lake Agassiz Regional Development Corp.
417 Main Ave.
Fargo, ND 58103
Phone: 701–235–1197 Fax: 701–235–6706
Service Area: Griggs, Bismarck, Mandan, Jamestown, and Valley City

Ohio

Community Capital Development Corp.
900 Michigan Ave.
Columbus, OH 43215-1165
Phone: 614–645–0387 Fax: 614–645–8588
Service Area: Franklin, Delaware, Fairfield, Licking, Union, Pickaway, Fayette, and Madison Counties

Enterprise Development Corp.
9030 Hocking Hills Dr.
The Plains, OH 45780-1209
Phone: 740–797–9646 Fax: 740–797–9659
Service Area: Adams, Ashland, Athens, Belmont, Brown, Carroll, Columbiana, Coshocton, Gallia, Guernsey, Harrison, Highland, Holmes, Jackson, Jefferson, Knox, Lawrence, Meigs, Monroe, Morgan, Muskingum, Hocking, Noble, Perry, Pike, Ross, Scioto, Tuscarawas, Vinton, and Washington Counties

Hamilton County Development Company, Inc.
1776 Mentor Ave.
Cincinnati, OH 45212
Phone: 513–631–8292 Fax: 513–631–4887

Service Area: City of Cincinnati, Adams, Brown, Butler, Clermont, Clinton, Hamilton, Warren, and Highland Counties

Kent Regional Business Alliance
College of Business #300-A, KSU
Kent, OH 44242
Phone: 330–672–1275 Fax: 330–672–9338
Service Area: Ashtabula, Geauga, Trumbull, Portage, Columbiana, Carroll, Holmes, Coshocton, Tuscarawas, Stark, and Harrison Counties

Women's Organization for Mentoring, Entrepreneurship, & Networking
526 South Main St., Suite 235
Arkon, OH 44311-1058
Phone: 330–379–9280 Fax: 330–379–3454
Service Area: Cuyahoga, Lake, Lorain, Mahoning, Medina, Stark, Summit, and Wayne Counties

Working for Empowerment through Community Organizing (WECO)
2700 E. 79th St.
Cleveland, OH 44104
Phone: 216–881–9650 Fax: 216–881–9704
Service Area: Cuyahoga County

Oklahoma

Greenwood Community Development
131 North Greenwood Ave., 2nd Floor
Tulsa, OK 74120
Phone: 918–585–2084 Fax: 918–585–9268
Service Area: Northwest Tulsa County

Little Dixie Community Action
502 West Duke St.
Hugo, OK 74743
Phone: 580–326–3351 Fax: 580–326–2305
Service Area: Choctaw, McCurtain, and Pushmataha Counties

Rural Enterprises of Oklahoma, Inc.
2912 Enterprise Blvd., P.O. Box 1335
Durant, OK 74702
Phone: 580–924–5094 Fax: 580–920–2745
Service Area: Statewide, excluding Adair, Canadian, Cherokee, Cleveland, Craig, Creek, Delaware, Haskell, Hayes, Hughes, Kay, Latimer, Leflore, Lincoln, Logan, McIntosh, Muskogee, Noble, Nowata, Okfuskee, Oklahoma, Okmulgee, Osage, Ottawa, Pawnee, Payne, Pittsburg, Pottawatomie, Rogers, Seminole, Sequoyah, Wagoner, Washington, and Wayne Counties, including the city of Tulsa

Tulsa Economic Development Corp.
907 South Detroit Ave., Suite 1001
Tulsa, OK 74120
Phone: 918–585–8332 Fax: 918–585–2473
Service Area: Adair, Canadian, Cherokee,
Cleveland, Craig, Creek, Delaware, Haskell,
Hughes, Kay, Latimer, Leflore, Lincoln,
Logan, McIntosh, Muskogee, Noble, Nowata,
Okfuskee, Oklahoma, Okmulgee, Osage,
Ottawa, Pawnee, Payne, Pittsburg,
Pottawatomie, Rogers, Seminole, Sequoyah,
Wagoner, and Washington Counties,
including the city of Tulsa

Oregon
Cascades West Financial Services, Inc.
1400 Queen Ave. SE, Suite 205c
P.O. Box 686
Albany, OR 97321
Phone: 541–924–8480 Fax: 541–967–4651
Service Area: Benton, Lane, Lincoln, Linn,
Marion, Polk, and Yamhill Counties

Sage Community Resources
10624 W. Executive Dr.
Boise, ID 83713
Phone: 208–322–7033 Fax: 208–322–3569
Service Area: Harney and Malheur Counties

Southern Oregon Women's Access to Credit, Inc.
33 North Central #209
Medford, OR 97501
Phone: 541–779–3992 Fax: 541–779–5195
Service Area: Jackson, Josephine, Klamath,
and Lake Counties

Oregon Association of Minority Entrepreneurs
Credit Corporation
4134 N. Vancouver Ave.
Portland, OR 97217
Phone: 503–249–7744 Fax: 503–249–2027
Service Area: Multnomah, Washington,
Clackamas, Columbia, Tillamook, Clatsop,
and Hood Counties

Umpqua Community Development Corp.
738 SE Kane St.
Roseburg, OR 97470
Phone: 541–673–4909 Fax: 541–673–5023
Service Area: Coos, Curry, and Douglas
Counties

Pennsylvania
Aliquippa Alliance for Unity and Development
392 Franklin Ave.
Aliquippa, PA 15001
Phone: 724–378–7422 Fax: 724–378–9976
Service Area: Beaver, Butler, and Lawrence
Counties

Community First Fund
44 N. Queen St., P.O. Box 524
Lancaster, PA 17608-0524
Phone: 866–822–3863 Fax: 717–393–1757
Service Area: Lancaster, York, Berks,
Dauphin, Lebanon, Cumberland, Perry, and
Adams Counties

Community Loan Fund of Southwestern PA, Inc.
1920 Gulf Towers, 707 Grant St.
Pittsburgh, PA 15219
Phone: 412–201–2450 Fax: 412–201–2451
Service Area: Allegheny, Armstong, Beaver,
Butler, and Indiana Counties

Northeastern Pennsylvania Alliance (NEPA)
1151 Oak St.
Pittston, PA 18640-3795
Phone: 570–655–5581 Fax: 570–654–5137
Service Area: Carbon, Lackawanna, Luzerne,
Monroe, Pike, Schuylkill, and Wayne
Counties

MetroAction, Inc.
222 Mulberry St., P.O. Box 4731
Scranton, PA 18501-0431
Phone: 570–342–7711 Fax: 570–347–6262
Service Area: Luzerne, Lackawanna, and
Monroe Counties

North Central PA Regional Planning and Dev.
Commission
651 Montmorenci Ave.
Ridgway, PA 15853
Phone: 814–773–3162 Fax: 814–772–7045
Service Area: Cameron, Clearfield, Elk,
Jefferson, McKean, and Potter Counties

Northwest Pennsylvania Regional Planning &
Dev. Commission
395 Seneca St.
Oil City, PA 16301
Phone: 814–677–4800 Fax: 814–677–7663
Service Area: Clarion, Crawford, Erie, Forest,
Lawrence, Mercer, Warren, and Venango
Counties

Philadelphia Commercial Development Corp.
1315 Walnut St., Suite 600
Philadelphia, PA 19107
Phone: 215–790–2210 Fax: 215–790–2222
Service Area: Philadelphia

SEDA-Council of Governments
RR #1, Box 372
Lewisburg, PA 17837
Phone: 570–524–9190 Fax: 570–524–449

Service Area: Centre, Clinton, Columbia, Juniata, Lycoming, Mifflin, Montour, Northumberland, Perry, Snyder, and Union Counties

Southern Alleghenies Planning & Development Commission
541 58th St.
Altoona, PA 16602
Phone: 814–949–6545 Fax: 814–949–6505
Service Area: Bedford, Blair, Cambria, Fulton, Huntingdon, and Somerset Counties

The Ben Franklin Technology of SE Pennsylvania
11 Penn Center, 1835 Market St., Suite 1100
Philadelphia, PA 19103
Phone: 215–972–6700 Fax: 215–972–5588
Service Area: Bucks, Chester, Delaware, Montgomery, and Philadelphia Counties

The Washington County Council on Economic Development
40 S. Main St., Lower Level
Washington, PA 15301
Phone: 724–228–8223 Fax: 724–250–8202
Service Area: Southwestern area of Pennsylvania, including Greene, Fayette, Washington, and Westmoreland Counties; Mongalia County in West Virginia

Puerto Rico
Economic Dev. Corp. of San Juan(COFECC)
1103 Avenida Munoz Rivera,
P.O. Box 191791
Rio Piedras, PR 00926
Phone: 787–756–5080 Fax: 787–753–8960
Service Area: Territory-wide

Rhode Island
Rhode Island Coalition for Minority Investment
216 Weybosset St., 2nd Floor
Providence, RI 02903
Phone: 401–351–2999 Fax: 401–351–0990
Service Area: Statewide

Saipan
Commonwealth Development Authority
P.O. Box 502149
Saipan, MP 96950-2149
Phone: 670–235–7147 Fax: 670–235–7144
Service Area: Saipan, Tinian, and Rota Counties

South Carolina
Business Carolina, Inc.
P. O. Box 8327
Columbia, SC 29202
Phone: 803–461–3800 Fax: 803–461–3826

Service Area: Abbeville, Aiken, Allendale, Anderson, Bamberg, Barnwell, Beaufort, Berkeley, Calhoun, Charleston, Cherokee, Chester, Chesterfield, Colleton, Darlington, Dillon, Dorchester, Edgefield, Fairfield, Florence, Georgetown, Greenville, Greenwood, Hampton, Horry, Jasper, Lancaster, Laurens, Lexington, Marion, Marlboro, McCormick, Newberry, Oconee, Orangeburg, Pickens, Richland, Saluda, Spartanburg, Union, and York Counties

Charleston Citywide Local Development Corp.
75 Calhoun St., 3rd Floor
Charleston, SC 29403
Phone: 843–724–3796 Fax: 843–724–7354
Service Area: City of Charleston

Santee-Lynches Regional Development Corp.
36 West Liberty St., P.O. Box 1837
Sumter, SC 29150
Phone: 803–775–7381 Fax: 803–773–6902
Service Area: Clarendon, Kershaw, Lee, and Sumter Counties

South Dakota
Lakota Fund
Trade Center, P.O. Box 340
Kyle, SD 57752
Phone: 605–455–2500 Fax: 605–455–2585
Service Area: Bennett County; Pine Ridge Indian Reservation; areas of Shannon and Jackson Counties, which are surrounded by Indian Lands and exclusive of Northern Jackson County

Tennessee
Economic Ventures, Inc.
P.O. Box 3550
Knoxville, TN 37927-3550
Phone: 865–594–8762 Fax: 865–594–8659
Service Area: Anderson, Blount, Campbell, Clairborne, Cocke, Grainger, Hamblen, Jefferson, Knox, Loudon, Monroe, Morgan, Roane, Scott, Sevier, Union, Greene, Hancock, Hawkins, Sullivan, Washington, Johnson, Carter, and Unicoi Counties

LeMoyne-Owen College Community Dev. Corp.
802 Walker Ave., Suite 5
Memphis, TN 38126
Phone: 901–942–6265 Fax: 901–942–6448
Service Area: Memphis and Shelby Counties

Southeast Community Capital
1020 Commerce Park Dr.
Oak Ridge, TN 37830
Phone: 865–220–2025 Fax: 865–220–2030
Service Area: Statewide

Woodbine Community Organization
222 Oriel Ave.
Nashville, TN 37210
Phone: 615–833–9580 Fax: 615–833–9727
Service Area: Cheatham, Davidson, Dickson, Houston, Humphrey, Montgomery, Robertson, Rutherford, Stewart, Sumner, Williamson, and Wilson Counties

Texas
ACCION Texas, Inc.
2014 S. Hackberry St.
San Antonio, TX 78210
Phone: 210–226–3664 Fax: 210–226–2940
Service Area: Arkansas, Atascosa, Austin, Bandera, Bastrop, Bee, Bexar, Blanco, Brewster, Brooks, Brownsville, Burnet, Carmeron, Caldwell, Calhoun, Comal, Concho, Corpus Christi, Crockett, Culberson, Dallas, DeWitt, Dimmit, Duval, Edwards, El Paso, Fayette, Fort Worth, Frio, Gillespie, Goliad, Gonzales, Green, Guadalupe, Harris, Hays, Houston, Hidalgo, Hudspeth, Irion, Jackson, Jeff Davis, Jim Hogg, Jim Wells, Karnes, Kendall, Kenedy, Kerr, Kimble, Kinney, Kleberg, Lampasas, Laredo, LaSalle, Lavaca, Lee, Live Oak, Llano, Loving, Mason, Maverick, Medina, McAllen, McCulloch, McMullen, Menard, Midland/Odessa, Nueces, Pecos, Presidio, Real, Reeves, Real, Reeves, Refugio, San Antonio, San Patricio, San Saba, Schleicher, Starr, Sutton, Tarrant, Tom Green, Travis, Uvalde, Val Verde, Victoria , Webb, Willacy, Zapata, and Zavala Counties

Business Resource Center Incubator
401 Franklin Ave.
Waco, TX 76701
Phone: 254–754–8898 Fax: 254–756–0776
Service Area: Bell, Bosque, Coryell, Falls, Hill, and McLennan Counties

BIG—Businesses Invest In Growth
4100 Ed Bluestein, Suite 207
Austin, TX 78741
Phone: 512–928–8010 Fax: 512–926–2997
Service Area: Travis, Williamson, Hays, Bastrop, Blanco, Burnet, Burleson, Milam, Gillespie, Lampasas, Lee, Llano, Mason, Mcculloch, and SanSaba Counties

Neighborhood Housing Services of Dimmitt County, Inc.
301 Pena St.
Carrizo Springs, TX 78834
Phone: 830–876–5295 Fax: 830–876–4136

Service Area: Dimmit, La Salle, Zavala Edwards, Kinney, Real, Uvalde, Val Verde, and Maverick Counties

Rural Development and Finance Corp.
711 Navarro St., Suite 350
San Antonio, TX 78207
Phone: 210–212–4552 Fax: 210–212–9159
Service Area: Cameron, El Paso, Starr, Hidalgo, Willacy, Maverick, Dimmit, Webb, Zapata, and Zavala Counties

San Antonio Local Development Company
215 South San Saba, Room 107
San Antonio, TX 78207
Phone: 210–207–3932 Fax: 210–207–8151
Service Area: Atascosa, Bandera, Bexar, Comal, Frio, Gillespie, Guadalupe, Karnes, Kendall, Kerr, Medina, San Antonio, and Wilson Counties

Southern Dallas Development Corp.
351 West Blvd., Suite 800
Dallas, TX 75208
Phone: 214–428–7332 Fax: 214–948–8104
Service Area: Portions of the city of Dallas

The Corporation for Economic Development of Harris County, Inc.
11703 ½ Easttex Freeway
Houston, TX 77039
Phone: 281–590–5600 Fax: 281–590–5605
Service Area: Brazoria, Chambers, FortBend, Galveston, Harris, Liberty, Montgomery, and Waller Counties

Vermont
Economic Dev. Council of Northern Vermont, Inc.
155 Lake St.
St. Albans, VT 05478
Phone: 802–524–4546 Fax: 802–527–1081
Service Area: Chittenden, Franklin, Grand Isle, Lamoille, and Washington Counties

Northern Community Investment Corp.
347 Portland St., P.O. Box 904
St. Johnsbury, VT 05819
Phone: 802–748–5101 Fax: 802–748–1884
Service Area: Caledonia, Essex, and Orleans Counties

Vermont Development Credit Union
18 Pearl St.
Burlington, VT 05401
Phone: 802–865–3404 Fax: 802–862–8971
Service Area: Addison, Bennington, Orange, Rutland, Windham, and Windsor Counties

Virginia

Business Development Centre, Inc.
147 Mill Ridge Rd.
Lynchburg, VA 24502
Phone: 434–582–6100 Fax: 434–582–6106
Service Area: Amherst, Appomattox, Bedford, and Campell Counties; cities of Lynchburg and Bedford; town of Amherst; and Altavista

Center for Community Development
440 High St., Suite 204
Portsmouth, VA 23704
Phone: 757–399–0925 Fax: 757–399–2642
Service Area: Chesapeake, Essen, Gloucester, Hampton, King and Queens, King William, Mathews, Middlesex, Newport News, Norfolk, Portsmouth, Suffolk, and Virginia Beach

Enterprise Development Group (*formerly Ethiopian Community Development*)
1038 South Highland St.
Arlington, VA 22204
Phone: 703–685–0510 Fax: 703–685–0529
Service Area: Prince William, Arlington, and Fairfax Counties; cities of Alexandria and Falls Church

Lightstone Community Development Corp.
HC 63, Box 73
Moyers, WV 26815
Phone: 304–249–5200 Fax: 304–249–5310
Service Area: Bath and Highland Counties

People Incorporated of Southwest Virginia
1173 West Main St.
Abingdon, VA 24210
Phone: 276–619–2228 Fax: 276–628–2931
Service Area: Bland, Buchanan, Carroll, Dickenson, Floyd, Grayson, Lee, Russell, Scott, Smyth, Tazewell, Washington, and Wise Counties; cities of Bristol, Galax, and Norton

Richmond Economic Development Corp.
501 E. Franklin St., Suite 358
Richmond, VA 23219
Phone: 804–780–3013 Fax: 804–788–4310
Service Area: City of Richmond

Total Action Against Poverty
210 South Jefferson St.
Roanoke, VA 24011
Phone: 540–344–7006 Fax: 540–344–6998
Service Area: Alleghany, Bath, Botetourt, Craig, and Roanoke Counties; cities of Clifton Forge, Covington, Roanoke, and Salem

Virginia Community Development Loan Fund
1624 Hull St.
Richmond, VA 23224
Phone: 804–233–2014 Fax: 804–233–2158
Service Area: Henrico, Chesterfield, Goochland, Hanover, and Powatan Counties; cities of Petersburg and Hopewell

Washington

Community Capital Development
1437 South Jackson, Suite 201
Seattle, WA 98144
Phone: 206–324–4330, ext. 104 Fax: n/a
Service Area: Adams, Chelan, Douglas, Grant, Kittitas, Klickitat, Okanogan, Yakima, King, Pierce, Skagit, San Juan, Snohomish, Island, Kitsap, and Whatcom

Oregon Association of Minority Entrepreneurs Credit Corp.
4134 N. Vancouver Ave.
Portland, OR 97217
Phone: 503–249–7744 Fax: 503–249–2027
Service Area: Clark County

Tri-Cities Enterprise Center
124 W. Kennewick Ave.
Kennewick, WA 99336
Phone: 509–582–9440, ext 108
Fax: 509–582–9720
Service Area: Benton, Franklin, Columbia, Garfield, Asotin, Whitman, and Spokane Counties

Washington CASH (Community Alliance for Self-Help)
1912 East Madison St.
Seattle, WA 98122
Phone: 206–352–1945 Fax: 206–352–1899
Service Area: Clark, Cowlitz, Island, King, Kitsap, Lewis, San Juan, Skagit, Snohomish, Thurston, and Whatcom Counties

Rural Community Development Resources, Inc. (*formerly WAME*)
24 South 3rd Ave.
Yakima, WA 98902
Phone: 509–453–5133 Fax: 509–453–5165
Service Area: Mattawa and Othello in Grant County; Moses Lake and Royal City in Adams County; Walla Walla County; Pasco in Franklin County

West Virginia

Lightstone Community Development Corp.
HC 63, Box 73
Moyers, WV 26815
Phone: 304–249–5200 Fax: 304–249–5310

Service Area: Statewide

Mountain CAP of West Virginia, Inc.
105 Jerry Burton Dr.
Sutton, WV 26601
Phone: 304–765–7738 Fax: 304–765–7308
Service Area: Barbour, Braxton, Clay, Fayette,
Gilmer, Lewis, Nicholas, Randolph, Roane,
Upshur Raleigh, Harrison, and Webster
Counties

The Washington County Council on Economic
Development
100 West Beau St., Suite 703
Washington, PA 15301-4432
Phone: 724–228–6949 Fax: 724–250–6502
Service Area: Monongalia County

Wisconsin
Advocap, Inc.
19 West 1st St., P.O. Box 1108
Fond Du Lac, WI 54935
Phone: 920–922–7760 Fax: 920–922–7214
Service Area: Fond du Lac, Green Lake, and
Winnebago Counties

Impact Seven, Inc
147 Lake Almena Dr.
Alemna, WI 54805
Phone: 715–357–3334 Fax: 715–357–6233
Service Area: Statewide, with the exceptions of
Fond du Lac, Green Lake, Kenosha,
Milwaukee, Oasukee, Racine, Walworth,
Waukesha, Washington, and Winnebago

Counties and inner city Milwaukee

Lincoln Neighborhood Redevelopment Corp.
2266 S. 13th St.
Milwaukee, WI 53215
Phone: 414–671–5619 Fax: 414–385–3270
Area Served: Greater Milwaukee SMSA

Northeast Entrepreneur Fund, Inc.
1225 Town Ave.
Superior, WI 54880
Phone: 800–422–0374 Fax: 715–392–6131
Service Area: Douglas County

Wisconsin Women's Business Initiative Corp.
2745 North Dr. Martin Luther King Jr. Dr.
Milwaukee, WI 53212
Phone: 414–263–5450 Fax: 414–263–5456
Service Area: Brown, Dane, Dodge, Jefferson,
Kenosha, Milwaukee, Ozaukee, Racine,
Rock, Walworth, and Washington Counties

Wyoming
Wyoming Women's Business Center
13th and Lewis Sts., P.O. Box 3661
Laramie, WY 82071
Phone: 307–766–3083 Fax: 307–766–3085
Service Area: State of Wyoming

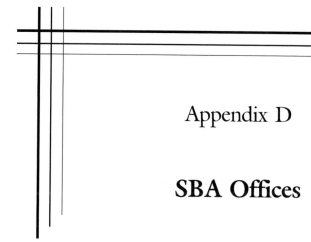

Appendix D

SBA Offices

Alaska
District Office, 510 "L" St., Suite 310
Anchorage, AK 99510-1952
Phone: 907–271–4022

Alabama
District Office, 801 Tom Martin Dr.
Birmingham, AL 35211
Phone: 205–290–7101

Arkansas
District Office, 2120 Riverfront Dr., Suite 100
Little Rock, AR 72202-1794
Phone: 501–324–5871

Arizona
District Office, 2828 N. Central Ave., Ste. 800
Phoenix, AZ 85004-1093
Phone: 602–745–7210

California
District Office, 2719 N. Air Fresno Dr., Ste. 200
Fresno, CA 93727-1547
Phone: 559–487–5791

District Office, 330 N. Brand Blvd., Ste. 1200
Glendale, CA 91203-2304
Phone: 818–552–3210

District Office, 650 Capitol Mall, Ste. 7-500
Sacramento, CA 95815
Phone: 916–930–3700

District Office, 550 West "C" St., Ste. 550
San Diego, CA 92101-3500
Phone: 619–557–7250

District Office, 200 W. Santa Ana Blvd., Ste. 700
Santa Ana, CA
Phone: 714–550–7420

District Office, 455 Market St., 6th Floor
San Francisco, CA 94105-2420
Phone: 415–744–6820

Colorado
District Office, 721 19th St., Ste. 426
Denver, CO 80202-2517
Phone: 303–844–6468

Connecticut
District Office, 330 Main St., 2nd Floor,
Hartford, CT 06106-1800
Phone: 860–240–4700

District of Columbia
District Office, 1110 Vermont Ave. NW, 9th Fl.
Washington, DC 20005
Phone: 202–606–4000

Delaware
District Office, 824 N. Market St.
Wilmington, DE 19801-3011
Phone: 302–573–6294

Florida
Dist. Office, 7825 Baymeadows Way, Ste. 100B
Jacksonville, FL 32256-7504
Phone: 904–443–1900

District Office, 100 S. Biscayne Blvd., 7th Fl.
Miami, FL 33131
Phone: 305–536–5521

Georgia
District Office, 233 Peachtree St. NE, Ste. 1900
Atlanta, GA 30303
Phone: 404–331–0100

Guam
Branch Office, 400 Route 8, Suite 302
Mongmong, GU 96927
Phone: 617–472–7319

Hawaii
Dist. Office, 300 Ala Moana Blvd., Box 50207
Honolulu, HA 96850-4981
Phone: 808–541–2990

Idaho
District Office, 1020 Main St., Ste. 290
Boise, ID 83702
Phone: 208–334–1696

Illinois
District Office, 500 W. Madison St., Ste. 1250
Chicago, IL 60661-2511
Phone: 312–353–4528

Branch Office, 511 W. Capitol Ave., Suite 302
Springfield, IL 62704
Phone: 217–492–4416

Indiana
District Office, 429 N. Pennsylvania, Ste. 100
Indianapolis, IN 46204-1873
Phone: 317–226–7272

Iowa
District Office, 215 4th Ave. SE, Suite 200
Cedar Rapids, IA 52401-1806
Phone: 319–362–6405

District Office, 210 Walnut St., Room 749
Des Moines, IA 50309
Phone: 515–284–4422

Kansas
District Office, 271 W. 3rd St. North, Ste. 2500
Wichita, KS 67202-1212
Phone: 316–269–6616

Kentucky
Dist. Office, 600 Dr. M.L. King Jr. Pl., Rm. 188
Louisville, KY 40202
Phone: 502–582–5761

Louisiana
District Office, 365 Canal St., Suite 2820
New Orleans, LA 70130
Phone: 504–589–6685

Massachusetts
District Office, 10 Causeway St., Room 265
Boston, MA 02222-1093
Phone: 617–565–5590

Branch Office, 1441 Main St.,
Springfield, MA 01103
Phone: 413–785–0268

Maryland
District Office, 10 S. Howard St., 6th Floor,
Baltimore, MD 21201
Phone: 410–962–4392

Maine
District Office, 68 Sewell St., Room 512,
Augusta, ME 04330
Phone: 207–622–8274

Michigan
District Office, 477 Michigan Ave., Room 515,
Detroit, MI 48226
Phone: 313–226–6075

Branch Office, 501 South Front St.,
Marquette, MI 49855
Phone: 906–225–1108

Minneapolis
District Office, 100 North 6th St., Ste. 210-C
Minneapolis, MN 55403-1563
Phone: 612–370–2324

Missouri
District Office, 323 West 8th St., Ste. 501
Kansas City, MO 64105-1500
Phone: 816–374–6708

Branch Office, 830 East Primrose, Suite 101
Springfield, MO
Phone: 417–890–8501

District Office, 200 North Broadway, #1500
St. Louis, MO 63102
Phone: 314–539–3785

Mississippi
Branch Office, 2909 13th St., Suite 203
Gulfport, MS 39501-1949
Phone: 228–863–4449

District Office, 210 East Capitol St., Ste. 900
Jackson, MS 39201
Phone: 601–965–4378

Montana
District Office, 10 West 15th St.,
Helena, MT 59626
Phone: 406–441–1081

N. Dakota
District Office, 657 2nd Ave. North, Rm. 219
Fargo, ND 58108
Phone: 701–239–5131

Nebraska
District Office, 11145 Mill Valley Rd.
Omaha, NE 68154
Phone: 402–221–4691

N. Hampshire
District Office, 143 North Main St., Ste. 202
Concord, NH 03301
Phone: 603–225–1400

N. Carolina
District Office, 6302 Fairview Rd., Ste. 300
Charlotte, NC 28210-2227
Phone: 704–344–6563

New Jersey
District Office, Two Gateway Center, 15th Fl.
Newark, NJ 07102
Phone: 973–645–2434

New Mexico
District Office, 625 Silver SW, Suite 320
Albuquerque, NM 87102
Phone: 505–346–7909

Nevada
District Office, 400 S. Fourth St., Ste. 250
Las Vegas, NV 89101
Phone: 702–388–6469

New York
District Office, 111 W. Huron St., Ste. 1311
Buffalo, NY 14202
Phone: 716–551–4301

Branch Office, 333 East Water St., 4th Floor
Elmira, NY 14901
Phone: 607–734–8130

Branch Office, 35 Pine Lawn Rd., Ste. 207W
Melville, NY 11747
Phone: 516–454–0750

District Office, 26 Federal Plaza, Ste. 3100
New York, NY 10278
Phone: 212–264–4354

Branch Office, 100 State St., Room 410
Rochester, NY 14614
Phone: 585–263–6700

District Office, 401 S. Salina St., 5th Floor
Syracuse, NY 13202
Phone: 315–471–9393

Ohio
Branch Office, 550 Main St.
Cincinnati, OH 45202
Phone: 513–684–2814

District Office, 1111 Superior Ave., Ste. 630
Cleveland, OH 44114-2507
Phone: 216–522–4180

District Office, 2 Nationwide Plaza, Ste.
1400 Columbus, OH 43215-2542
Phone: 614–469–6860

Oklahoma
District Office, 210 Park Ave., Suite 1300
Oklahoma City, OK 73102
Phone: 405–231–5521

Oregon
District Office, 1515 SW Fifth Ave., Ste. 1050
Portland, OR 97201-5494
Phone: 503–326–2682

Pennsylvania
District Office, 900 Market St., 5th Floor
Philadelphia, PA 19107
Phone: 215–580–2722

Branch Office, 100 Chestnut St.
Harrisburg, PA 17101
Phone: 717–782–3840

Dist. Office, 1000 Liberty Ave.
Fed. Bldg. Rm. 1128
Pittsburgh, PA 15222-4004
Phone: 412–395–6560

Branch Office, 7 North Wilkes-Barre Blvd.
Wilkes-Barre, PA 18702
Phone: 570–826–6497

Rhode Island
District Office, 380 Westminster St., Rm. 511
Providence, RI 02903
Phone: 401–528–4561

Puerto Rico
Dist. Office, 252 Ponce De Leon Ave., Ste. 201
Hato Rey, PR 00918
Phone: 787–766–5572

South Carolina
District Office, 1835 Assembly St., Room 358
Columbia, SC 29201
Phone: 803–765–5377

South Dakota
District Office, 110 S. Phillips Ave., Suite 200
Sioux Falls, SD 57104-6727
Phone: 605–330–4243

Tennessee
District Office, 50 Vantage Way, Ste. 201
Nashville, TN 37228-1500
Phone: 615–736–5881

Texas

District Office, 10737 Gateway West
El Paso, TX 79935
Phone: 915–633–7001

Branch Office, 3649 Leopard St., Suite 411
Corpus Christi, TX 78408
Phone: 361–879–0017

Dist. Office, 4300 Amon Carter Blvd., Ste. 114
Dallas, TX 76155
Phone: 817–684–5500

District Office, 222 E. Van Buren, Suite 500
Harlingen, TX 78550
Phone: 956–427–8533

District Office, 8701 S. Gessner Dr., Ste. 1200
Houston, TX 77074
Phone: 713–773–6500

District Office, 1205 Texas Ave., Suite 408
Lubbock, TX 79401-2693
Phone: 806–472–7462

District Office, 17319 San Pedro, Suite 200
San Antonio, TX 78232-1411
Phone: 210–403–5900

Utah

District Office, 125 State St., Room 2227
Salt Lake City, UT 84138
Phone: 801–524–3209

Vermont

District Office, 87 State St., Room 205
Montpelier, VT 05602
Phone: 802–828–4422

Virginia

District Office, 400 N 8th, Fed. Bldg., Ste. 1150
Richmond, VA 23240-0126
Phone: 804–771–2400

Virgin Islands

Post of Duty, Sunny Isle Prof. Bldg., Stes. 5 & 6
St. Croix, VI 00802
Phone: 340–778–5380

Post of Duty, 3800 Crown Bay
St. Thomas, VI 00802
Phone: 809–774–8530

Washington

District Office, 1200 6th Ave., Suite 1700
Seattle, WA 98101-1128
Phone: 206–553–7310

District Office, 801 W. Riverside Ave., Ste. 200
Spokane, WA 99201-0901
Phone: 509–353–2800

West Virginia

Branch Office, 405 Capitol St., Suite 412
Charleston, WV 25301
Phone: 314–347–5220

District Office, 320 West Pike St., Suite 330
Clarksburg, WV 26301
Phone: 304–623–5631

Wisconsin

District Office, 740 Regent St., Suite 100
Madison, WI 53715
Phone: 608–441–5263

Dist. Office, 310 W, Wisconsin Ave., Ste. 400
Milwaukee, WI 53203
Phone: 414–297–3941

Wyoming

District Office, 100 East B St., Room 4001
Casper, WY 82602
Phone: 307–261–6500

Appendix E

SBA Loan Forms and Requirements

SBA Business Loan Forms		
Form Name	**Description**	**Web Location (URL)**
SBA Form 4	Business Loan Application	*www.sba.gov/sbaforms/sba4.pdf*
SBA Form 4: Schedule A	Schedule of Collateral	*www.sba.gov/sbaforms/sba4_a.pdf*
SBA Form 413	Personal Financial Statement	*www.sba.gov/sbaforms/sba413.pdf*
SBA Form 912	Statement of Personal History	*www.sba.gov/sbaforms/sba912.pdf*
SBA Form 159	Compensation Agreement	*www.sba.gov/sbaforms/sba159.pdf*
SBA Form 652	Assurance of Compliance for Nondiscrimination	*www.sba.gov/sbaforms/sba652.pdf*
SBA Form 1624	Certificate Regarding Debarment	*www.sba.gov/sbaforms/sba1624.pdf*

SBA Loan Package Checklist

Personal Financial Information

❏ 1. SBA Form 413: Personal financial statement. Form 413 should be completed for each stockholder with 20 percent or greater ownership. A form should also be completed for every partner, officer, and owner. (Forms must be signed and dated.)

❏ 2. SBA Form 912: Statement of personal history.

❏ 3. Detailed list of collateral. Include a legal description of real estate offered as collateral.

❏ 4. Resume of all people listed under management. Include education, technical and business background.

Business Information

❏ 5. Business plan.

❏ 6. Brief history of the company. Include a paragraph describing the expected benefits the company will receive from the loan.

❏ 7. Articles of Incorporation and By-Laws.

❏ 8. Balance sheet, income statement, reconciliation of net worth, and a summary of accounts receivable and accounts payable for most recent three years. For each year all statements must have the same date. All information should be signed and dated. If the last three years of financial statements are not available, projection of earnings by month for at least one year and by quarters for the second and third year.

❏ 9. Key assumptions for financial projections.

❏ 10. Copies of business income tax returns.

❏ 11. Lease agreement on existing facility.

❏ 12. Schedule of all term debt, including notes, contract, and leases payable.

❏ 13. Aged accounts receivable.

❏ 14. Aged accounts payable.

Collateral Requirements

❏ 15. Schedule of fixed assets to be acquired and their costs.

❏ 16. Real estate appraisals, if applicable.

Franchise

❒ 17. Franchise agreement.*

Construction

❒ 18. Construction contract.*

❒ 19. Copy of performance bond.*

Additional Information:

❒ 20. Any Buy-Sell agreements and copy of escrow instructions.*

❒ 21. Partnership agreements.*

Note: The SBA may not guarantee a loan if a business can secure a loan at reasonable terms from a bank or private institution. A borrower must first seek private financing and show evidence of refusal. In cities with populations of [more than] 200,000, two such letters must be obtained. The refusal letter(s) must state the reason(s) for refusal of credit, the date of refusal, and the amount and terms requested.

A free directory of Small Business Administration publications may be obtained from the SBA Answer Desk (1-800-8-ASK-SBA), or from any regional SBA office.

*If applicable.

Source: United States Small Business Administration

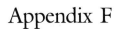

Appendix F

Everyday Business Math

Finding a Percent of a Number
To find the percent of a number, first change the percent to a fraction or a decimal and then multiply.

Example: Find 25% of $150,000 by changing the percent to a fraction.

Change 25% to a fraction.

(Place the number over 100): $\quad\quad\quad$ 25% = 25/100

Multiply: $\quad\quad\quad\quad\quad\quad\quad\quad\quad$ 25/100 × $150,000 = 37,500.00

Finding What Percent One Number Is of Another Number
To find the percent one number is of another, divide the smaller number (the part) by the larger number (the whole), then move the decimal point two places to the right.

Example: 75 is what percent of 400?

Identify the numbers: $\quad\quad\quad\quad\quad\quad\quad$ 75 = part and 400 = whole

Divide: $\quad\quad\quad\quad\quad\quad\quad\quad\quad\quad$ 75 / 400 = .1875

Convert .1875 to a percent.

(Move the decimal point two places to the right): .1875 = 18.75%

Calculating Simple Interest
Formula for simple interest: I = P × T × R

Example: Find the amount of simple interest due on $5,000 borrowed for 6 months at 8 ½%.

Convert 8 ½% to a decimal, which is .0850.

6 months converts to ½ year (6 months/12 months)

Plug the amount information into the formula. I = $5,000 × 6/12 × .0850 = $212.50

Everyday Business Math Problems (With Step-by-Step Solutions)

1. Change the decimal .325 to a percent.
    Move the decimal point two places to the right: $\quad$ .325 = 32.5%

2. Change 45.7% to a decimal.

Move the decimal point two places to the left: 45.7% = .457

3. What is 43% of 280?
    Convert 43% to a decimal: 43% = .43
    Multiply: .43 × 280 = $120.40

4. What is the percent equivalent 3/8?
    Convert 3/8 to a decimal.
        (Divide the numerator by the denominator):   3 / 8 = .375
    Move the decimal two places to the right: .375 = 37.5%

5. 20% of what number is 1,250?
    Convert the percent to a decimal: 20% = .20
    Divide: 1,250 / .20 = 6,250

6. A BESt Company's sales have increased from $150,000 to $205,000. What is the percentage increase?
    Find the difference between the beginning amount
        and the ending amount: $205,000 – $150,000 = $55,000
    Divide that difference by the beginning amount: $55,000 / $150,000 = .3667
    Convert the decimal to a percentage: .3667 = 36.67%

7. A BESt CEO buys an item for $30 and wants to make a 40% Gross Profit Margin. What is the selling price?
    Convert the desired Gross Profit Margin percentage
        to a decimal: 40% = .40
    Subtract the desired Gross Profit Margin from 1.00: 1.0 – .40 = .60 (conversion factor)
    Divide the item's cost by the conversion factor: $30 / .60 = $50.00 (selling price)

8. A BESt CEO purchases an item for $30 and wants to sell it for $75. What is the Gross Profit Margin percentage?
    Find the difference between the selling price and cost, then divide by the selling price.
        (Selling Price – Cost) / Selling Price = Gross Profit Margin percentage
            ($75 – $30) / $75 = Gross Profit Margin
                $45 / $75 = .60 (or 60% expressed as a percentage)

9. A BESt CEO purchases an item for $25 and sells it for $60. What is the Markup percentage?
    Find the difference between the selling price and cost, then divide by the cost.
        (Selling Price – Cost) / Cost = Markup Factor
            ($60 – $25) / $25 = Markup Factor
                $35 / $25 = 1.40 (or 140% expressed as a percentage)

10. Average monthly expense for supplies decreased from $1,200 per month to $900 per month. What is the percentage decrease?
    Find the difference between the beginning amount ($1,200) and the ending amount ($900). Then divide that difference by the beginning amount ($1,200).
        $1,200 – $900 = $300
        $300 / $1,200 = -.25 (or -25% expressed as a percentage).
    Because the amount decreased, the answer (both decimal and percentage) will be negative.

Appendix G

Glossary

Accounts payable: Money that is owed to suppliers for goods and services purchased on credit with an agreement to pay within a specified period of time.

Accounts receivable: Money that is owed to a business by its customers.

Advertising: A dynamic, ongoing communication effort designed to get the attention of potential customers and persuade them to purchase products and/or services.

Advertising copy: The persuasive words written to encourage a targeted customer to develop interest in a business and its products and/or services.

Amortization period: The length of time that it takes to completely pay off a mortgage through repayment of the principal and the accumulated interest.

Angel investors: Private individuals or small groups who invest in business opportunities by taking on large risk with the prospect of earning a higher return than more traditional investments.

Bad debt: Accounts receivable and other debts to a business that are either uncollectible or have a high probability of becoming uncollectible.

Balance sheet: A financial statement that includes a listing of a business's assets, liabilities, and net worth on a specific date.

Business plan: A planning document that describes a business, its marketing and management objectives and strategies, and its financial forecast. Used to attract outside financing and as a benchmark for operations.

By-laws: The operating rules that a corporation establishes to guide the actions of its shareholders, officers, and directors. One of the first documents created when forming a corporation.

Calendar year: An accounting period consisting of 12 consecutive months that ends on December 31.

Capital: Wealth, in the form of money or other assets, that is owned by a person or a business.

Cash flow: The inflows and outflows of cash in a business over a specified period of time. If more cash is coming in than going out, the business has a positive cash flow. If the business has more cash going out than coming in, cash flow will be negative.

Certified Public Accountant (CPA): An accountant licensed by the state after passing a rigorous, national, standardized examination.

Cash discount: An amount that a firm allows a customer to deduct from an invoice as an inducement for prompt payment.

Collateral: Assets pledged as a security for the repayment of a loan.

Corporation: A distinct, legal entity organized under state law and separate from the individuals who own it; it can be considered an artificial person.

Credit limit: The amount of purchasing power a vendor is willing to extend to a customer so that merchandise can be conveniently ordered without having to pay before shipment is made.

Current assets: Cash and other assets that are likely to be converted into cash or used to benefit the company within one year; examples include cash, inventory, and accounts receivable.

Current liabilities: Liabilities that are likely to be paid with cash within one year; examples include accounts payable, wages payable, and accrued taxes.

Demographic relevant range ("DRR"): A manageable geographic area consisting of potential customers that a small, home-based business could effectively serve.

Depreciation: The process of expensing the purchase price of a fixed asset over its estimated useful life.

Employer Identification Number ("EIN"): A nine-digit number assigned to all companies, including corporations, partnerships, and limited liability companies. The IRS uses this number similar to the way it uses social security numbers for individuals.

Entrepreneur: A person who takes a risk in starting a business to earn a profit.

Entrepreneurial inertia: The tendency of a business idea to remain just an idea until some force moves upon it to make it become a reality.

Entrepreneurship: The process of starting, organizing, and managing a business.

Equity: The amount of ownership a person or entity has in an asset or entity.

Expediting: The process of contacting a supplier to determine where an order is in the delivery process and moving the process along if it has stalled.

Expense: The cost that a business incurs in the process of producing or selling goods or services as well as the cost of managing that business.

Extended maintenance contract: An agreement with a software vendor to continue providing software support service beyond an initial maintenance period.

Financial statements: Financial reports that allow a business to determine its worth and to assess its performance.

Fiscal year: An accounting period of 12 months that ends on any date other than December 31st.

Fixed assets: Assets that generally have a useful life greater than one year and are depreciable; also called long-term assets.

Freight: The cost of getting goods purchased from a vendor's location to your location.

Freight collect: A type of delivery where the buyer pays shipping charges to the freight company upon receipt of merchandise.

General and administrative expenses: All salaries, indirect production costs, and general expenses necessary to operate a business; also called G&A.

General liability insurance: Insurance that covers the business against claims for bodily injury or property that occurs on or away from the premises; it also protects a business against risk associated with its products.

General partnership: A form of partnership in which each partner is an owner in the business and shares all the privileges and risk of ownership.

General ledger: A book of accounts that includes all of the accounts shown in the financial statements.

Globalization: The expansion of economic opportunities made possible by technology that spans borders and reduces or eliminates cultural barriers that hinder commerce as well as competition.

Goodwill: The intangible value of a business beyond the value of its "hard assets." Goodwill comes as a result of better business processes, strong customer service, industry reputation, customer loyalty, etc.

Home-based business: Any operation that sells goods or provides services for profit from a private residence.

Home business (or home office) deduction: A series of smaller deductions that may include such items as a portion of utility bills, mortgage interest, repairs, and depreciation. These expenses are totaled together to get an overall deduction called *Expenses for Business Use of Your Home.*

Income: The money earned from products sold, work performed, or investing activities.

Income statement: The financial statement reports the revenue, expenses and net income or loss for a specific period of time. It answers the question: "Is my business operating profitably?"

Information packet: A collection of various documents, generally prepared in-house, that are intended to convey a substantial amount of information about the company. Usually given to third parties, including customers, bankers, etc., who are imminently interested in doing business.

Inventory: Goods held for resale.

Inventory turnover: Measurement of how quickly a company sells 100 percent of its products.

Liability: An amount that a business owes to another.

Limited Liability Company or ("LLC"): A hybrid type of legal entity. It has qualities of both a corporation and a partnership.

Line of credit: An arrangement in which a lender makes available a specified amount of credit to a borrower for a specified period of time. In accordance with the company's needs, the borrow can draw against available credit or make payments to reduce the outstanding balance.

Local planning commission: A local governmental entity that is responsible for enforcing zoning laws and planning community growth and development.

Management: The process of using financial resources and human effort to accomplish a business's objectives.

Market: The world of commercial activity where competition drives the buying and selling of goods and services. Without competition, there would be no market.

Market analysis: The process of determining the characteristics of potential customers, what their needs are, and how to best serve their needs in a competitive environment.

Market research: Research that seeks to determine customers' characteristics and needs.

Market share: A company's share of the total sales of all products or services within a particular brand category.

Marketing: The process of analyzing buyers and the business environment in order to favorably position goods and services in the marketplace.

Marketing concept: The idea that a business must position and promote products and/or services that customers demand through a lan that takes into account all of the company's objectives (not just its sales goals).

Marketing mix: The combination of the four marketing elements designed to meet the needs of the target market. The four marketing elements are product, place, price, and promotion.

Markup: The process of pricing an item for resale by applying a certain percentage to its cost.

Minority Business Enterprise ("MBE"): A business that is owned by a minority entrepreneur. Generally businesses obtain a MBE certification by allowing a certifying agency to examine its organizational structure and corporate records.

Net profit: The excess of income and gains over expenses and losses for a specified period of time.

Net worth: The difference between assets and liabilities; also called owners' equity.

Notes payable: A formal promise to pay a specified amount at a stated interest rate by a stated date. May be secured by collateral.

Operating cycle: The time span between the purchasing of inventory through the collection of receivables.

Operations: The actions and transactions that a business is involved in during its day-to-day pursuit of profit.

Owner's equity: The difference between a company's assets and liabilities.

Partnership: An association of two or more persons who own and operate a business for profit.

Product mix: A specific assortment of products offered by a company to its customers.

Projected financials: Financial statements that show what is likely to occur in the future based on a set of key business and financial assumptions.

Purchasing: The process of determining the specifications of what to buy, who to buy it from, soliciting prices, comparing prices, placing the order, and receiving the order.

Retained earnings: The amount of net income retained in a business.

Replacement cost: The amount of money necessary to replace property damaged as the result of an insured peril, without regard to the age of the property.

Revenues: Income from all sources before any deductions.

7(a) loan guarantees: An SBA loan program designed to encourage banks to lend money to small business by providing a government guaranty that shifts a percentage of the risk from the lender to the federal government.

Small Business Development Centers (SBDCs): A program administered by the SBA that consists of a network of easily accessible branch locations that provide management and technical assistance to current and prospective small business owners.

Small business: The SBA defines small business in one way; planning agencies or banks may use another definition. Generally, it is the commercial effort of one person or a small group to operate a business profitably.

Small Business Administration ("SBA"): An independent government agency that was created to promote small business. Has many programs to assist minority-owned companies.

Shipping: The process and logistics of getting products to customers.

Sole proprietorship: A business owned and operated by one person.

Storefront: The physical presence (brick and mortar) that a business occupies other than the owner's home.

Tax year: Usually a period of 12 consecutive months for which a company or business calculates earnings, profits, and losses.

Term loan: A fixed amount at the beginning of the borrowing period and monthly payments of principle and interest are made over the life of the loan.

Trade show: A large collection of vendors "under one roof." These vendors disseminate information about their particular company and demonstrate their products or educate prospective customers about their services.

Unique selling proposition ("USP"): A phrase explaining why a potential customer should do business with a particular company rather than its competitor. A USP can focus on products, services, or business methods.

Umbrella coverage: An extra layer of insurance protection that covers a business when liabilities are greater than existing coverage or not covered by other policies.

Value-added services: The freebies that "business associates" are willing to give away at no additional cost in order to build goodwill with their customers.

Venture capital: Investment in an early-stage or growth-stage business that is considered to have an excellent chance at success but may not have ready access to conventional financing sources.

Vertical analysis: A technique that expresses each item within a financial statement in terms of a percent of a base amount; sometimes referred to as common size analysis.

Workers' compensation insurance: Workers' insurance coverage that is required by law in all states. Pays medical cost and lost wages for employees injured on the job.

Working capital: Current assets minus current liabilities. Measures a business's ability to meet current obligations with its current assets.

Recommended Reading

Accounting

Bookkeeping the Easy Way, Wallace W. Kravitz, Barron's Educational
Series, Inc.

*Financial Statements: A Step-by-Step Guide to Understanding and Creating
Financial Reports,* Thomas Ittelson, Career Press, Inc.

*Keeping the Books: Basic Recordkeeping and Accounting for the Successful
Small Business,* Linda Pinson, Dearborn Trade.

Publication 334: Tax Guide for Small Business (IRS Publication),
www.irs.gov/publications/index.html

Publication 583: Starting a Business and Keeping Records (IRS
Publication), *www.irs.gov/publications/index.html*

Advertising

*Capturing Customers.com: Radical Strategies for Selling and Marketing in a
Wired World,* George Colombo, Career Press, Inc.

50 Powerful Ways to Win New Customers, Paul R. Timm, Ph.D., Career
Press, Inc.

Funding

*Every Business Needs an Angel: Getting the Money You Need to Make Your
Business Grow,* John May and Cal Simmons, Crown Publishing Group.

*Financing the New Venture: A Complete Guide to Raising Capital from
Venture Capitalist, Investment Bankers, Private Investors, and other Sources,*
Mark H. Long, Adams Media Corporation.

Management

Black Enterprise (Magazine), Earl G. Graves Publishing Company.

Business Etiquette: 101 Ways to Conduct Business with Charm and Savvy, Ann Marie Sabath, Career Press, Inc.

CEO Logic: How to Think and Act like a Chief Executive, C. Ray Johnson, Career Press, Inc.

FSB: Fortune Small Business (Magazine), Time, Inc.

Manage Your Payables and Fuel Your Growth, Robert A. Cooke, Career Press, Inc.

101 Ways to Make Every Second Count: Time Management Tips & Techniques for More Success with Less Stress, Robert Bly, Career Press, Inc.

Positive Cash Flow: Powerful Tools and Techniques to Collect Your Receivables, Manage Your Payables and Fuel Your Growth, Robert A. Cooke, Career Press, Inc.

Organizing

101 Best Home Businesses, Dan Ramsey, Career Press, Inc.

Planning

Business Plans Kit for Dummies, Steven Peterson and Peter E. Jaret, John Wiley & Sons, Inc.

SBA Funding

SBA Loan Book: How to Get a Small Business Loan Even with Poor Credit, Weak Collateral and No Experience, Charles H. Green, Adams Media Corporation.

SBA Loans: A Step-by-Step Guide, Patrick D. O'Hara, John Wiley & Sons, Inc.

SBA Loans Made E-Z, Lew Gaiter and Roberta E. Lonsdale, Made E-Z Products.

Index

A

accounting software, 114-117
accounts payable, 119, 164
accounts receivable, 119, 164
actual cash value, 49-50
ad valorem. *See* inventory taxes
advertising copy, 127
advertising, 57, 68-69, 125-131
    brochures, 130
    business cards, 128
    direct mail, 126
    flyers, 130
    internet, 127-128
    newspaper ads, 126-127
    packets, 129
    television commercials, 126
    trade shows, 129-130
all-risk insurance coverage, 49
amortization period, 94
angel investors, 86-87
Apple Computers, 17
articles of incorporation, 38
attorney, hiring a, 39
auto insurance, 48-49

B

balance sheet, 117, 154-155, 160-163
bank loans, commercial, 85
benefits, fringe, 20
BESt Principles, 12, 16, 19, 22, 24, 53,
    116, 120, 133, 175-176
brochures, 130
business cards, 33, 128
business etiquette, 171-173
business insurance, 47-52
business license, 46
business opportunity specialist (BOS), 109
business plan,
    defining, 53-54
    developing, 54-55, 56, 60
    elements of, 56-60
Business Plan case study,
    advertising and promotion, 68-69
    company overview, 66-67
    competition, 70
    executive summary, 63-65
    financial plan, 73-79
    industry analysis, 65-66
    management and operations, 70-73
    products, 67
    sales strategy, 69

About the Author

BILL BOUDREAUX, CPA, MBA, has worked with small, minority businesses for more than 20 years. He has worked in many varied industries, including oil, education, transportation, industrial safety, healthcare, and marine transportation. He was one of the youngest African-American CPAs in the United States at the time of his certification. At 25, he became the treasurer of an international marine transportation firm with offices in the United States, Germany, and Brazil. He has an ongoing relationship with an information technology firm that develops software solutions to track marine vessels in the inland waterway system. He is also a member of the adult education faculty in Terrebonne Parish.

Bill has a B.S. in accounting and a masters of business administration from Nicholls State University and is a Certified Public Accountant in the state of Louisiana. He is the president and founder of Minority Business Options, LLC, a company that is dedicated to helping small minority companies succeed in their effort to do business in both the public and private sectors. With his wife, Linda, he works tirelessly with juvenile offenders and other at-risk students.

Bill is an adventurer who enjoys canoeing and primitive camping throughout the Gulf South.